The Edge of Forgiveness on Blue Mountain

BOOK TWO: THE LOST IN THE ADIRONDACKS SERIES

By

Heidi Sprouse

1

THE EDGE OF FORGIVENESS ON BLUE MOUNTAIN.

ISBN-13: 978-1533327307

ISBN-10: 1533327300

"Not all who wander are lost."—J R. R. Tolkien

For Sara Anne, Suzanne, and Kellisue…your candles will always burn bright.

Other Works by Heidi Sprouse

The Lost in the Adirondacks Series

Adirondack Sundown

The Cordial Creek Romances

All the Little Things: Book One

Lightning Can Strike Twice: Book Two

Aging Gracefully: Book Three

Sunny Side Up: Book Four

Wander Back in Time Series

Whispers of Liberty

Free on smashwords.com to see the birth of a writer:

Lakeside Magic

Deep in the Heart of Dixie

"The weak can never forgive. Forgiveness is an attribute of the strong."
—Mahatma Gandhi

Prologue

NEW YEAR'S DAY. GRAHAM SCOTT WAS AWAKE long before sunrise. This time, he wasn't up for a run; he only ran now for the sheer pleasure of it. Right now he wanted to be still and savor the approaching dawn.

The map of the Adirondacks was torn down off the wall, the search for Sarah ended. Only the calendar remained. Lila, her five-year-old daughter, had made a big, yellow smiley face on today's date to make sure it stood out as special. Extra special. Today was the beginning of Graham's life, their new life. Nothing mattered before this day. It was his wedding day. It was all he could do not to pinch himself, afraid this was a dream and he'd wake up to find himself still combing the Adirondack wilderness for Sarah.

The back deck was slippery with a new layer of snow that had fallen in the night, making the world look like it had dressed up for the occasion. Graham traced the steps they would take to marry. Off the deck. Down the bank. To the end of the dock where their mothers had put up an arbor, interwoven with pine boughs and white lights.

He was shaking by the time he stepped under the archway, his teeth chattering and his breath a fog swirling around him; he'd forgotten his coat and didn't care. To feel alive again!

Graham didn't know what he would have done if Sarah had wanted to wait. If he could have eloped with her the moment he brought her out of the woods, he would have, to make certain she was his. He would never let her go again.

He hit his knees, oblivious of the cold or the snow, and let the glory of the sunrise wash over him. "Thank you, God, I can never thank you enough for bringing her back to me. I will do my best to do something good with this gift You have given me."

IT WAS HER LAST MORNING that she would wake up in her hometown, Johnstown, and the Gingerbread Cottage, bringing with it a hint of sadness. This had been Sarah's home with Lee before war tore him away from her. Their time together in this house had been all too brief; it was Lila's place more than anything else and the keeper of so many memories made with and by her daughter. The little house had weathered many storms in Sarah's life and it held much love. It was a parting and felt like saying goodbye to a loved one, even if it was a building made from brick and wood.

Happiness, shining and bright like the sun, was strong enough to wipe away the shadows of leaving. Sarah was about to start her new life with Graham. His name meant home and it was fitting. Each time she saw him again felt like a homecoming. She had come to the realization that it would not matter where they went. Graham *was* home.

The phone rang, pulling her away from her musings. She stretched lazily like a cat and picked up without needing caller i.d. "Good morning."

"It is because of you. I've been up for over an hour and can hardly stand myself. We should have had a daybreak ceremony." It was her groom-to-be, exuberant, bubbling over with excitement like a child, his impatience making him breathless.

Sarah snuggled in the covers and felt her own anticipation rising to meet his. "I can't wait either. Just a little while more. Do you think you can hang on?"

There was the pitter patter of tiny feet and a flurry of motion. Lila burst into the room and jumped into bed. "We're getting married today, we're getting married! Is that Crackers? 'Morning, Crackers! I wish you could come have breakfast at Nana's and Pop Pop's, but Mommy says you can't see the bride before the big moment. Wait until you see her dress!"

Graham's laughter carried over the line. "I wish I could be there too, Lila my lovely, but after today we'll have breakfast together every day. Love you, sweetie, and I love you, Sarah.

I'll see you in a few hours. Did I tell you I can't wait?" The phone disconnected.

Sarah wrapped her arms around her daughter and tipped her head against Lila's, one shining curtain of hair spilling into another like sunshine falling down. "It's our new beginning, Lila. Today we write the first chapter in the storybook of our life together with Graham!"

THE SUNSET CREATED A PERFECT BACKDROP for their vows, a splash of color streaking across the sky as Graham stood with Sarah under the archway of pines, white lights, and a dusting of fresh snow. They were a contrast of black and white, the groom in his tuxedo and dark head bent to the bride's fair hair and ivory gown. Pleasant Lake, a stand of trees, and the mountains spread beyond. Everyone held their breath, witnesses to an answer to their prayers in the wedding kiss.

Now, darkness had fallen. Jim Pedersen sat in an Adirondack chair by the large, outdoor fireplace, his wife, Jeanie, on his lap. The newlyweds were on their dance floor, a cleared area on the ice lit by torches. They held each other close, spinning round, their laughter drifting on the air.

"Look at them! They're not even wearing coats. They're crazy!" Jim shook his head, smiling at his best friend of over twenty years. He had never seen Graham this happy.

"Crazy in love! Do you remember when we were like that? It's been fourteen years since we said, 'I do.'" Jeanie stared into her husband's coffee-colored eyes, the reflection of the fire flickering in her dark gaze.

Black wisps of hair escaped from a green beret to match her jaunty coat. A short stretch of legs in black tights was capped off by shiny knee-length boots, making her cute as a button. She was Jim's Italian spitfire, spicing up their lives in more ways than her husband could count.

Jim's hand rested on the slight swelling that was their child and thought his heart couldn't stretch any bigger trying to hold his love for her. "It's still like that for me, Jeanie-girl, every day that I wake up next to you."

He planted a kiss on her forehead and tucked her in under his chin. Their attention turned to the young couple on the ice, a mirror image of the pair shining with happiness on the dark surface of the frozen lake. All the wrongs of Sarah's abduction had been made right on this night.

No one saw the uninvited guest, concealed in the trees, his white-streaked, sandy hair wild as rage lit a fire in his golden eyes.

1

THE CEREMONY TOOK PLACE AT SUNDOWN on Pleasant Lake, at the home that was now theirs. Surrounded by family and their closest friends, Graham and Sarah exchanged vows under the snowy arbor on the dock. It looked like the stuff of fairytales covered in pine boughs and the twinkle of white lights.

Lila's ice rink made a perfect dance floor. Laughter echoed all around, breath a mist floating on the air, everyone bundled up like Eskimos. Sarah's father and Jim took turns pulling Lila on a sled. Guests milled around the outdoor fireplace, drinking hot cocoa or coffee flavored with liqueurs, toasting with champagne, and eating cake. Finally, the newlyweds were left alone.

The Scotts had moved their celebration inside. The fire had died down to a dim glow, candles were scattered around the room, and the lights were turned down low. John Denver's, "Rocky Mountain High" played softly on the stereo as Graham moved back and forth in a slow sway with the new Mrs. Scott.

A flash of memory surfaced in his mind of his mother and father dancing in the kitchen to the same music. Her arms had been looped around his neck and they were laughing, slightly tipsy from a bottle of wine for their anniversary. They thought their young son was sound asleep, but Graham had been lying at the top of the stairs caught in the wonder of their love.

It was bittersweet, making his heart ache. He gathered his *wife*—savored that word, could never get enough of it—closer and buried his face in her hair. "This was my father's favorite music."

Sarah's hands drifted upward, skimming up his strong chest and sturdy arms before entwining in his hair. "Your father and mine would've been good friends. Daddy loves John Denver too. That's part of the reason I put it on. I can still remember him swinging me around the living room to 'Thank God I'm a Country Boy' when I was little." She sank into Graham's body and rested her weight on him with a sigh. "I wish your dad could've been here today."

The song came to an end and moved on to a slow ballad, making Graham feel a little melancholy. The hole left by his father's death felt deeper and darker on this most important of days in his life, a milestone meant to be shared by a father and son. "Me too. You would've liked him. He was my rock."

Sarah stood up on tiptoe to take her husband's face in her hands. Her eyes held the light of the sky and promise for the night to come. "Like you are mine."

She took his hand and pulled him toward the bedroom. A quick glimpse in Lila's room proved the little girl was sound asleep; it had been a long, full day for a five-year-old. Sarah pulled her door shut and gave a tug until they were in Graham's room—correction, *their* room.

Sarah had already placed candles on all of the available surfaces. Their firefly flickering was the only light, making shadows dance on the walls. She turned her back to her husband now, her message clear as she lifted her hair away from her neck. Graham reached up with fingers made clumsy in his anticipation, fumbling with her zipper. It felt hard to breathe and his heart began to race as the gown slipped from her shoulders, falling in a puddle of satin on the floor. Sarah stepped out and turned to face her husband. The invitation in her eyes made him melt.

His jacket dropped to the floor first. He tugged at the tie, closing his eyes while her fingers did magic, letting it slip out of fingers that tingled. Graham's skin warmed with the touch of her hands. His pulse started to throb, fluttering as she pressed her lips against his neck. His hands came up with a will of their own, knowing exactly what to do as they removed the small excuse of material that was a substitute for underwear.

His breath caught in his chest at the sight of her. "God, you're beautiful…so beautiful."

Sarah looped her arms over his neck and buried her head in his chest. "So are you. Don't make me wait any longer, Graham. You and I have been apart for a lifetime. It's time to be one."

In answer, he scooped her up into his arms and carried her to the bed. He laid her down on thick, warm blankets and proceeded to worship the temple that was his wife.

Graham lost track of time. Sarah was nestled in his arms, her heart thumping under his arm draped across her chest when he felt her shiver. He grazed her hair with his lips.

"What's wrong, baby?" He whispered, his voice gone hoarse from a night that had worn them both to the point of exhaustion, a feeling neither regretted.

"I don't know. I just had that eerie sensation of being watched. I'm just paranoid, I guess." Sarah turned over and buried her head in his chest.

Graham stroked her hair, hoping to calm her fears. A slow unraveling began in his arms until she slept. It was a long time before sleep came for him, doubt stabbing at his peace of mind. Eventually, the warmth of his wife's body and her breath kissing his skin was enough to help him tumble off into fitful dreams.

IT FELT GOOD TO WEAR HIS UNIFORM AGAIN. The sturdy, deep green of the forest ranger steadied him and made him feel grounded. No longer a reminder of the all-consuming search for Sarah, it gave him back his purpose.

Graham had gladly taken the regional director's offer to go on vacation. He had been desperately in need of a break after over six months of scouring the vast Adirondack Park. A little over a month had passed, a time to recuperate, refuel, and renew his life. It was time to get back to work.

Besides, Sarah was returning to school to teach her kindergarten class for the first time since her disappearance and Lila would be in the room across the hall from her mother. Graham might as well be useful and hit the woods again.

Sarah's arms came up around him in the mirror and he could hear the sound of her inhaling deeply. "Mmm, you smell and look good enough to eat. Are you sure we don't have time to go back to bed?"

Her body leaned up against his, her head resting on his back. It felt good. They fit together, two halves of a whole. It explained why there had been such a gaping emptiness in each when Sarah was missing.

Graham turned around and wove his fingers in the sunshine of her hair. Her blue eyes were lit with pleasure; they warmed him like nothing else could, filling all those empty spaces that had gnawed inside of him for too long.

"You have a classroom of munchkins waiting for you. You look incredible. If all of my teachers had looked like you growing up, I never would've learned anything. I'd be too busy falling in love." He dipped his head to steal a kiss when a little windstorm in the form of a five-year-old arrived.

"Look, Daddy! Look! Mommy and I match! We picked out our outfits last night!" Lila did a little twirl in her red dress with black spots and white puffs for sleeves. She called it her

15

ladybug dress. "Red's Mommy's favorite and we thought these were perfect for good luck on her first day back to school. Doesn't she look really pretty?"

Lila was practically quivering with her excitement, almost tripping over her tongue. School had been torture for the little girl, something she dreaded and could barely manage, staring across the hall at the room where she knew Sarah was supposed to be. Now she could look forward to being there because her mother was there too.

Sarah did a little spin in her red dress that tapered to her ankles. It was covered with little black polka dots and a black jacket belted at the waist to make her look very classy. "What do you think? Too much?"

Her uncertainty tugged at Graham's heart. Her life had been turned topsy-turvy over the course of the past, several months and it would be strange for her, this period of readjusting. Terrifying, but at the same time she couldn't wait.

Graham pulled her close, dipped her back, and planted a long kiss that should've turned her insides to liquid; he knew that his were. "You're perfect. I don't know how I'll get through the day thinking about my two ladies in red."

His girls walked him to the door, sent him off with hugs and kisses, Sarah lingering with her body pressed against him, the scent of her shampoo and perfume making him dizzy. Graham pressed his forehead to hers and let loose a groan. "You do not know how hard you are making it for me to leave."

16

Her giggles bubbled over and she rose up on tiptoe to kiss his ear, whispering playfully, "Just giving you something to look forward to. Have a good day, Mr. Scott."

"You too, *Mrs.* Scott." One last round of kisses topped off his leaving with a big smacker planted on the top of Lila's golden head and Graham stepped out the door, whistling cheerfully. He climbed into his forest ranger's truck, cranked the engine, and pulled out. His hand hung out the window as he waved until he rounded the bend in the driveway when they couldn't see him any longer.

Graham took a long draw from the thermos of coffee that Sarah pressed in his hand, a bit of heaven on earth. He closed his eyes for an instant, opened them, and slammed on the brakes. Something grabbed at him, something out of place. Slowly, he crept forward a few more feet and set the coffee down, leaning on the steering wheel to get a better look. The hair rose up on the back of his neck and a curse slipped from between gritted teeth.

A set of footprints made a serpentine path, cutting through the woods to a stand of pines that provided a bird's eye view of his home. Graham left the truck running and got out to follow the trail. There was no doubt the prints were fresh. Snow had fallen on New Year's Eve, making the entire world look brand new. Pristine. Except for these marks that were a scar on his personal landscape. He placed himself beside the prints, eyed the house, caught a glimpse of red passing by his bedroom

17

window. Graham's stomach clenched and he almost lost his coffee.

He turned around and tracked the prints through the woods until they stopped at the road…only to resume on the other side. Graham's heart began to pound. He wanted nothing more than to follow those prints, see where they would lead, but Sarah and Lila came first.

As he sat back down in his seat, his hands tightened on the wheel, and he slammed it with his fist. Snow was sprinkling down overhead. According to the weather update on the radio, at least half a foot would fall before nightfall. Enough to hide the mysterious footsteps. To cover Kane's tracks.

SHE LIT UP LIKE A CANDLE. There was no better way to describe the moment when Sarah's students first arrived and she shook their little hands on their way in her door. Graham had always thought that children were like bees to honey when they were around her. It was no different for these little ones even though they didn't know his wife yet. It was her element, where she belonged.

Her best friend, Melissa Ashley, beamed as she stood at her post across the hall. They had exchanged tearful hugs and smiles when Sarah walked in. Now Lila stood next to Ms. Ashley and gazed at her mother. It was as if the little girl was drinking her in and couldn't get enough of her.

Graham knew the feeling well. If he lived to be one hundred and spent the rest of his days with Sarah by his side, he would still want more. After having her stolen away and given back by some miracle, his heart swelled to bursting and learned to beat again.

Watching Sarah with the boys and girls, seeing the simple pleasure on Lila's face to have her mother in her place again, Graham's eyes began to burn. He gave his girls a wobbly smile, a wave, and turned away. He'd turned his truck around and insisted on taking them to school, claimed he missed them too much already, unable to bear sending them off on their own after seeing those footprints.

Not now that they'd had a mysterious visitor. One Sarah had sensed on their wedding night. Had *he* been watching then? Graham pushed those thoughts away and headed for the door. His girls were content to be back where they belonged. It was time for Graham to return to the place that was like a home and a chapel—the woods.

He ducked outside and sucked in the cold air, filling his lungs and blinking to clear his vision. The snow continued to fall, making the whole world look like a snow globe. His mind turned to the wilderness. No longer a torment to him when they withheld the secret of Sarah's whereabouts, the Adirondacks were once again the air that he breathed. If only they didn't harbor Kane.

Graham had to lose himself in their midst. Feel the presence of the mountains towering above him. Be surrounded by the scent of the pines. Walk their trails and marvel at the life held within. Time to be their guardian again rather than try to take back what did not belong.

As his truck turned toward the woods, the knots slowly unwound and Graham's anxiety began to abate. He was being unreasonable. Someone was probably going for a walk. One of their wedding guests may have gone to the trees to get a picture of the house. There were plenty of reasons why someone might go on a trek through the woods. Kane was long gone; he had promised to leave Sarah alone if Graham repaid the favor in kind. *Easier said than done.*

Where to start? He'd pondered it for the last few days. Part of him resisted, but his gut overruled any hesitation. Graham decided to stay close to home and face the place where Sarah's disappearance began—Rockwood State Forest. He needed to make peace with it and put it behind him.

They'd gone together, Sarah, Lila, and Graham, but he needed to do this on his own. Otherwise, it would always hurt to be here, like a cancer or a thorn that gnawed at him and had to be pulled out. He had to work through his fury at Kane Johnson, buried but always simmering deep within, ready to erupt at the slightest provocation. Time would be the only way to curb his anger, time and patience. Hopefully, Graham would be granted enough of both.

It was only a ten minute drive and his truck seemed to find the way to the parking area on its own. There was no other car which was just as well. Graham wanted to go it alone. He strapped on his cross country skis and glided over the trails. Snowshoes would have worked but they were slower; facing his fears didn't mean he had to drag it out any longer than necessary.

The options were numerous. Graham branched off to the right, looped around, and ended up where he started. Winded but feeling stronger after the first round, he took a different path. This one led him to the spot where he met Sarah and Lila. That trip was welcome no matter how many times he traveled its path.

It was making his way out of the trails that hit him hard, made his mouth go dry, and his heart start to trip. It would be a long time coming before Graham would get over the total dread that took hold of him at the sight of Sarah's empty car in the lot, locked, with all of her things still inside, but no sign of her.

He sat in his truck, leaning on the steering wheel, and pulled it together. It was still early. His father's words came to him, reminding him of what he already knew. *You have to finish what you started.* There was one other place he had to return to today. Rockwood took Sarah away from him. Kane Mountain gave her back.

Thirty minutes later, Graham made his way up the slope, snowshoes the only way to tackle the incline. The seasonal campers and hikers were gone. The path was unbroken. It would be too difficult to walk up in boots and Graham didn't feel like fighting with skis even if the incline was not extreme. Skis were meant for going down, not up.

He was glad for the exertion and challenge. His emotions were still churning from the excursion into Rockwood. It was cold, with a bite to it, but Graham didn't mind. It was a reminder that he was alive and should be thankful.

The spot was quiet, mainly visited during the other seasons, especially summer. Graham was fortunate to be able to face the past without intrusions or distractions. Cardinals and blue jays winged from bough to bough in the evergreens, the wind shook the tree limbs, a shimmer of snow breaking loose to drift in the air as the tops of the pines swayed and creaked. A soft snowfall continued to drift down, shutting him off from the rest of the world.

Otherwise, it was calm. The trees rose up around him, quiet companions. His guardians. Graham took his time making his way to the top, took it all in, let the woods be his cure as they soothed all of the rough and raw places.

He crested the top of the mountain trail, a little short of breath, sweating even in the chill. His body had worked hard. The old ranger station was the perfect stop off point, a place to drop on the porch and drink down the next dose of his most essential medicine—coffee.

It was peaceful this time of year, sitting on the porch of the cabin, with nothing but the breeze and the occasional animal for company. Graham scanned the interior; the two rooms remained empty and unharmed. It was an unspoken rule that this place was not to be molested in order to be enjoyed by all. Many a hiker or spontaneous camper had taken refuge under its roof.

Graham deliberated a few minutes before gearing up for the last leg of his journey. He had a final duty to perform here in order to close the door on Kane Johnson, a door in his memory he planned on locking. Time to steel his mind.

Procrastination had never been his way. Graham slammed down the last of his coffee, removed his snow shoes, and mounted the steps. Inhaling deeply of the frigid air, he didn't hesitate to go the final stretch of this journey. His blood started humming in his veins, his heart thumping erratically. At the top, Graham took out his binoculars and scanned the woods. This time he found it easily—Kane's cabin, where Sarah had been held prisoner. Where the torment finally came to an end.

The woodsman had lived there all his life in a home built by his father, meant to be kept secret. For over 45 years, his father had been successful in avoiding the outside world. As a Viet Nam veteran, he'd wanted to escape civilization and had managed to keep his family there in peace without intrusion upon or from others. But Kane's parents died and the all-consuming loneliness destroyed that peace, followed by his sister's terminal illness. The hermit was driven out of the woods in search of a companion and helpmate. He had taken Sarah for his own.

Inexplicably, through snippets of memory and vivid dreams, Graham had been drawn to the tower on a wintry day in November. Had it been mere coincidence or something more when Sarah tried to escape on the same day, revealing her presence? For a man of faith, it had been strengthened one hundred fold when Graham laid eyes on her.

He'd created a diversion, fought off Kane, and brought his Sarah home. In the long months, an eternity, of her abduction, he'd never faltered in the effort to make that goal happen. His determination had been rewarded.

There was no sign of life in the cabin now. It was easier to pick it out, dusted in snow. When Kane's father had built his home, he'd created a masterpiece in woodwork, disguising the cabin with the trees, rocks, and surrounding landscape. It had been carefully tended to remain camouflaged, its owners making certain it blended in throughout the seasons. Signs of a guardian were no longer evident.

Graham resisted the temptation to bridge the gap and look inside again. It felt like trespassing. Odd that he would respect the personal property of someone who had violated their lives in the deepest sense. Deep down in his bones, he knew. Kane wasn't there. Graham prayed to God that he would never see the man again.

The survivalist was somewhere in the wilderness that he knew best. Graham felt a prickling on his neck and glanced over his shoulder. Would he feel Kane's eyes on his back for the rest of his life?

2

MOST OF THE OTHER TEACHERS HAD LEFT.
Graham leaned against his truck in the school parking lot,
waiting for his girls. He tried to look casual, but his nerves were
strung tight. No matter how illogical, his palms were actually
sweating from a wave of anxiety, fearful that something might
have happened to Sarah and Lila.

Get a grip! What could possibly happen to them at an
elementary school? Images of Columbine and Sandy Hook
flashed through his mind. He ruthlessly squashed them. *Nice
job. Now you've ruined this place too.*

The door opened and out walked his ladybugs, holding
hands while the snow sprinkled down on two blonde heads.
Like rice tossed at a wedding. The part of Graham that had been
suffocating could finally breathe easy again.

Lila saw him and came running. "Crackers! I mean,
Daddy, we had the bestest day ever!"

Graham grabbed hold and swung her around in a circle,
his smile mirroring hers. "Really? What did you do?"

He held Lila on one arm and opened the other to pull
his wife in to smell the apple scent in her hair, reassuring
himself that she was warm. Solid. Not a dream. Graham could
never get enough of her. "Hello, Beautiful," he murmured.

"We had a 'Welcome Back, Mommy Day.' Well, they didn't call her Mommy. You know what I'm talking about, right Daddy? All day long, our two classes did special things together. We had games in the gym, we watched a movie and ate popcorn, and we had make your own sundaes. I wish every day could be like today."

She took a break to come up for air, looking closely at Graham. "Have you been sitting here all day waiting for us?"

He laughed and kissed her cheek. "No, Sillybilly. I went to the woods and did my job. Then I came back. Remember, I dropped you off. How else would you get home?"

Sarah was a bit wistful beside them as she glanced down the road toward her parents' home. A wedding gift from her parents, her first husband, Lee, had agreed that the Gingerbread Cottage next door would be the perfect location for their first home. She and Lila used to walk to the school on a daily basis.

"Lila was ready to head to Nana and Pop Pop's. Old habits are hard to forget." She leaned into Graham and gave him a kiss. "I missed you today. How was your first day back to work?"

His mood darkened and he began to stiffen. He made an effort to force himself to ease up, keep his tone light. It was over. *It will never be over.* "Just fine. It felt good to be back in the saddle again. What do you say we walk over to your Mom and Dad's? I'm sure they'd like to see you and we can catch up on how your day went."

If Sarah noticed Graham avoiding the topic, nothing was said. Lila's tongue didn't stop running for the walk home. He feared it might break at such a fearsome pace.

Sally Anderson's face lit up like the sunrise when she opened her door. "Well, if it isn't the Scott family! Come in! Come in!"

She made sure to divvy out hugs for everyone when they stepped inside. Sarah had not only inherited her mother's eyes that held the sky and hair that held the sun. A big heart had also been passed down.

"Steve and I were just talking about school going back in session. It's so strange not to have you next door anymore. I suppose you'll have to keep visiting to make sure we don't get too lonely." Sally bustled around her kitchen while the three sat at the table, putting on hot water for hot chocolate for the girls and pouring Graham's coffee before setting out a plate of cookies.

Graham caught her hand and pulled her close for a kiss on the cheek. "Good job on the coffee, Sal. You and your daughter have the magic touch. Where's Steve?"

There was no sign of his father-in-law. Steve could be out running errands or taking a nap, although the latter was unlikely. Sleeping in and daily naps had been a means of escape while Sarah was missing. Those coping methods quickly ended upon his daughter's safe return.

"Oh, he's out puttering in his woodshop. Why don't you invite him in for a cup of coffee and let him know that his girls are here?" Sally didn't even wait for an answer. She reached up to pat his cheek as Graham slipped into his coat. "Married life must be treating you well. You're starting to get rid of those sharp edges. You're not so thin any more. Are you happy, Graham?"

He glanced at his wife and Lila, their heads nearly touching as they fiddled with a jigsaw puzzle set out on the table. Their laughter, a blend of Lila's high pitched notes blending with Sarah's lower ones, made him smile. Somewhere inside, a part of him that had remained frozen during his journey, into the woods and within himself, thawed.

"What else is there? I'm the luckiest man on earth." Graham took a sip of his coffee and headed outside.

A rush of cold air followed him inside the cozy woodshop. The wintry blast pushed past Graham and made the wood chips rise into the air, transforming into a small twister that traveled across the floor. It was warm inside, suiting the preference of its owner and his older bones.

The scent of wood, polyurethane, and smoke from the woodstove met Graham and hit him hard. His father had loved to work with wood. It only took closing his eyes to imagine Dylan Scott standing in the room. When he opened his eyes, the illusion intensified. If only Graham could step back in time to the days when he could open a door and find his father standing there.

Steve Anderson had his back turned to his son-in-law. He had the same dark hair speckled with gray, wire frame glasses that glinted in the light, and held himself in such a way that one would have thought he and Dylan were the same person…until he turned around and Graham had to remind himself. His father was dead.

The draft pulled Steve's attention away from the wood he was cutting on the band saw. Catching sight of his son-in-law, his face creased in a smile, adding the kind of wrinkles anyone would want. "Graham, this is a nice surprise! We didn't expect you this evening. I was just finishing up a sign for your place. Does Sally know you're here?"

Graham's eyes stung and he gave his father-in-law a hug to hide the longing for his own father. Steve might not be his dad, but he was definitely up there, a close second-best.

"It was the girls' first day back to school and they've been missing you two. Besides, Lila's bursting with new information. She's been chewing my ear off for the last twenty minutes or so. I figured it was Pop Pop's turn for a nibble. Sally's making coffee. You up for a cup?"

Steve set his project aside, an intricate carving of *The Scotts*, to hang on Graham's front door. "Sounds good. Let me get my coat. That air's bitter out there, enough to take a nip out of your skin, no doubt about it."

After shrugging into the welcome warmth of a gift from his wife, he inspected his son-in-law more closely. Eyes like slate bored in deep, the tools honed by a father. "Is something bothering you? You seem like you're on edge. Trouble in paradise? That can't be possible for you two love birds. Are there money problems?"

Steve's forehead furrowed in concern as he reached for his back pocket, ready to grab his wallet. That was his way, always prepared to give anything he had—his money, his time, a sturdy shoulder, or a listening ear. Even while his own world was crumbling, he had been a constant for Graham during Sarah's disappearance.

Graham shrugged off his concern. "It's nothing, really. Just missing my dad a bit. Some of Sal's coffee will cure me."

He slung an arm around the older man's shoulders and they made their way inside, Graham shaking off the blues with the cold. His whole world was sitting at the kitchen table, laughing and talking with Sally. There was no reason to let the past bring him down. He had the here and the now.

Sarah was nibbling on a cookie when her face brightened at the sight of the two most important men in her life. She stood up to give her father a hug and a kiss. He let her go, only to allow her to be swept off her feet as Graham spun her around in a circle and dipped her down low. "Did I miss anything while I was gone? How about another kiss? I was in withdrawal all day. Driving away from my girls was near impossible this morning."

Sarah humored him with an all too brief taste of her lips and sank back down in her chair on unsteady feet. Graham was pleased to have that power over her. Would those feelings ever wear off or would they only grow stronger? "Behave yourself, Mr. Scott. My affections will have to wait until later."

Graham's insides turned to gel. That was the kind of hold *she* had on *him*. He pulled up a chair beside her and rested his hand on hers. This need to be close to Sarah—after nearly losing her—intensified every day. If there was a way to be with her 24/7, he would be more than willing. Since that wasn't a possibility, he made most of moments like these.

He lifted a strand of hair from her face, watched the color bloom as his finger brushed her cheek, and gave her a crooked smile. "Oh, I can wait. I'm an extremely patient man."

The sound of a throat being cleared reminded Graham of the fact that there were other people in the room. He directed his attention back to his in-laws and his daughter.

Steve nodded his head, amusement making his eyes sparkle. "Enough of this lovey-dovey business. Let's get to what's really important—Lila's day at school! How was your day, Ladybug?"

He patted his knee in invitation and was rewarded with the welcome weight of his granddaughter on his lap. Her arms came up around his neck and she gave him one of her "squeeze the stuffing right out of you" hugs, like he had taught her. "So, out with it. Graham tells me you're just chock full of news. Tell me everything."

Lila gave him a big grin, all the more endearing with one of her top teeth missing. "Oh, Pop Pop, it was the bestest day ever. We celebrated all day long. We spent the whole time with the other class and we watched a movie and ate popcorn and had ice cream too! I made my sundae just like you like it, Pop Pop, vanilla with chocolate sauce, peanut butter, whipped cream, and nuts too. I would have brought one home for you, but Mommy said the ice cream would have turned to soup. How could the sundae have melted, Pop Pop? My breath was a frozen cloud on the way home. If I could have put a stick in the middle, it would have been a popsicle!"

Laughter was her answer, a rumble deep down in Steve's belly. That was Lila's specialty—filling their lives with joy. "I think Mommy was worried about when the ice cream was still inside school. Besides, you might not have been able to resist. That would have meant two sundaes and one, big tummy ache. How about Mommy? How was your day, Sarah?"

His daughter's smile, the glow in her eyes that had been missing during her ordeal, said everything. "Wonderful, Dad. It's funny. I was so nervous since I haven't been with this class since the beginning of the year. I was afraid I'd be like a substitute to them and that I would forget what to do. But the second I walked in that door, I felt like I had never left."

33

Steve leaned over and pecked her cheek. "That's good, Sarah-girl. I didn't think things would go any other way. That leaves you, son. Did you keep yourself out of trouble today?"

Graham busied himself with preparing another cup of coffee and worked his way through a cookie, striving for calm. His lingering unease made him feel anything but. "I went here and there, nothing out of the ordinary. The woods welcomed me back. It felt good to get to work, do something useful."

Sally picked up on her son-in-law's tension. They'd come to know him well, better than most in-laws would. During his intense, drawn-out search for Sarah, Graham had been a regular in their home, sharing his progress and his pain, a pain that was a burden shared by all. "Where did you go? I didn't catch that."

Inwardly cursing her perceptiveness, Graham took another sip of coffee and decided to bite the bullet. "Rockwood and Kane Mountain. There wasn't much time for anything else. I'm slower going on snowshoes." He stared back down into his coffee cup. Otherwise, his mother-in-law was sure to see into his heart.

Sarah took hold of his hand and gave a good squeeze, forcing her husband to look into her gaze. "Graham, I'm here now. I'm not going anywhere. You need to put the past behind you."

A bob of his head and he was up out of his seat. "That's what I was doing, saying goodbye to my memories. Excuse me for a moment."

He strode off to the bathroom and splashed some cold water on his face. Any reference to the time before, that gaping hole when Graham didn't know if he'd ever crawl his way out if he didn't find Sarah, still shook him. Hard. He needed a moment—to remember how to breathe again. To stop his insides from shaking. To slow down his heart. When would these feelings stop? When would it finally be over and done?

Collected again, Graham opened the door. Sarah was leaning against the wall. Waiting for him. Thank God. She was standing there. She was real. Not a memory or a dream.

She opened her arms and her heart was in her eyes. He stepped into her embrace and felt a fluttering in her chest, like a hummingbird. Sarah felt the same way that he did. "Graham, it's okay. Everything will be all right now. You don't have to keep secrets from me to protect me. It's hard to talk about what happened, but I can take it. Don't hide things from me and don't torture yourself anymore, okay? You need to let yourself heal, not open up all the raw places again."

Graham dropped his head to her shoulder, a shudder running through him, and held on tight. "It's just…I can't shake being afraid you're a dream and then…here you are. How did you get so good at taking care of me, Mrs. Scott?"

"I learned from the best. That means you." Sarah stood on tiptoe and gave him another kiss. "Come on, Graham, before they think we're up to no good."

Lila found them first and grabbed hold of Graham's hand. "Come on, Daddy! Let's go play in the yard!"

Those baby blues stared imploringly up at him, irresistible in that sweet face. The little slip of a girl had a hold on him that said she meant business. Already geared up, she made a beeline for the back door, towing Graham behind her. He glanced at the others and shrugged. Everyone knew "Crackers," now renamed Daddy, was wrapped around this little one's finger.

He had the presence of mind to pull on his winter cap and gloves before a barrage of snowballs hit him. The little munchkin didn't stay focused on any activity for long, moving on to snow angels, King of the Hill, and marching through the snow banks, climbing them like a mountain. They were perched at the top of the highest peak, Graham taking a breather, when the Snow Queen joined them.

Sarah was in her glory, eating up every second, trying to catch each twinkling with her girl. Her bright red cap and gloves reminded Graham of cardinals, her favorite bird. A splash of color, against a puffy, white coat and the surrounding snow, bobbed wherever she went.

With a war whoop reminiscent of the Dukes of Hazard and a scramble to the top, the hill was conquered with ease, the

Snow Queen enthroned, while her subjects lay at the bottom. Her reign didn't last. Unable to resist joining her husband and daughter down at the bottom, Sarah rolled down until they were a tangle of limbs, giggling together until they ran out of breath.

LILA WAS TUCKED IN BED. Sarah sat on the edge, her hand resting on her daughter's head while she whispered a prayer. Graham had already read to the little girl and leaned against the doorway, watching the two of them. He always gave them a private moment between mother and daughter.

They had belonged to each other, were each other's world for the first four years of Lila's life. Graham was grateful the door had opened and they'd pulled him in, but respected their special bond, especially since that bond had nearly been broken.

Sarah bent down low and kissed her daughter's hair gleaming in the moonlight. Graham felt a tugging on his heart, watching them, both so similar, both his. His wife stood and padded softly across the room, taking his hand. They walked quietly to the bedroom.

No words were necessary. Nothing more of Graham's day had been mentioned after their earlier discussion. It was a dance between them, this love they had. First to move in close, then step back. To hang on tight, then let go. To hold each other up when necessary, but let them stand alone when that was needed more.

Graham stretched out on the bed, head propped on his hand, as he watched his wife. When he was in his nineties, old and gray, barely able to move, he would never tire of watching her. The ritual of a woman getting ready for bed was mesmerizing.

The fall of Sarah's hair down her back, the dip of her head teasing him with a glimpse of her neck, her bare skin as her clothes dropped to the floor and she slipped on some sort of filmy, light material over her head that seemed to float around her. Lotion with a scent that nearly drove him crazy as her hands danced over her skin, making his own fingers itch to take over the job. No, Graham would never get enough of this.

He prayed they'd keep on this way until their bones were creaking almost as loud as the sway of their rockers. There was that familiar stab of fear that it could all be ripped away in an instant. Curse Kane Johnson for placing a shred of doubt in Graham's mind about growing old with Sarah.

"When does it get easier?" Unable to stop himself, the words stabbed the air while Sarah finished her preparations.

She sank onto the bed and lay down next to him, resting a hand on his, waiting with questions in her gaze. Graham closed his eyes to keep her from seeing the darkness that still lurked within. "I know I'm irrational. A part of me doesn't ever want to let you go. If I could be your shadow, I would. It killed me walking out of there this morning, leaving you and Lila, and

38

in the afternoon while I was waiting in the parking lot...I nearly called in the search and rescue dogs."

Sarah's hand pressed his and he felt the weight of her stare, forcing him to look at her. Her eyes were calm and steady, a place where he could always find his way. "There's an irrational part of me that wants *you* to stay by my side all of the time, like my own, personal bodyguard. Since we can't live our lives that way, we have to have faith, to put complete trust in God to keep us safe. We were brought back together and nothing on this earth has the power to keep us apart, not really. Even when I was in that cabin with Kane, my heart was always with you."

Graham pressed his forehead to hers, too overcome to speak. Her hand ran through his hair and became entangled. She was beside him and wasn't going anywhere. "I think I felt your presence, something that kept me believing you were alive and nearby. Every day that you were gone, I wouldn't give up and my heart was yours. Only yours."

With a little sound that was almost a cry, Sarah tucked herself in beside him as if she couldn't get close enough. They held on tightly and drifted off entwined in each other's arms with the light still on. With a sigh and a sudden loosening of all of his limbs, Graham welcomed a good night's rest.

Sleep came quickly, pulling him under while in his wife's embrace. It didn't last. He awoke with a start, his heart pounding, jittery with a nerves that jangled. At least there weren't any shreds of bad dreams this time, not that he could remember. The only cure—to get up and walk through the house, run his fingers over familiar objects, make sure things were undisturbed.

Room by room, he found nothing out of place, only moonlight and shadows. He paused to stand by a window in the kitchen, staring out into the darkness, wondering if Kane was out there watching them. A shudder ran through him and Graham drank a glass of water in long, deep swallows to steady himself when he heard crying.

"Mommy! I want Mommy!" Lila's voice drifted down the hallway, tearful and shaking.

Graham was there in an instant, sitting on the side of the bed, stroking her hair. Her little arms came up around his neck, holding on as tight as she could. She buried her head in his chest and he could feel her trembling. "Daddy, I dreamed I couldn't find Mommy. I went through every room. First, we were here, then the Gingerbread Cottage, then in the woods. I kept calling and calling, but I never found her!"

The cracks in Graham's heart, only just healed, split wide again. Without a word, he scooped up the little girl that had become his and carried her to their bedroom. "She's right here and she's not going anywhere. It was only a dream. We all have bad dreams sometimes, but you don't need to be scared anymore, Lila my lovely. You're safe and so is Mommy. I'll make it so."

He lifted up the covers and slipped the little girl into bed. Sarah's arm reached out—even in sleep a mother sensed her child—and pulled her daughter close. Lila burrowed down with a sigh, relaxing in the safety and warmth of her mother's presence. Graham stretched out next to them, propped on one elbow, watching. All the while, he continued to picture the footprints in the woods. Close to his home. Too close for comfort.

How long would it take for Kane's damage to be done? When would his touch no longer reach them in their dreams? Questions that couldn't be answered, but Graham lay awake asking them anyway, finally dozing off in fitful spurts until waking in the dark on the brink of dawn.

He was out of sorts after his unsettled night, holding his head in his hands while he sat on the side of the bed. Maybe a run would help clear his mind and ease the tension. A warm touch on his arm startled him. "Graham, what is it? What's wrong?"

He turned and absently stroked Sarah's hair, brushed a hand over Lila's head poking out of the covers. "Nothing, it's nothing. I didn't sleep well, that's all. It's really early. Go back to sleep." His voice was a whisper, not wanting to disturb Lila after her nightmares.

Graham knew from his own experience, Lila's, and he was certain Sarah's as well, that Kane was tiptoeing in, insinuating himself into all of their dreams. He suspected

Sarah's abductor interrupted her sleep often—how could he not?—even though she kept her fears to herself most of the time. It bothered him to no end that Johnson still had the power to steal their peace of mind.

"It's because of me and what happened with Kane, isn't it?" Sarah could step inside Graham's mind. Her voice trembled and that bothered him even more, that she was upset, to the point of making him angry.

"Can't a guy just have a rough night? Maybe I couldn't sleep because of feet jabbing me in the back." There was a sharp intake of breath in the darkness and her hand dropped, leaving a chill in its place.

Graham could feel her drawing away from him, the bloom of hurt between them, and an instant regret filled him. Sarah and Lila had suffered a lifetime's worth of hurt. To cause more was unacceptable. "I'm sorry, so sorry for snapping. You're right—Kane's shadow won't go away. It's not your fault, never yours. This is *his* fault. Lila had a bad dream thanks to the bastard and I was done for. I wish I could fix this for all of us."

There was a shifting of the covers and the weight on the bed. Graham felt pressure on his legs and Sarah was on his lap, arms looped over his neck. "You fix everything because you're here. Piece by piece. After every bad dream. Each time that you listen. Whenever we see you waiting for us."

42

They sat that way, holding on to each other until Kane's presence faded from their minds, replaced by the love they felt for each other. Love won out, every time.

3

HOLDING ON A LITTLE LONGER, GRAHAM FELT SARAH GO LIMP, her limbs heavy with sleep. Carefully, oh so carefully and quietly, he stood and slipped Sarah back under the covers next to Lila. He tiptoed out, intent on taking a run and then a shower when his cell rang.

"Graham Scott here. What's up, Laura?" The caller i.d. showed the number of the regional office. Laura was the morning dispatcher. She didn't call him often. Usually Graham checked in at the beginning of each week. If the office called, it was due to an emergency or something out of the ordinary.

"Hi, Graham. You're sounding chipper. Listen, we got a call of shots fired in the woods near Murray Hill Road and Mud Road in Ephratah. I figured that's your old stomping ground. Can you check out the place before we call in the local authorities?"

"Sure. I need a few minutes to get ready and I'll head right out." She disconnected and Graham hit the shower. Five minutes later, he was in his uniform, hair combed, and teeth brushed. Uneasiness rattled him, paranoia creeping in. Who lurked in the woods?

He jotted a note for Sarah and drew a doodle for Lila while he waited for the coffee to perk. A granola bar made for a quick departure and he was warming up his truck.

A tapping on the window gave him a start while he was fiddling with the defroster. Being on edge pushed him to half-expect Kane to be standing there with his face pressed to the glass. Instead, Sarah was waiting outside in her robe and boots, shivering. She pulled the door open and handed him a travel mug full of coffee.

"Here. I know you like mine better than yours." She stood on tiptoe to plant a long, hard kiss on his lips. "That's to keep you warm while you're out in the woods today. Be careful. I love you and thanks for the little note."

Graham shook his head and pulled her up inside the truck, closing the door after he had her settled on his lap. "Baby, you are making it really hard to leave this morning. I'm sorry I bit your head off earlier. What can I do to make it up to you?"

Sarah fiddled with a strand of his hair and stared into his eyes. Mission accomplished—he was back on steady ground again. "Oh, you really didn't do anything, but I wouldn't mind some attention tonight when you get home. How about you cook dinner?"

There was time for one more hug, to breathe in the scent of her, and steal another kiss to tide him over. "Years of bachelorhood gave me plenty of practice. I'll make you a meal you won't forget. Now go in before Lila wakes up looking for you. Love you."

 He watched her until she made it inside, carrying her smile and the warmth of her touch with him on the twenty minute ride to Ephratah.

Habit made his truck drive as if the trusty, hunk of metal had a will of its own, carrying him to his childhood home. Ephratah held countless memories, most of them good ones, until his father spent his last days dying of cancer within the walls where Graham had grown up. After his death, his mother couldn't bear to live in the house she'd shared with her husband. Graham couldn't even set foot inside until it was time to pack it up when she moved. Now he found himself parked in the driveway, staring at what had once been Home Sweet Home.

Although he'd prefer happy thoughts, flashes of the end crowded his mind and still overpowered all of the rest. Hospice workers and round-the-clock nurses helped Dylan Scott make the transition from the land of the living to the great beyond. Graham and his mother, Pamela, kept vigil by his side, counting each breath that became far and few between.

The night that Dylan crossed over, it was a little past midnight with a clear sky and a full moon, light bathing the shell of a man in a soft glow. There were no final words. He'd been unable to speak for the last few days and had said his "love you's" when it was still possible. They had fiercely tried to hold on to Dylan Scott. Now they helped each other learn how to let go.

Graham wiped at his eyes and pulled out of the driveway. As painful as those memories were, they gave him strength. The drive to Mud Road was brief as the colors began to bleed into the sky, announcing the sunrise. He shrugged into his winter coat and hat, checked his 357 pistol, and slipped on his gloves.

His breath formed a cloud the instant it hit the air. The temperature had to be hovering around zero. A great day to be hanging out in the woods in search of a poacher. Even though there were other possible reasons for shots being fired, illegal hunting was most likely.

Anything bagged now was against the law, a law Graham was required to uphold. As an environmental conservation officer for New York State, he had the authority and jurisdiction to uphold all of New York State's laws. However, poaching was under his area of expertise.

Slipping on snowshoes, he let the woods take him, their branches closing in and the scent of the pines strong enough to be a barrier to the rest of the world. It was quiet, unnaturally so with no sound of bird chatter or the rustle of leaves in the bitter chill. Graham's guard came up. Silence suggested something had already disturbed the wilderness. Its inhabitants were taking caution. Motionless. Watching. Waiting.

He followed nature's lead, took cover behind a stand of evergreens, and remained still. His pulse had kicked it up a notch, his nerves strung tight. One never knew what to expect or how many might be in the woods, armed, possibly dangerous or worse—stupid. For all he knew, his nemesis, Kane Johnson *could be* in these parts. Graham couldn't erase those footprints from his mind.

Rage, red hot and stoking the fire always at a low burn in the pit of his stomach, made it hard for Graham to concentrate. He had to work at yanking his mind off that track to calm himself. When the silence continued with no signs of activity, and Graham could think clearly again, he moved on in search of his perpetrator.

It didn't take long and was foolishly easy. Nearby, there was the loud crack of a rifle, snatching Graham's breath and making his heart stop. When it was beating again, he moved in the direction of the shot, taking care to lay low. Some idiot might take him for a deer even though he wore green and fluorescent orange. Worse yet, someone might want to take him out. *Someone like Kane.*

The footprints were next, leading the way in the fresh snow, followed by a trail of blood. There had been a hit. About a mile in—there was some satisfaction that the deer put up a good fight and a chase—Graham came to a small clearing. A buck of a respectable size lay in the snow, a pool of brilliant red beneath him, his eyes already glazed over. A man bent over him

48

with a large, hunting knife, his rifle lying beside him in the snow.

For an instant, Graham pictured sandy hair threaded with steaks of white. Golden eyes that burned with a quiet fury of their own. He blinked hard to clear his vision. Took a deep breath. Pulled off his gloves and took out his pistol, centering himself.

When his aim was set on the hunter, he sent up a prayer for a level head and spoke in a loud voice that rang out clearly in the silence. "Put the knife down and put both hands in the air where I can see them."

The man jumped and dropped the knife with hands that shook. Slowly, he turned to face the source of the command. He blanched visibly, the color spilling from his face, and began to sway.

"Officer, I'm sorry. Please don't shoot! It's my…my family needs to eat. I didn't know any other way." The air filled Graham's lungs in a rush. It wasn't Kane.

He approached the hunter slowly, never dropping his gaze. Graham pushed the gun away from the poacher's foot, knelt down, and picked up the knife, slipping it in his belt. The man's pallor was alarming, like he was going to pass out.

"Whoa, hold on. Sit down and put your head between your knees."

The man acquiesced all too willingly, dropping down like a stone. Graham knelt beside him and pressed his head down. "Breathe in deeply through your nose and let it out slowly. Give it a minute." He could feel the man trembling. His fear was not an act.

"Whew…okay, I'm okay. I thought I was a done for a moment. You scared the crap out of me, Graham." The man glanced up and looked Graham directly in the eye. He even managed a weak smile as fine tremors ran through his body beneath the forest ranger's intense gaze.

Graham studied the face in front of him. Now that all threats had been removed, he could study him more closely. Flipping through his mental file, Graham pulled out a picture from high school of a black-haired teen with eyes that were a bolt of blue, bordering on purple like Elizabeth Taylor's legendary gaze. He'd been slight of build then, still in that awkward stage between childhood and adulthood.

The man beside him now had broad shoulders and a sturdy build, but the bones in his face were too close to the surface. Going hungry appeared to be a valid excuse. "Danny? Danny Rogers? The last time I saw you, you were at your graduation party. You were getting ready to join the army. What happened?"

Danny's forehead creased in a frown and he looked away. "Life happened. I went to the service, put in my four years, and got out—it wasn't pretty. I went for forestry at FMCC and got my associate's. I meant to go on for four years, but my wife had a baby. You know how that goes. I took a job

50

in one of the leather mills. It sucked, but the pay was decent and I had benefits until they closed a year ago. I'm about to run out of unemployment and I didn't know what else to do. My wife works part time. It's still not enough. I've been going for jobs *every day*, Graham. Nothing's come up. My wife and son have to eat and I'll be damned if I'll let them starve. If I have to take a deer, by God, I'll do it. Are you going to lock me up? If you do, at least let them have the deer."

His head snapped up at the end, facing Graham head on, fury and hopelessness marring his features.

Graham shook his head and squeezed Danny's shoulder. "Take it easy, Danny. I'm not going to let you starve. I'll let you off with a warning this time. If you'd been near other homes, I'd have no alternative. If I catch you again, I'll have to take you in and you'll be fined."

Danny pulled away and turned around. "Then you might as well take me in now because I'm going to have to do it again and I don't have any money to pay the fine. Jail is warm and there's food. Maybe my family will get social services. They say we don't qualify now." His frustration was almost tangible, shoulders slumped in dejection.

Graham paused in consideration, hoped old times were enough, and put an arm around the other man's shoulders. He could feel something give and Danny's face crumpled. "Danny, I'm not taking you in. Calm down. Tell me—you said you have your associates in forestry?"

At a nod, he plowed on. "We need someone—an assistant ranger. It's not great pay, but it's decent and there are benefits. It will be better than where you are now or the leather mill. If you want, I'll put in a word for you. I'll even go with you to the regional office today if you can get it together. What do you say?" The gratitude that poured out of those blue eyes and the bear hug that followed said more than any words ever could.

GRAHAM REFLECTED ON HIS DAY on the drive home after dropping Danny off at his house. They'd taken the deer to the Rogers' household. The ranger sat at their kitchen table, was graciously offered coffee which he accepted, and bounced little Danny Junior on his knee. The man of the house showered, dressed in his best clothes quickly pressed by his wife, and they drove in Graham's truck to the regional office.

After a brief conversation with the director, John Christopher, Danny was hired on the spot. His military service in addition to his associate's degree had tipped the balance, Christopher had the utmost respect for the nation's veterans and he had complete trust in Graham Scott's judgment. No mention was made of the deer.

The Rogers' heartfelt thanks, from Danny and Diana, his wife, had sent Graham home on an emotional high. Pulling into his driveway, seeing his wife and daughter building a snowman, pushed him over the edge. He sent up a prayer of thanksgiving and asked for forgiveness for his dark state of mind that morning.

His family was happy, healthy, and well-fed. Moreover, they were his and they were waiting for him. Kane Johnson remained an obstacle in their lives, one Graham was uncertain he could ever get past, but the woodsman wasn't here now. It would have to be enough.

4

*SHE WAS RUNNING…*faster than she had ever run in her life, branches slapping at her face, the slippery leaves beneath her making her lose her footing, and there was an explosion of color everywhere. The cover of foliage was too thick to see through.

No matter how fast Sarah ran or how far, she wasn't getting anywhere. Not daring to look behind her for fear of what she would see, she plowed ahead. Her breath came in gasps like a sob and there was a fierce cramping in her side. No matter. She had to get away.

A hand shot out of nowhere, whipped her around, and he was there—Kane, her personal nightmare. There was steel in his grip and unbending tone. "*You are mine*. Did you really believe I would *ever* let you go?" She opened her mouth to scream her heart out…but there was no sound.

Sarah's eyes snapped open. She was breathing hard and two, strong hands *were* holding on tightly to her arms. Graham. Graham held her and no other. Her eyes closed in relief and she wilted against the pillows as the tears spilled from her eyes. She was home. In her bed. With her new husband.

It had only been a dream,—not the kind she would have asked for on a school day when she would have to face the kindergarten—but not the living nightmare. That was over. Or was it?

Until he truly lost his hold on her, the time with Kane would never be over. Sometimes she wondered if she needed to see him, confront him, dredge up forgiveness if it could be found. The mere thought of being in the same room with the man made her tremble.

"You were screaming." Graham's face was bleached of color in the moonlight, eyes dark. "Kane again, right?" He swallowed hard and released her arms to pull her against him.

"When is he going to be gone for good? Will he haunt us forever?" A fine tremor ran through his rigid frame. "*Damn it*, why did I leave first that day? If I could turn back time, I would."

Sarah reached up and pressed a finger to his lips. "*Stop.* Right now. None of this was your fault. It was never your fault. Not once did I blame you and neither should you."

She laid her head on Graham's chest and felt a hammering beneath her ear. Her hand found its way to his hair and began to stroke in a soothing motion meant to make him relax and sleep.

"What can I do to make it better, baby? You know I'd take all those hurts away if I could." His voice was rough, his body tense. Even at rest, Graham never let down his guard. He would always be on watch for Sarah and Lila for the rest of his life.

"You've already done it, Graham. You brought me home. I'm here, in this bed with you, in this house with my little girl. That's all I could ask for. Every moment spent with you heals me and makes up for the time away. What I need right now is for you to hold me and let the quiet settle, let us just...be. I love you."

Graham's arms came around her and held tight enough that they almost hurt. "I love you too."

Sarah closed her eyes and listened as his breathing evened and his heart slowed its pace. She could kick herself for waking him with her dream. He did not need reminders of the time all of them were trying to forget. Sarah's abduction had been hard. Although she had never been harmed, the pain of being separated from her loved ones had been unbearable.

What had bothered Sarah the most was knowing that her loved ones were going through a living hell, with no inkling of her whereabouts or that she was alive. Those close to her had been changed by the hardship of her absence. Her parents had aged in the months she was held captive. Her daughter was fearful that her mommy would disappear again and was reluctant to let Sarah out of her sight.

Graham had been hit the hardest. Her disappearance had made its mark physically, whittling him down, making him all edges and hard where he used to be soft. There was a shadow in his eyes yet to go away. Emotionally and mentally, he was still raw, his feelings always close to the surface, the strain of the search reluctant to let him go.

Sarah tucked herself in next to him. She'd crawl under his skin if she could, the need to be close was that powerful. His breathing, slow and steady, and the beat of his heart, sure and strong, lulled her to sleep with him.

NIGHTS AND WHAT HAPPENED in her dreams were beyond her control. During the day since Sarah returned home, she made a conscious effort to simply ride the wave of happiness she felt and take everything for what it was worth. The door was slammed shut on her months spent in captivity with Kane and she did her damnedest to pretend nothing ever happened.

For the most part she was successful until something would trigger a memory and the door would be blasted open. Mentally, Kane was unwilling to give her up, still trying to lay stake to his claim.

Driving into work, listening to Lila's chatter, with Graham's arm draped across the back of the seat to allow his hand to brush her shoulder, Sarah sealed that door in her mind with sheer grit. Her mother would call that quality pigheadedness. Graham's presence was enough to give Sarah the last shove needed to put her nightmare behind her and start her day with a clean slate.

Count her blessings—that was how she had to start each morning. At the top of that list: Graham and Lila. Her parents, of course. Her work. Friends. Coming home. Sarah thought back to the night before and Graham's recounting of Danny Rogers' plight. She reminded herself again. *My cup runneth over*.

"Hello…where did you go, Sarah Scott? You looked like you were miles away." Graham tapped her shoulder and gave her his typical crooked smile.

There were shadows under his eyes. Her heart ached because he lost sleep because of her. She'd have to go the extra mile when they were back home to make up for that.

"I was just thinking how lucky we are, especially compared to people like Danny Rogers. I'm so glad John gave him the job. It sounds like he really needed that extra nudge."

She turned and smiled at Graham, then Lila, as one of her favorite songs came on the radio and her little girl really started to bop to the music. Her spirit was contagious, forcing both parents to sing along.

Sarah looked forward to the daily drives into work and home again. Graham had made an unspoken arrangement. He would take her unless his job made that impossible. When he had to leave early yesterday, she had dreaded the trip on her own, even with Lila as company, only to see Jim pull in with his police cruiser.

At the end of the day, Jeanie picked them up. She stayed for decaffeinated tea, which she despised but anything for the baby, and caught up on the news. Sarah knew it was crazy—she could drive herself and they were spoiling her. Regardless, she'd let them continue until she was ready to go it alone. Until then, she'd draw strength from the rock beside her in Graham.

The song came to an end all too soon. They pulled up at the front door of the school. Graham reached over to unhook Lila's booster seat only to have her scrambling into his arms. "Hey, Monkey! Have a good day, you hear me? Love ya, Lila my lovely."

Lila rubbed noses with the only father figure she'd ever known and squeezed him until he hollered that he'd had enough. "I love you too, Daddy. Did I squeeze your stuffings out?" She waited patiently only to have him growl and hug her back, making her squirm and giggle in his grasp.

"Yes, my stuffings are out! How about my bear hug? Did it work?" He tapped her on the nose, eyes shining and laughter close to bubbling over the surface. Lila had that effect on people.

"It was perfect. Your turn, Mommy." Lila moved over to the side to allow Sarah to slide in as close as she could get to give her new husband the kind of kiss that would keep him coming back for more. His hand came up to cup her neck and Sarah lost her train of thought.

"Have a good day, Sarah. I'll see you both before you know it. Love you, babe." Graham's voice went hoarse and the look in his eyes nearly sent her to her knees. He certainly was not in the driver's seat when it came to the heat they felt at that moment. It would probably take him a while to bring his heart rate back down to a safe level. Maybe a dip into a cold river to cool down…

Sarah leaned in to drop one more kiss on his lips before forcing herself to pull back and get out. "Love you too. Be safe."

Lila held out her arms so that her mother could lift her down from the truck. Graham reached across to close the door and they waved him off. Sarah couldn't help but notice the rush of color that had flared in his face. No, it wouldn't be easy for either of them to concentrate.

Once inside, it was business as usual. Lila went to Melissa Ashley's room across the hall while Sarah made last minute preparations before her students began to trickle in. Coming back to school had been like riding a bicycle. She fell into the routine with ease, enjoying the ebb and flow of a kindergarten class. There had been a few bumps. The children missed the teacher they had for the first half of the year, but Sarah addressed that by having occasional visits to aid in the transition. Otherwise, it felt like she'd never left.

Today was one of her favorite days—Fridays. Every Friday, the two classes came together to do fun activities after a week of working hard. Being best friends with her co-teacher made it a true success. They began their day with stories and songs, a snack that they prepared together, and rounded out the morning with a project. The divider between the two rooms had been opened, turning it into one happy, melting pot. A few aides came in to help make everything run smoothly and it was already time for lunch.

Melissa and Sarah sat together in the staff room, catching up on the latest news. All too soon, the free period was over. Sarah set up the movie and settled everyone on the rug while Melissa popped popcorn and poured drinks. The lights were off and the movie theater was open for business.

Sarah was just about to sit down when she had to go to the bathroom. She'd had to do that unusually often lately. "Hey, Mel, I have to go to the bathroom *again*. I'll be right back."

Melissa waved a hand dismissively. "Don't worry, take your time. We've got a captive audience here. They've been fed, they have drinks, and there's television. That about covers all bases." She gave her friend a nod of her head with a bounce of her brown curls and a flash of her green eyes.

Sarah made it in the nick of time to the staff bathroom next to the principal's office. Doing her best to be speedy, unwilling to keep Melissa waiting on her own, she washed her hands and grabbed for the door handle. It wouldn't budge.

"Silly, dry your hands," she whispered to herself. A quick blast of the hand blower and she tried again. Still nothing.

There was a tightening in her chest as her heart began to pound and her breath caught in her throat. Sarah tried again, tugging as hard as she could. When that didn't work, she started to bang on the door and shout weakly. "Help! I'm stuck in here!" Never a fan of being in close and confined places, she despised them after her experience at the hands of Kane Johnson.

Panic was quick to overtake reason and Sarah started to pound her fists on the door. "Please get me out of here!" She called in a voice that was not her own, the tears starting to come and her throat choking up.

Couldn't they hear her?! If there were a fire alarm inside the bathroom, Sarah would have no qualms of pulling it even though she warned her students never to touch the red box.

There was the sound of rattling as someone tried the knob on the other side. "I hear you! Calm down. A custodian's on the way. Who's in there?" The reassuring, deep voice of Andy Vicenza, their principal, rang out. Sarah pressed her forehead and both hands up against the wood and tried to settle nerves gone haywire.

"It's me, Sarah Scott. I don't know why I can't get the door open. I've tried everything," she called out, ending in a sob and covering her mouth to hold back her cries.

There was the sound of voices outside and a quick consultation, then tools rattling around. An instant later, the door was opened, revealing a rather flustered and disheveled woman wiping at her face. The whole ordeal had taken about ten minutes. It felt like an eternity.

"The lock jammed. Are you all right, Sarah?" Andy took her arm. As she stepped out of the bathroom, Sarah started trembling uncontrollably. The principal nodded to the custodian to allow him to repair the doorknob and walked by his teacher's side to reassure himself she was fit to return to the classroom.

Sarah attempted to smooth her hair and dab at her cheeks. "Yes, yes, I'm fine. It just startled me. I know you're busy, Mr. Vicenza. I'd best get back before Ms. Ashley gets worried." It was already too late for that. The moment Mr. Vicenza walked Sarah to the classroom door, Melissa was up out of her seat, concern written all over her.

"Sarah, what happened? You're white as a sheet! Are you ill?" Melissa brought her to a chair and knelt down beside her, holding her friend's hand.

"It's silly. I got locked in the bathroom and I guess I lost it a little bit. I'll be fine. Let's just watch the movie." Sarah closed her eyes and fought to calm her breathing. To slow the rapid staccato of her heart. Nothing helped. It only seemed to get harder until the children were staring at her.

"Sarah, *look* at me. You are going to go down to the nurse right now. You are *not* okay. Do you hear me? I'll be fine here. We have two helpers and everything is under control except you. Go. *Right now*." Melissa stared her down and motioned for Kathy, one her aides, to go with her friend.

Not willing to argue and starting to feel scared, Sarah stood on shaky legs. She leaned on Kathy for the entire trip down the hallway. As soon as they hit the nurse's office, she burst into tears. Kathy whispered to Cindy, the nurse, to appraise her of the situation and left them in privacy. Fortunately for Sarah, she'd chosen a slow day for a meltdown of sorts. No students were there.

"Sarah, come lie down. Relax, honey. You will be all right." Kathy was soothing and reminded Sarah of her mother with her gentle ways and caring manner.

The nurse wore a crisp, white jacket, her gray hair in a twist. Her wire-rimmed glasses perched on the end of her nose could not hide brown eyes filled with concern. She settled Sarah on the bed and continued to murmur calming words while taking a pulse and blood pressure reading. "Everything's a bit high, right now, sweetie, but not in a dangerous way. Tell me. What set you off?"

Sarah closed her eyes and breathed in slowly through her nose, then out, counting to ten. When it no longer felt like her heart was going to leap out of her chest, she told the nurse about the bathroom incident. "It's ridiculous. I knew I wouldn't be stuck there forever. That's what the logical side of my brain said. The crazy side said I might be in there for the rest of my life!"

Kathy patted her arm. "You relax here a moment, sweetie. You've had yourself a panic attack. It's a normal reaction, especially when someone's been through an ordeal like yours. Rest and I'll be back in a jiff."

True to her word, the nurse popped out and returned with Dana Bowers, the school psychologist. She'd already brought her up to speed and retreated to her office to give Sarah some time alone with Dana.

Dana was in her fifties with hair that had transitioned to that beautiful white-silver that others found in a box. Her eyes were a pale green, lighter than Graham's, lovely in their own right. The psychologist was no nonsense and always got straight to the point as she sat down beside Sarah on the nurse's bed.

"Kathy told me what happened. It's natural to become panicked when trapped. All of us have a little claustrophobia. You've had some experiences that are pretty rough, worse than most. Have you considered counseling?"

Anger replaced fear, bringing Sarah to a sitting position as the heat rushed from her chest all the way to her face. "What, you think I need a shrink? I don't think so. I'm doing all right."

Dana took her hand in her cool grasp, her gaze steady. "Sarah, you don't need a 'shrink.' You and your family have been through something really tough. It would be good for you to find someone to talk to so you can work through any difficult memories you have. I'm sure Graham and Lila could use some help dealing with the emotional aftermath as well. Think about it. In the meantime, you can come see me anytime."

Ashamed by her outburst, Sarah gave her co-worker a brief hug and pulled back. "Thank you. I'm really not ready to talk about what happened. When I am, I'll think about your advice. I'm sorry I gave you a hard time." She accepted a drink of water, a pat on the back, and returned to her classroom to finish her day. It would be a while before she'd use that bathroom again.

5

SHE DIDN'T MENTION THE INCIDENT to Graham or Lila. No need to upset them, not with the prospect of the weekend ahead. Besides, Sarah was embarrassed. Anyone could have a breakdown after being trapped, right? No reason to raise the alarm.

After Lila went to bed, Sarah kept Graham up late, fulfilling the promise of the kiss she'd given him that morning. The late hour and some wine made drifting off easy, wrapped up tight in a tangle of limbs and covers. For once, she slept like the dead.

"Mommy, Daddy! Wake up! I'm going to Nana and Pop Pop's for the weekend, 'member? Wake up!" Something was pouncing on the bed, more than one something. There were little paws walking all over their bodies and Sarah felt a wet tongue mopping her face. Lila started to giggle when Dale, the golden retriever puppy and Graham's inseparable tagalong, climbed onto his head.

"Off! Somebody get the little monster off of me!" A muffled voice called from beneath the furry, fluff ball doing his best to burrow a path under the covers.

Sarah could be of no help. She had her hands full with Chip, the black Labrador. There was an explosion of covers and limbs as Graham erupted from beneath the pile. He launched a tickle attack on Lila and the puppies.

Sarah knew when it was wise to retreat. Otherwise, her husband would get his hands on her too. A hasty escape to the kitchen meant putting on coffee for a man that lived for *her* coffee and hers alone. With the pot perking cheerfully, she set the kettle on the stove for her daily dose of tea and began preparations for French toast.

By the time the puppies scampered in, pulled by their noses and the scent of bacon, the table was laid. Sarah leaned against the counter, sipping her hot brew, reveling in the bustling of activity and the pure happiness of being…together.

"Faster, Daddy! Faster!" Lila's voice rang out from the hallway along with the pounding of feet on the hardwood floor. Graham burst into the room, their little girl perched on top of his shoulders. She resembled a princess on her noble steed with her blond locks falling into her eyes.

Graham reached up and lifted Lila over his head, settling her in a chair at the kitchen table, and dropping a kiss on the top of her crown. "I'd better start working out! Otherwise, I am never keeping up with you."

He transferred his attentions to his wife, pulling her close and planting a kiss on her cheek. "As for you, you are sending me to heaven! This breakfast smells to die for."

Sarah dug her fingers in his shirt and inhaled the blend of pine, deodorant, and something that belonged to Graham alone. She could never get enough of waking up to this man, cooking for him, and standing with him, lost in his kitchen and the forest within his eyes.

"Why don't you try sticking around? They'll be plenty more where this came from." She pulled herself up on tiptoe to steal a kiss and sent him to the table, hungry for more than breakfast.

It was nothing special, nothing different from millions of other households in America but it was family time, made precious because they had almost lost the chance to wake up together.

When everyone had full bellies, including the puppies, Lila cleared the table while Graham washed the dishes, allowing Sarah to slip into the shower. Graham's turn came next, giving the girls time to put the bedrooms to rights. They were out of the house and on the road, filling the truck with conversation and the hum of anticipation. Lila was spending the night with her grandparents, Graham was going to an outdoors exhibit with Jim, and Sarah was having a girls' day with Jeanie.

With a little tug on her heart, Sarah gave Lila a hug and a kiss send-off at her parents. Graham expected the same before climbing in Jim's SUV.

Sarah's kiss lingered long enough that Jim had to clear his throat and divert his gaze. "It's getting a little steamy in here. Do you two need some privacy? A hotel room perhaps?"

Laughing and blushing hotly, she gave her husband a little push. "Go on or he'll leave without you. Love you." Sarah stood and waved. When she turned around, Jeanie was waving off her husband from the living room window. Sarah was comforted to know she wasn't the only woman crazy in love.

"Get in here before you turn into an ice sculpture! It's freezing out here!" Jeanie stood in the open door way, waving her friend inside. Sarah didn't have to be told twice. She hustled up the steps, giving the tiny woman a hearty hug . "Let me take your coat. I'm so excited about our girls' day! I can't remember the last time I did something like this without one of the guys around! Your hands are like ice, honey! Come in and I'll get you something hot to drink."

Life was always the same with Jeanie, being caught up in the whirlwind speed of her tongue, her warmth, and larger than life presence even though she was a little spitfire of a woman. What she didn't have in size she made up for in heart.

Sarah followed her into the kitchen and watched Jeanie closely while preparing tea. There was a glow to her skin and dark eyes, a little more fullness in her face, and the swelling of her stomach was growing. The wonder of a mother-to-be.

Sarah reached out and laid a hand on the warm, reassuringly hard bump to feel a kick as a reward. "Motherhood is looking good on you, Jeanie-girl. You're making me want one again too."

Jeanie's happiness was unmistakable, yet worry hovered nearby. "I feel good. I'll just be happy when the little question mark gets here. This waiting is killing me!"

They sat down at the table and sipped tea, making quick work of a plate of chocolate biscotti and talking babies. Sarah shared some of her memories and was a good sounding board for her friend, letting her know her nerves and preoccupation were completely normal. Soon they were laughing over some of the more embarrassing moments they had in common.

They moved on to pampering one another, turning the bathroom into a spa. Pedicures and manicures came first. Hair and make-up were next until they were giggling like teenagers while the radio played and they sang along.

Jeanie made a heaping bowl of popcorn, ice cream sodas, and they propped themselves up on her bed to watch chick flicks, alternating between tear jerkers and a comedy. It was in the middle of the lighter choice that Jeanie let out a cry of pain, pressing her hand to her side.

"What is it?" Sarah took her hand and received a bone-crunching squeeze in return. Jeanie might be little, but she was strong as a whip. Her friend had paled and her eyes were wide with fear. Sarah felt her own pulse begin to race.

"It's nothing, I'm sure—oh!" Jeanie called out again and bit down on her lip, tears brimming and threatening to fall.

She pushed herself up off the bed and rushed to the bathroom. Sarah followed close behind and stood pressed against the door, listening, wanting to come in, unsure if she should. Thoughts of Jeanie's miscarriage came unbidden to Sarah's mind and she forcibly shoved them down. She could hear the hitch in her friend's breathing from crying and that settled it.

Jeanie was sitting on the closed toilet seat, holding her middle, rocking back and forth. The tears streaked down her face, unchecked. Sarah knelt down beside her and laid a hand on her friend's middle. "What is it, honey? Are you having contractions again?"

At the jerk of Jeanie's head in the affirmative, Sarah stood and wrapped an arm around her shoulders. "Listen to me. I want you to relax. Breathe in slowly. Count to ten. Do the same as you let it out. Remember that Braxton Hicks contractions are common and they are completely normal. I'm *sure* that's what this is. Come with me. I want you to lie down."

Sarah kept her tone light and steady, outwardly calm when her insides were a mess. What if she was wrong?

With Sarah's arm supporting her, Jeanie went back to the bedroom and stretched out on the bed. As she propped her feet on a pillow, Sarah pulled a warm comforter up to her neck. Once Jeanie had a few minutes to lie with her eyes closed, she visibly relaxed. "Okay…I'm okay. It's over." She looked up at her friend and gave her a tremulous smile. "Thank you, Sarah. I was so scared. Promise you won't say anything to Jim. He's worried enough as it is."

Sarah didn't like keeping anything from Graham's best friend. Jim would want to know everything—good and bad— when it came to his wife. However, one look at Jeanie's burning gaze and she nodded. "All right, but if this happens again or goes on longer, I want you to call your doctor and tell Jim, got it?" Her friend agreed and they settled back into their movie although they both had a hard time focusing after their scare.

They'd started another, this time a favorite each had seen a million times, when Jeanie turned to Sarah and took her hand again, gently this time. "Okay, you know one of my secrets. Time to spill yours. What's going on? I can tell— you're not yourself. You're good at covering up, but something's bothering you."

Was she that obvious? If so, it was only a matter of time before Graham cornered her next. "It's nothing really. I've been having bad dreams and yesterday, I was stuck in the bathroom at school. I had a panic attack. The whole thing was silly. Really."

Sarah raced over the words. If she spoke quickly, maybe she wouldn't have to think about the muddle of nerves and snippets of nightmares that threatened to pull her under.

Jeanie turned off the television, leaving them in silence with only the sound of their breathing. When Sarah could no longer avoid the tug of her friend's gaze, she looked up. The face beside her was open, a book to be read and shared. "Sarah, you were abducted and held captive for over six months. I cannot even begin to fathom what you endured and I don't think you can either. Panic attacks and dreams—they're your mind's way of dealing with the intolerable. I'm going to give you your advice—if they get worse or last longer, or you find yourself in a place where you can't stand it, you *need* to ask for help."

Sarah let out a great gust of air, blowing her bangs out of her eyes. Her knuckles had turned white as she gripped the blanket. It took a conscious effort to loosen her hold. "I do my damnedest not to think about it at all, to not even give *him* the time of day—any time out of my day, but he keeps coming back. Kane and that blasted cabin."

Her voice shook and her hands clenched again. Jeanie's small fingers began to knead at her fists until they finally lay open and motionless. "I wish I could reach inside my head and pull out every memory of that man, all of those moments that were stolen away from me." Her head tilted to the side and leaned against Jeanie. Her eyes closed and she willed the tension away, but Kane Johnson still tied her in knots.

"It *will* be all right, Sarah. You're back where you belong now. The rest will work itself out. I wish that Kane Johnson would show up here now. I'd tell him a thing or two and then—he'd be swimmin' with the fishes."

Her impression of a mobster and accompanying glare were so fierce in that tiny frame, Jeanie had Sarah rolling with laughter. The girl could always cut her problems down to size.

A DAY APART MEANT MAKING UP FOR LOST TIME. With Lila at her grandparents, Sarah and Graham had the rare luxury of a night alone, their first since the wedding. A honeymoon had not been an option what with Sarah returning to school and the thought of being separated from Lila again brought on a pain that was physical, like ripping her in two.

Even now, she felt a tugging on her heart when her mind turned to her little girl. Captivity with Kane had felt like a lifetime. Never again would Sarah be separated from her daughter. If Lila moved across the world, she would follow. There was no other way Sarah could live.

Now was not a time to think about Lila. Her daughter was in good hands. Sarah needed to devote her full attention to her husband. Graham leaned against the stone fireplace, eyes reflecting the soft candlelight creating a warm glow in the living and dining room. He looked good in jeans and a dark, green sweater—good enough to make her want to forget about dinner and skip right to dessert.

"Come sit. Dinner's almost ready." Sarah pulled out a chair and poured two glasses of wine.

In answer, Graham took the bottle from fingers gone loose and pulled her into an embrace. Music was playing on the radio, something soft and jazzy, something from long ago. As he began to dance with her in front of the fireplace, Sarah felt like she had stepped back into the past when the world was much simpler.

There was no boogeyman, real or imagined, to taint anyone's dreams. Graham's hands were warm, his body hard and durable. Unbreakable. Slowly but surely, a little bit of meat was coming back on his bones, giving her something more substantial to hold on to. A voice, deep and rich, welled up in song and flowed around them. With a start, she realized it was Graham.

"I didn't know you can sing. There's so much I still don't know." Closing her eyes, Sarah imagined it was long ago and she was Ginger Rogers to Graham's Fred Astaire.

It didn't matter—swept into the past or in the midst of the here and now, she had her homecoming in Graham. The significance of his name would never be lost on her.

"We've got a lifetime to find out everything there is to know. Right now, I hate to tell you this. I'm not hungry, at least not for food." He had one arm around her waist, another holding her hand. As if in slow motion, Graham spun her around, pulled her close, and dipped her down low. His lips pressed to hers and she could swear, for one instant, fireworks flashed across her mind.

"Dinner can wait. I'm willing to do something else. Did you have anything in mind?" Sarah asked him playfully.

She gave a little shriek when he picked her up and carried her off to the bedroom. Their clothing became a puddle on the floor and a soft place to fall. There was no patience for making their way to the bed.

Sometime past midnight, after working up a good sweat and an appetite, Sarah sat on Graham's lap and they polished off dinner. A few glasses of wine and they fell into bed, feeling as unwound as two people could be. So mellow the act of breathing was a challenge.

Tranquility didn't last. Sarah awoke in darkness, filled with an indescribable terror although she didn't know why. Clouds pressed down on the night, snuffing out the light of the moon. The blankets were twisted around her body, restraining her, while the walls of the bedroom were pressing in. Closer. *Closer*.

Breathing in short pants, Sarah fumbled her way out of the bed, tripping in her haste to get out of the covers that had snared her. Practically sobbing, she made her way to the bathroom and began to splash cold water on her face. She was shaking so hard, her teeth were chattering and her heart was ready to burst, pounding at a fearsome pace. She slid down on the floor, propped against the wall, and began to cry.

It felt like falling from an impossibly high place with no landing in sight. An irrational fear took her breath away and put her mind in a tailspin of panic with no way out. Until someone threw her a rope.

Strong arms wrapped around her, catching her and drawing her into their shelter. Graham was there, tucking her head under his chin and whispering words of comfort, soft nothings that helped her to find her way out of the darkness.

Sarah let herself sink into him as her heart slowed and she could breathe easy again. A hand came up to brush hair from her face and gently wipe away her tears. "Can you tell me about it? Nightmares again?" Graham's voice was low, reaching out to her in the dimly lit room, a balm to nerves worn ragged.

The moment of truth. Sarah had known all along she would have to confess. There could be no secrets between them. "No, at least not that I remember. I woke up and I was afraid. I couldn't breathe and my heart was pounding. I don't even know why!"

The rest spilled out, about the incident in the bathroom at school and other moments of intense anxiety. "The nurse told me I'm having panic attacks and Dana, the school psychologist, suggested counseling. Great, huh? I'm losing my mind or maybe it's already gone."

Graham shifted his hold on her to cup her face and force her to look up into his eyes. They were her calm in the storm, steady as the wilderness that embraced him every day, unwavering as the line he walked to live his life—strong and true. "You are *not* crazy. You've been through hell. We all have. I think Dana is right. We should all go—together. I don't want to admit it, but Lila and I need help too. She's not sleeping well and clings to you in a way she never had before. I can't stand to let you out of my sight. If counseling means figuring out how to deal, how to find a way to get past this, let's go for it. Otherwise, I'm afraid I'll commit unspeakable violence on Kane." He laughed softly, a sound without humor.

A shiver ran down Sarah's spine at his weak attempt at humor. Graham was a peaceful man. If he felt the urge to lose control, it was time to get help. He nodded as the light of comprehension dawned on her face. "If it's the three of us, it won't be so hard will it? We're going to be all right if we do this together."

The next time Sarah awoke, she felt cold and unsettled. The dim light of dawn, making everything look black and white, revealed an empty space beside her in their bed. She hated waking up alone and never slept well when Graham was not by her side.

Stepping out of bed, she slipped on her robe and searched the house, beginning with the ritual of checking in Lila's room. Sarah had to reassure herself, countless times, that her daughter was safe and sound. Often, she would find Graham keeping watch over his little ladybug too. Not this morning. Lila was at her grandparents.

The rest of the house proved empty, quickening Sarah's pulse. A quick glance in the driveway proved both vehicles were there. He hadn't been called to work. Could Kane have…the thought came unbidden and made her mouth go dry.

The only other possibility was the deck. Sometimes Graham would go outside and simply stand there, drinking in the beauty of the lake and the Adirondacks that stood as guardians over the land. Sarah fought the urge to run and went to the large picture window that treated them to an incredible view. On this morning, as shades of pink and purple streaked across the sky as a precursor to day, the welcome sight of her husband made her nearly deflate in relief.

He was ruthlessly and methodically clearing an ice rink in front of their dock on Pleasant Lake, his motions sharp, sending the snow flying behind him. Graham must have been at it for a while because there was an area large enough for an Olympic skating competition.

His breath steamed around his head, proving the thermometer was correct—ten degrees Fahrenheit to be exact. The temperature didn't appear to faze him. He had shed his coat and worked only in a long-sleeved shirt with no hat on his head and no gloves. Sarah shook her head and moved on to the kitchen to prepare reinforcements.

Minutes later, she stood on the dock, bundled up in Graham's spare winter coat, a silly hat with ear flaps that reminded her of Elmer Fudd, gloves, boots, and a tall thermos of coffee in her hands. She didn't call to him. There was no need.

Graham stopped mid-shovel and turned toward her as if pulled by a string. "Good morning, Mr. Scott. You're bright-eyed and bushy–tailed this morning. Working hard I see."

He jabbed his shovel in the snow on the side of the rink and cautiously made his way across the ice, a hint of a smile tugging at his mouth, although his eyes were dark with some inner source of irritation. "Good morning, Mrs. Scott. Don't you look sexy in that get-up. I'd like to strip you out of it right here, right now, but then we'd both be freezing."

Graham took the thermos from her with fingers that were like ice when they brushed her skin, a fine shiver running through his frame as he sucked down the steaming beverage, heedless of scalding his tongue. "Sweet heaven, there is a God. I expected you—no, I wanted you—to sleep late after your rough night, but I will be forever grateful for the miracle of your coffee."

He pulled her close and planted a kiss on her lips, lingering long enough to make her mouth taste the brew and chill her cheek with the touch of his skin. "Man, you're nice and warm. Just let me hold on to you." He burrowed his hands under her coat, making her shriek.

"Graham Dylan Scott, what is *wrong* with you? It's just shy of zero and you're out here with almost nothing on. You're supposed to be the expert on avoiding exposure to the elements.

81

Can you explain yourself?" Sarah pulled back and put her gloved hands on his cheeks. There was no way of escaping her. He had to face his wife.

He closed his eyes for a moment, gathering his thoughts. "After we came back to bed, I couldn't fall back to sleep. I kept thinking about Kane, all that he's cost us, especially you. The more I thought about him, the angrier I became."

His grip on her waist, under her coat, tightened to the point of being painful and he forced himself to ease up. "I know they say you're supposed to find forgiveness for others, but I'm having a really tough time finding any mercy for Kane. So, when I'd worked myself up to the rabid-dog stage, I figured I had to do something about it. Wa la!" He waved at his efforts.

Sarah pressed herself up close and wrapped her arms around his neck. Graham was shaking so hard he couldn't stop. "Come on, silly. Let's get you inside and warmed up before you catch pneumonia and can't enjoy the fruits of your labor. You know Lila will expect you out there with her." They turned away from the lake, arms around each other's waist, and returned to the inviting warmth of the house.

As for Lila, always up with the birds, she was back home from her grandparents, and on the ice in the early afternoon. Sarah joined her daughter and Graham stepped off the ice, moving to the dock to sit on the edge. He swung his legs back and forth, watching his girls.

When invited him to join in, he waved them off, said he was taking a breather. Sarah knew the truth. Ever since the beginning of their relationship, Graham had always respected her time with Lila. Before he came into their lives, there had only been the two of them and now that they were a unit, he still made certain to give them time and space for each other.

Sarah spun round and round with her daughter until both were rosy cheeked, golden hair flying out from underneath heavy, woolen caps. They managed to flop down on to the ice at the same time, laughing in a pile of limbs. Lila looked at her mother, Sarah looked at her daughter, and they turned in unison to call out to Graham. "Help!"

In quick, long glides of his skates, he was at their side, lifting them to their feet. They formed a trio, traveling in a line and then a circle, faster and faster until they all landed on their bottoms with a thump and more laughter. Just what the doctor ordered. As they lay on the ice, their giggles echoing around them, Sarah held on tight to the moment. If only she could pluck out all of the bad memories. The best she could do was make new memories of happy times, together, strong enough to put the bad to shame.

6

JIM WOKE UP WITH WORRY WORKING AT THE EDGE OF CONSCIOUSNESS. It settled as a painful knot in his stomach. He figured this was what an ulcer felt like. Maybe this stabbing sensation *was* an ulcer.

Lately, it was his lot in life to have worry as a constant companion. He worried on the job as a police officer keeping Johnstown safe. He'd spent over six months worrying about Graham and Sarah. Now his worry was for Jeanie to the point that he was having trouble finding his characteristic good humor.

His wife was having a difficult pregnancy. They'd tried for years, been given a brief flicker of hope, only to have a miscarriage the last time. Jim prayed this time around would go smoothly, that his wife would make it through until the end, but he saw the fear in her eyes. Fear that she'd lose one again.

Jim wasn't sure Jeanie could make it through another miscarriage. His wife was made of strong stuff, but how often could a heart be broken? His mind wouldn't erase that day when he found her sobbing in the bathroom and the blood—there'd been so much blood! All over her. Spilling out on the bathroom floor. He'd rushed her to the emergency room. Too late. Pray and worry were the best a man could do.

If he could trade places with her, he'd gladly do so, in a heartbeat. It grated on the nerves that as a man, Jim had to sit and watch his wife go through something so big and beyond their control. The baby, that little mystery that already ran their lives, couldn't get here soon enough so Jim could stop worrying about his wife. Of course, he'd worry about the baby for the rest of his life.

Odds and ends around the house were a daily task, something useful that Jim could do besides worry. He might not be able to carry their child, but he could carry his weight with the housekeeping and then some.

Coffee. He needed it like a man needed air, something to give him that morning jolt, but his stomach couldn't take it, not yet. A shower would have to suffice. Next, he ran through what had to be done around the place. The garbage was a must. Every bin in the house had to be emptied otherwise she would do the job herself and the doctor had been explicit. *No heavy lifting.* Jim dragged the large cans out to the curb, moving quickly in the brisk, morning chill.

Back inside, he swept and mopped. The noise of the vacuum would cue Jeanie in on the fact that someone horning in on her turf. He finished with his least favorite chore—laundry. Lugging clothes down to the basement and up again was a pain in the butt. Whoever designed homes with a downstairs laundry hook-up should be shot. Jim had only come to truly appreciate that fact when the job became his chore. He'd have to look into adding on a washroom upstairs after the baby was born. One thing at a time.

Nudging the bedroom door with his toe, he made an attempt at being quiet while dropping off a basket filled with clean clothes. All good intentions were shot to hell. His toe rammed into the dresser, hindered by the lack of light.

"*Dammit!*" He cursed under his breath, a long string of colorful words, dropping the basket with a thud and grabbing hold of his foot.

"Jim, what's going on?" Jeanie's voice, still heavy with sleep, drifted out of the darkness and there was a shifting of the covers.

Her hand was too quick for him, flipping on the light, leaving them both squinting in the sudden brightness. "And I thought we'd acquired a laundry fairy." She shook her head with a smile. "You know you don't have to do that. I'm not an invalid. I can handle the clothes."

Jim sank down on the edge of the bed and cupped her cheek with his hand. "Let me do these little things for you, okay? It's the least of it compared to what you're doing. You're growing a new person in there! If you can do that, I can help out. Besides, the doctor said you shouldn't strain yourself. So, if I catch you dragging around laundry, or anything heavy, I will personally…give you a spanking."

Her lips curled up in a devilish grin and mischief lurked in those dark, Italian eyes. "Is that a threat or a promise, Officer Pedersen? Either way, it makes me want to be a *very* bad girl."

Jim leaned in close and locked his lips over hers. When they both had to come up for air, he growled playfully, "Be good or *else*. Now try and go back to sleep. I'm sorry I woke you."

He turned off the light and went into the adjoining bathroom to get changed. When he came back out, the bed was empty. Shaking his head, he went to the kitchen and found breakfast waiting for him along with his wife, impossibly sweet and sexy at the same time in her short, red robe and matching, fluffy slippers. "I thought I told you to go back to sleep."

Jeanie shrugged and handed him a cup of coffee. "I wasn't tired anymore. Eat before your breakfast gets cold."

Waffles and eggs waited on the table. She sat down across from him and nibbled toast while sipping her tea, keeping morning sickness at bay. It troubled him that the nausea held on, made him wonder if her struggle was another harbinger of doom. His own stomach gave a jab, hard enough to make him shut that train of thought down.

Jim ate first and managed half a cup of coffee before his stomach protested again. At least he got the food down. He'd never hear the end of it if he didn't eat. That was a requirement in this house. His wife embodied her heritage when it came to eating what was put on the table.

He carried his dishes to the sink and grabbed an antacid out of the cabinet when Jeanie wasn't looking, hoping to settle the uncomfortable burning that happened more and more often lately.

She was there, behind him, her arms coming up around him as he drank a cool glass of water to wash the chalky flavor out of his mouth. "Your stomach's bothering you again, isn't it? Go to the doctor, Jim. You're worrying yourself sick and there's no reason for it. Take care of yourself so I don't have to worry about you instead."

He turned around and gave her a hug. "I don't need to go to the doctor—your morning sickness is probably worse than the way I feel, really. It's just pre-baby jitters. I'll be fine in…oh, four months or so. I've got to get going. Take it easy, all right? If you need anything, call me. Love you, babe." Jim shrugged into his coat and received a kiss in return.

"I love you too. Be careful and have a good day." Jeanie walked him to the door and waved him off, something she had done every day since he started working as a police officer twelve years ago.

The sight of her standing in the doorway, hair mussed from sleep and cheeks flushed, made him want to turn around and call in sick. He dug down for his willpower—it took every ounce—to give a wave and keep on driving. The prospect of coming back to her at the end of his shift would have to tide him over.

The day started out quiet, typical for historical Johnstown. Dating from colonial times, it boasted several famous landmarks, including the oldest, working courthouse in the state. The town was quaint with tiny shops on Main Street and a modest population, small town America in a nutshell. Jim had spent his whole life there. It was a part of him and in his blood. He was called to serve and protect its residents, thankful to take care of his own.

An early morning shift meant a few speeders in a rush to get to work on time. Jim let them off with a warning, intent on returning to the same spot the next day. If he caught them again, no more Mister Nice Guy. Sometime around midmorning, he was sent to a gas station for shoplifting. It was a crime of monumental proportions; an elderly woman had slipped a donut into her purse.

After a brief conversation with the offender, Jim slipped her the money for the donut and made sure the cashier was appeased. As soon as she walked out, Jim gave the attendant a twenty for future visits along with his card when the woman's tab ran out.

What could he say? He had a soft spot for old ladies. They reminded him of his grandmothers, two great women. Jim bought a dozen more donuts and tracked down the hardened criminal a short distance away on the sidewalk. He received a kiss on the cheek for his troubles.

"Thank you, young man." A nice, warm spot lingered on his cheek and in his heart for the rest of the morning. Jim even felt up to a cup of coffee.

A call for a domestic dispute came next, turning his stomach sour again. He hated these calls. One never knew what would go down and the sight of women or children that had been hurt by another human being made Jim feel sick. This time it was a young couple with financial troubles. The husband lost it when he found out there wasn't any money for cigarettes. What began with shouting ended with hitting.

Jim arrived to find the woman sitting on the front steps in the cold, trembling, without a jacket. She was rocking back and forth, cupping her face. He sat down next to her and spoke very quietly.

When he sensed something in her give, he gently moved her hand to see an eye already closed with swelling, a nasty black and blue mark covering half of her face. She burst into tears and fell against him. His arms came up instinctively to form a shelter for her.

"Hey, get your damn hands off of my wife!" A slurred voice shouted from the doorway.

Jim turned and ducked just in time to miss the swing of a beer bottle from the man responsible for the damage. Her husband wasn't in much better condition himself, hair disheveled, his face covered with stubble. His shirt was filthy and looked like he'd worn it for a week. A bath and a change of clothes, along with his attitude, would do him a world of good.

Jim stood up and made himself a shield for the crying woman beside him. She had begun to shake uncontrollably. "Listen, *buddy*, you'd better calm yourself down. You touch me and I'm bringing you in for assaulting an officer. Believe me. If I charge you, it *will* stick."

The cool voice of authority, learned through training and experience, came in handy, not to mention a gaze of steel. Jim glanced over his shoulder at the man's wife. "Do *you* want to press charges?"

"No, it will only be worse," she whispered and curled into herself. Jim's frustration and anger nearly boiled over. If she wouldn't let him help, there was nothing he could do. He turned back to see an ugly sneer on the guy's face. That was all it took.

Jim grabbed hold of her husband and slammed him up against the door, hard enough to make the porch windows rattle. Fear replaced the cockiness and the beer bottle slipped to the floor, shattering to bits. Alcohol splashed on their legs, only intensifying the officer's rage. "I want you to take a good look at my face. Remember me. If I ever get called here again because you hurt this woman, or *any* woman, I will make sure you pay for it before you ever get to the station."

He dragged the man by the collar and yanked him down on the step, shoving him close to get a good view of his handiwork. "Now, *look* at your wife. Look at her eye and her cheek. *Look at what you did to her*! Are you proud of yourself?"

The man's face caved in when he saw the harm that had been done in the heat of the moment. He reached out tentatively. She shrank away from him. "Kathy...I'm sorry. Oh baby, I'm so sorry. I don't know what came over me. Please, honey, believe me when I say I'm sorry."

She looked up at him, eyes red from crying and her husband became a sniveling wreck beside her. By the time Jim left the scene, they were huddled together with a pamphlet in the man's hand for counseling. On that promising note, Jim headed to the Railside Café for lunch in search of some peace and quiet. Maybe he'd find his appetite.

He was sitting at a table in the corner by a window when he saw a familiar figure in a dark green uniform walk in. "Hey, Scottie! Why don't you join me?" He waved to the empty chair across from him and dug up a smile from somewhere way down deep.

Graham made his way through the lunchtime crowd and slipped his jacket over the chair before dropping down into the seat. He eyed his best friend's bottle of antacid with raised eyebrows. "Are you still popping those like candy? You really ought to think about seeing a doctor." He gave his order to the waitress and waited, watching him intently.

Jim cleared his throat and chewed on another tablet. "I started on these when Jeanie began having problems with her

92

pregnancy and today didn't help. I just had to deal with a domestic. I can't stand it when men use women for punching bags." His stomach did a mean twist, calling for another antacid.

Graham shook his head. "I don't blame you for being mad. You want me to go beat up the guy for you? He doesn't know me. You can swear you know nothing. I could even make it look like an accident. I have my ways." He wiggled his eyebrows suggestively just as their food arrived.

Jim found himself feeling better already. Graham had a way of doing that. "Thanks, but I don't need to hire any hits today. I think I've got it handled. So, how's married life treating you?"

Graham's face softened even though there were still shadows darkening those green eyes that made Jim think of a summer storm rolling in. "The best, but the girls are having bad dreams. Sarah's having panic attacks. It's going to take a long time to undo the damage Kane has done to us. I only hope I'm up to it."

Jim locked eyes with his friend and nodded sharply. "You better believe you're up to it. You never gave up on Sarah and look what happened. Give yourself time. They'll be all right and so will you."

Jim wondered how long it would take before Kane Johnson would become nothing more than a faded memory. They looked outside to find a rain shower under way.

Conversation turned to other topics in spurts between bites to eat until it was time to go.

Graham picked up the tab at the register, nudging his friend out of the way. "I've got this today. You look like you can use a pick-me up. You can catch the tab the next time. It's the least I can do after all the times you picked me up in the past year, okay?"

Jim put his hands up in surrender. "Hey, I'm not arguing with you. Thanks, buddy."

He went back to the table to set down a tip and glanced out the window. *Great, just what I need. An ice storm.* In the short time they'd been at the register, the fine misting rain had changed over. A sheen of ice covered the parking lot and the trees. A driving disaster.

Graham came up behind him and took a good look outside. "Nice. Maybe we should sit back down for chocolate pie and forget about venturing out."

Jim shook his head. The recently unraveled knots in his stomach were tightening up all over again. "Crap! I hate ice. It brings out the stupid in people! You be really careful, Graham. There are a lot of idiots out there." They went out the back and took it slow going down the steps to the parking lot. Jim almost wiped out twice.

Graham moved with due caution and skidded his way to his truck. "You watch yourself, too, you hear?" He hopped in and gave his friend a wave.

Jim pulled out, taking caution. Limbs were down and power lines wouldn't be far behind. Cars were already off the road, only fender benders, but worse would be on the way. Common sense flew out the window when it came to ice.

He pulled up at an intersection only to watch a car slide through on red, nearly missing a collision and ending up in a field. Jim shook his head with a groan. The whole thing would have been avoided if the driver had been going an appropriate speed for the conditions.

He was out of the car and at her side in an instant. "Mam, are you all right?"

An older woman sat trembling behind the wheel, gripping it tightly in her hands. "I couldn't stop. The ice made me go out of control." She bowed her head and tears started to fall. Her body was shaking, but she appeared unharmed.

Jim sighed. Another woman to comfort—the story of his life. "It's all right, mam. Nobody was hurt. It happens to everyone."

Suddenly, a horn blared. Jim looked up just in time to see a car hurtling straight for him. Something fast and red. He leaped out of the way and dove to the ground. The car just missed him, giving Jim the shakes. The horn was from Graham, who by the grace of God, had decided to follow him after lunch. Jim had never been so happy to see that uniform and friendly face before in his life.

Oblivious to everything else around him, Graham was out of his truck and sliding across the road like he was on ice skates. He wiped out and crawled the rest of the way until he reached his best friend and grabbed hold of him.

His eyes frantically scanned Jim's body, looking for blood, while his hands patted him down. "My God, Pete, that was close. Too close. Are you hurt?"

Jim took stock of himself and shook his head. "No, just scared the hell out of me. Thanks for saving my life." He closed his eyes and took a moment to collect himself, waiting for his heart to stop galloping before it leaped out of his chest. "We'd better check on everyone else."

The car that almost hit Jim had been the end result in a chain reaction involving at least five other cars. Graham skated his way to an SUV farther back in the line. Jim took a deep breath and managed to get his legs underneath him. He went to the red Monte Carlo that had nearly taken him out and peered inside the window.

It was bad. A young girl, probably a teenager, was trapped behind the wheel. She was caught in a tangle of seat belt and mangled interior with glass everywhere from a broken windshield. The first thing he noticed was her eyes—piercingly bright and blue, the color of the ocean scene Jeanie had painted in the nursery. *Cerulean, that's what she called it.*

Inane trivia floated to the surface of his mind, a coping mechanism to deal with the blood. Too much blood. A shard of glass was protruding from a gash in her neck. The cut was small, almost inconsequential, but a crimson fountain spurted with each pump of her heart which could only mean one thing. A severed artery.

Jim fought with the door which didn't want to cooperate. With a final wrench, he yanked the mangled metal open far enough to slip inside. "Hey, hang in there. You're going to be all right. We've just got to stop the bleeding." The girl's eyes followed him, wide and wild in a face gone paper white, a contrast made sharper by a curtain of dark hair falling to her shoulders.

He shoved glass out of the way, heedless as it sliced his hands and arms, looking for anything to fill the wound. Seeing no other solution, Jim closed his eyes to say a hasty prayer for strength and guidance, then stared into her eyes. "Okay. I'm going to remove the glass in your neck and use my finger as a plug, like the little Dutch boy in the wall. On three. One, two, three!"

She squeezed her eyes shut and let out a little cry of pain when he pulled the glass out to plunge his finger in, creating a stopper. He could feel the hot pulsing as her blood rushed through the artery. Sweat broke out on his forehead, but he forced a reassuring smile. "There. You'll be all right. Don't try to talk and don't move. Stay still as can be. Help is coming, I promise."

Oblivious to the wintery blast coming in through the windshield or the freezing rain pelting his skin, Jim focused on the girl next to him, the silent tears making tracks down her face, the reassuring rise and fall of her chest as her breath came in shallow gasps. What else could he do? He couldn't hold back the blood forever. She had already lost so much. *Somebody help us. God, please send someone.*

Inexplicably, Graham was there. "Jim, what can I do?" He asked, immediately assessing the severity of the situation. He struggled with the door, put all he had into it, and managed to open it all the way. Leaning in close, he eyed the girl with a critical gaze. "Do you want me to take over?"

Jim glanced over his shoulder and shook his head. "No—too risky. Call 911 and tell them the situation, that this girl takes top priority. When someone gets here, you send them our way, okay?"

Graham gave him a jerk of his head and was gone. The two were left alone together, shivering with the cold and staring into each other's eyes. Both were scared. Both were trying not to show it.

The sound of sirens came closer and closer, from different directions as a variety of rescue vehicles arrived on the scene. "Here comes the cavalry," Jim told the girl.

She gave him a slip of a smile. Graham flagged down an ambulance, stubbornly insisting the driver follow him, using the brute force of his personality. He wore his authority well. Jim could hear his voice, loud and clear, refusing any arguments. Because of his best friend, rescue workers had the girl out of the car and into the ambulance with someone else's finger doing the job of being a plug. Everything was over within minutes.

The moment the ambulance was out of sight, Jim lost his lunch in the ditch where he'd nearly lost his life and had watched a girl on the brink of losing her own. Graham was there again, hand on his back, rock solid. He spoke quiet, soothing words, although Jim couldn't process them at the moment. A numbness had come over him and his mind was in a haze.

Jim marveled at how Graham had always been there in his life, through thick and thin, since they were boys. It was the way they were for each other, through the highs and the lows. Somehow, his best friend instinctively knew where he had to be. Right now, it was in the wet and the cold, on the side of the road, a flash of lights washing over them with sirens clamoring loudly in their ears as another victim was carried away.

Slowly, Jim made it to his feet although he swayed a little. "Pete, you're not looking so hot. Do you want me to give you a ride?" Graham remained at his side, holding him steady. His summer eyes were calming in the midst of all the craziness around them.

"I'll be all right. You'd best be getting home. Lila and Sarah are probably worried about you. Thanks for everything, Scottie. Take it easy. I don't want you ending up like anyone here today." Jim heard himself saying the words. It was as if he was standing next to himself, watching himself talk.

He barely felt a pat on his back, the freezing rain on his skin, or the slippery pavement beneath his feet. Somehow, he bridged the gap to his car, turned the key, and headed home.

Jim didn't remember the drive or finding his way to his driveway in front of his cozy, inviting home in town. He wasn't sure he could get inside the house. A crushing fatigue made his body too heavy to move. He slumped against the steering wheel, in his driveway, while the freezing rain pinged off the roof and the blood thundered in his ears.

7

JEANIE WAS IN THE KITCHEN, fiddling with a dish for dinner. She'd chosen something complicated with lots of steps to occupy her hands and her mind. Cooking was good therapy every time she worried about Jim while he was out on the job. The kitchen was called for on a day like today when the weather took a nasty turn for the worse.

The sound of the door opening and closing, followed by heavy footsteps, stopped her mid-stir. Jeanie closed her eyes and sent up a prayer of gratitude. He was home.

"Jim Pedersen, there had better be a good reason why you did not call me. You know I worry something fierce on days like today. You should have…" Jeanie broke off the moment she stepped in the living room.

Her husband sat on the couch, head bowed and pressed to his hands. There was blood—on his uniform, his arms, smeared on his face, and in the tangle of his hair. When she wrapped an arm around him, she could feel his trembling. "Sweetheart, what happened?" Her voice crept upward in fear.

Jim's body started to shake. "It was an accident…out on the arterial. I was helping a woman that slid off the road when a car almost hit me. It probably would've killed me if Graham hadn't been there, blaring on his horn. When I was able to get up and look inside the vehicle, I found a young girl. Blood was gushing from her neck. I ended up being her plug; I had no other choice. I almost lost her, Jeanie. If I'd found her a few minutes later, she would have been gone. There was so much blood. It was everywhere." His hands dug down to his scalp and he squeezed his eyes shut tightly.

"It's all right. You're all right. The girl is too. Come with me now, Jim. Let's get you cleaned up." She took her husband's hand and gave it a gentle tug.

Jeanie led the way into the bathroom and turned the water up as hot as he could take it because Jim's teeth were chattering. His body was quaking so hard with an inner chill and his hands felt like ice. With fumbling fingers, she managed to take off his clothes and get him under the hot, steaming spray.

Without hesitation, she stepped out of her own dress and climbed in with him. While Jim braced his arms against the wall and hung his head down low, Jeanie lathered his body with soap. She wrapped herself tightly around him until the tremors stopped.

Once out of the shower, Jeanie slipped on her robe and toweled her husband off while he stood with his hands pressed to the edge of the sink, as if holding him up. She ran her fingers over the cuts on his arms and hands, pressing kisses to them before attending to them with ointment and bandages. She darted into the bedroom, found sweats and a t-shirt, and helped him dress. It was as if Jim moved in a fog, allowing his wife to lead him to the couch where he laid down without protest.

She pulled up the blanket and stretched out beside him. "It's all right now. Everything is all right. You're safe. You're where you belong. You're with me."

Something broke loose inside of Jim and he was sobbing, taking in big gulps of air as he struggled to speak. "I'm sorry, Jeanie. I don't know what's wrong with me."

He buried his head in her shoulder. She gave him the magic in her hands, the solid warmth of her body, and the sweet music of her voice to wash over him to fill in the cracks.

"Shh. You have no reason to say I'm sorry. Let me hold on and help put you back together." Jeanie whispered in his ear. Dinner would have to go on a back burner. Her husband came first.

SOMETHING SMELLED GOOD and it was coming from the kitchen. Something over the top. Slice of heaven good. Jim followed his nose to find his wife in the middle of a dance. There was no other way to describe her moves. She was humming to the music on the radio, swaying from one dish to the next, flitting to the counter and back. Her cheeks were rosy from the warm oven and her dark eyes had regained their sparkle. She'd slept well and finally awoken without feeling queasy. Things were looking up.

Jim tiptoed up to the stove and slipped his arms around her waist. He surveyed the various concoctions bubbling on the stove and his eyes closed in ecstasy. "Are you making what I think you're making?"

He dropped to his knees and raised his hands in the air. "All hail the kitchen goddess! My absolute, all-time favorite is in the works, I just know it. It's your lasagna, isn't it? Don't tell me this is a tease, baby, please! I can't take it!"

Jeanie turned away from the stove, shaking with laughter, and tapped her husband on the head with a kitchen mitt. "Get off the floor, you fool! Yes, it's your lasagna with the salami, pepperoni, and itty, bitty, pain in my butt meatballs. I can't keep any secrets with you poking around in my domain."

The doorbell rang, making her jump. "Will you get that? I ordered some things for the nursery. Maybe it's UPS.".

"Did anyone say there was an Italian festival going on at the Pedersen residence?" Graham stood on the step, Lila in one arm, his other hooked loosely around Sarah's neck. Looking at the three of them together, there was one word to describe them: happy.

Jim turned and shook a finger at his wife, although he couldn't hide his pleasure. "All right, someone's being sneaky around here. How long have you been cooking *this* up?"

It was exactly what Jim needed. He'd been shaken, badly, from the accident two days ago, followed by a visit to see the girl who nearly died in his hands. Company with his best friends, friends that had gone through hard times and made it through to the other side, that was his cure.

Jeanie stepped up and wrapped an arm around his waist, leaning in to drop a kiss on his cheek. "I was in the mood for a full house and thought you might be too."

Everyone stepped inside, shutting the door on the breath of winter that arrived with them. Hugs and kisses were swapped while Jeanie took care of coats. Boots were shed and they padded on silent, sock feet to settle in the family room.

It was the heart of the house, bright and spacious with a high ceiling. Large windows lined the walls, letting in the day and the view. "Mommy, Mommy, can I give Jeanie her present? I can't wait! I *really* can't wait!" Lila hopped up and down in front of her mother, as excited as if the gift was for herself.

Sarah laughed and lifted a strand of Lila's hair, a fall of sunshine that rained down on her shoulders. "Yes, Ladybug. I couldn't put you through the torture of waiting." Graham gave her a tug and they snuggled in the recliner, basking in their daughter's excitement.

"What have you got for me, munchkin?" Jeanie knelt down at Lila's level. She had a knack about what worked best with children. She would make such a good, little mother. Jim cast up his daily prayer. Her body *had* to hang on a few more months.

Lila pulled out a colorful gift bag from behind her back. "Open it, Jeanie, open it! It's exactly what you need!" She was practically trembling in her eagerness. Jim came up behind the little girl and put an arm around her. He couldn't help but smile. Her eagerness was contagious.

Jeanie ended the suspense, pulling out a box of scented candles, bath gel, and lotion. A reverent expression lit her face while Lila's face fell. "Ooh, these are just what the doctor ordered. I can really use them at the end of the day when my back and feet are killing me. Thank you, sweetie."

Sarah waved a hand dismissively. "Those are a little something extra that I threw in. I knew you could use a little pampering. Make sure you use them after the baby is here too." She pointed to the bag. "Lila's present is still waiting for you. Hers is the big deal, not mine."

Jeanie blew Sarah a kiss and pulled out the next gift. Her eyes filled and she swallowed hard. A dolphin rose out of the waves with a sea shell for a light, the perfect match for their ocean-themed nursery. She wanted her baby to be reminded, "Life's a beach," every time it opened its eyes. "Lila, this is beautiful. Did you pick this out yourself?"

Jim's eyes began to burn as his wife opened her arms wide and the little girl came to her, a warm and welcome weight, a reminder of the reward she would soon be able to hold in her arms. *God's will be done.*

"Yup. We were looking in a catalog and I told Mommy that the baby had to have a night light. The dolphin lights up too, along with the shell. At night you can just leave the dolphin on and everything looks blue and soft and glowy. I had my night light on every night that Mommy was gone, plus her candle, and they were good luck so you'll have good luck too." She hooked her arms around Jeanie's neck and hugged her, hard.

Jeanie held on tight. "I love it, honey. Every time I I see this sweet, little dolphin, I'll think about you." She pressed a butterfly kiss to Lila's nose. Jim marveled at the little girl's glow. Would they have a little pixie of a girl like Lila? Or a mischief maker of a boy? He didn't care. *Please God...give her a healthy child.*

Graham cleared his throat behind them, drawing Lila back to his side. "Oh yeah, Daddy has something for Jim, too." She took a little bag that her father had carried in and brought it to their host. "Here, Jim. Daddy says we got something Jeanie needed and for the baby so you had to have something too. I don't get it. Maybe you will."

Jim eyed his best friend, expecting some kind of trouble. He reached inside and pulled out a lacy apron and a feather duster. "What's the meaning of this?" He asked with a little bit of fire. His housekeeping had been mentioned in confidence. He'd never expected Graham to make fun of him.

Graham raised his hands in surrender, a little bit of the devil making those summer green eyes shimmer. "Hey, I figured if you were going to be June Cleaver, you'd better dress the part. Anything else I should pick up for him, Jeanie-girl?"

Jeanie took the dust mop and tickled her husband behind the ears. "No, I think this will do." She gave Jim a little wiggle and a wink with a promise. Feather dusters could come in handy for more than cleaning. She crossed over to Sarah to give her a hug, followed by Graham. As she leaned up against him, the baby gave a hearty kick.

Jim watched his best friend's eyes widen in amazement. His wife smiled and took his hand, pressing it to her belly to let him feel the next one. Graham lit up at the life moving under his fingers, getting a taste of their anticipation. "Oh baby, Jeanie-girl. It looks like you've got a firecracker in there. I bet it's a little spitfire of a girl like you."

Jim watched the exchange, saw the longing in his best friend's gaze. It hit him; Graham wanted a child of his own, maybe as badly as the Pedersens. There was no doubt that he loved Lila, had from the start, and was the only daddy she had ever known. But to have one of his own, to start a life, Jim knew—there was no better way of grabbing hold of all that was good that God had to offer.

"Can I interest anyone in something to drink?" Jim asked while Jeanie bustled off to the nursery to find a place for her lamp, Lila tagging along to be a consultant. Sarah trailed behind them.

Graham joined his friend in the kitchen. Jim pulled out sparkling grape juice for the girls and handed a beer to Graham. Another beer found its way to his own hand. A pop of the top and a good swallow went a long way's toward cooling him down in the steaming kitchen.

Graham jostled his arm with his elbow in camaraderie. "No hard feelings about the gag gift, right? I'm just busting on you. It's really cool how you're there for Jeanie." He took a swig of his drink and sighed in ecstasy. "There isn't much that tastes better when you're hot. What is it—150 degrees in here?"

"You come to expect a sauna in this house when Jeanie is in her glory." Jim led the way back to the living room which was cooler and they kicked back in the recliners. "That's what it's all about, beer, comfy chairs, and a game. What game do you want to watch? We have about 100 sports channels..."

Graham gave him a shrug of the shoulders. The more he drank, the more mellow he became. "Who cares. Just pick one. Let the girls yammer and we can veg." Channel surfing produced a football game. Within minutes, Lila came capering out of the baby's room and launched herself on Graham.

Luckily he had good reflexes and set the beer down before her landing. "What's up, Lila my lovely?" He tucked her in close. Jim always melted inside at the sight of them together. Soon. God willing, he'd make such a bond of his own.

"Let's go outside and play. Jeanie says dinner won't be ready for a while and I don't want to stay inside. Come on! Let's get moving. Time's a wastin'!" The little girl tugged Graham out of the chair first and moved on to Jim.

THE BOYS WERE GOOD SPORTS. They suited up and trailed after Lila for a backyard adventure. Sarah stood at the sliding glass doors, hands pressed against the glass, watching a snow war. It would never grow old watching them, *being able* to watch them again.

Laughter gurgled over while Jeanie washed dishes. "They make quite a crew, our very own Three Musketeers." Her eyes softened and grew moist from emotions that were always brimming at the surface these days. "He's going to make a good father, isn't he?"

Sarah joined Jeanie at the sink and gave her shoulders a squeeze. "The best. Like Graham, I expect."

She pulled a towel out of the drawer and the two women fell into the easy rhythm of washing, stacking, and drying. Finally, the last dish was done. Jeanie stood with a hand pressed to the small of her back.

Sarah poked her chin toward the cozy, little table tucked in by the windows with a view of the backyard. "Let's sit.

110

Everything's ready for dinner and you've earned a rest after all of your hard work."

With a sigh that travelled all the way from her toes, Jeanie plopped herself down and put her feet up on another chair. They already looked swollen. She blew hair off her forehead and closed her eyes. "You don't know how good this feels. How can I be this tired and feel this *huge*? I'm only five months along! I'll be a house by the end!"

Sarah set a cub of herbal tea in front of her friend and rubbed her feet in sympathy. "You may feel that way but you are by no means huge! You've got the cutest, little baby belly. We all feel this way. Make sure you don't over-do and listen to your body. If it says rest, don't argue."

They sat in companionable silence, watching the merrymakers outside, enjoying a bit of peace. It felt good to share each other's company again. Sarah giggled as she saw Jim drop to the ground in exhaustion with Lila stretched out on top of him. Her daughter wore a grin that stretched from ear to ear and his matched.

"How's Jim doing? Graham told me about the accident the other day."

Jeanie stared into her tea cup and took a sip, shuddering as she did. "He's all right now. That was cutting it really close—first, to almost be hit by a car, then to be the lifeline for the teenage driver that nearly took his life. He visited her yesterday and that helped. Picking himself up again took a little time. He's like Graham. They keep on going."

Jeanie paused, then pushed forward. "I've watched them both work through tough times, but your disappearance hit all of us hard. Other people would have caved. Not Graham. He kept on doing what had to be done. He never gave up on you, the same way Jim won't give up on me."

Sarah felt Jeanie's hand on hers and held on tight, surprised by the strength in such a tiny package. There was a lump in her throat that was hard to swallow as her eyes followed her man in the back yard. "I never gave up on him either."

8

THE DARKNESS WAS SMOTHERING, pressing in until he felt like he couldn't move. He shot out of the covers, slamming against the unyielding, cement wall in his rush to feel his way to the window. To climb up to the sill. *To get out.* Bars stood in his way, solid and inescapable. They would not budge no matter how hard he pulled. Frantic, he banged and scratched until his fingers bled.

Breath coming in harsh sobs and his heart threatening to make its way out of his chest with the mad flurry of its beating, he hung on the bars in defeat. Nose pressed to the small opening, striving to capture the outdoors in his lungs, he sought his beloved woods. But the night wore a shroud of black clouds, holding back the light of the moon and stars as surely as the iron in his hands held him hostage.

His was an immense sorrow, daunting in its depth and power. Death was a welcome alternative. The only alternative. He removed his shirt. Shredded it down the middle. Twisted it into a rope. Tied it to the bars. Tears falling freely, he whispered, "Mama, Daddy, Caroga...*My God*, forgive me," and stepped off the end of the bed.

Kane Johnson snapped awake, gasping as if choking with his hands clawing at his neck. The last scraps of the nightmare faded as he wiped at his face, wet from weeping. He stumbled out of bed, shivering with an inner chill, and threw open the door of his new home.

The snow was so cold it hurt his bare feet, the air stabbed at his lungs, and the fury of a winter storm whipped around him. Arms spread wide with his head tilted to be baptized in the bitter wind, he breathed deeply and opened himself to the great outdoors, let it restore his equilibrium. It had been nothing more than a dream.

There had been a flood of dreams since his escape from prison, inundating him in the beginning, ebbing to a trickle as time went by. Each time he awoke, Kane took stock of himself and his surroundings, recovering because the heart of the wilderness was his home once again.

It hadn't been easy. After the heady relief of eluding his jailors on Thanksgiving night, he had fled to the surrounding forest that bordered the town before civilization surrendered to unsettled wilderness. Crushing anxiety of being taken nearly paralyzed him and with it grew a fury fast approaching an inferno.

The focus of that blaze: Officer Graham Scott for taking it all away from him—Sarah, his home, his liberty. Risking everything, Kane made a brief excursion into a minimart in the middle of the night, found the ranger's address in a phone book, and made his way to Pleasant Lake.

Two days later, after foraging for clothing and food in seasonal camps, he secreted himself in a stand of trees that bordered Scott's home. *Pretty as a picture,* a voice in his mind taunted. Lying in wait gave Kane plenty of time to lick at his emotional wounds only to make them fester. His mind was a dangerous place when a green truck pulled in the driveway and three people climbed out.

Catching sight of the forest ranger took all of Kane's resolve to remain crouched beneath the trees. He had to dig his fingers into the bark and cling to two trunks that sheltered him. The urge was nearly overpowering to burst forth, take the man down, and reclaim Sarah.

A delightful pixie of a child, a miniature of Sarah, dashed across the snow and was swept up onto Graham's shoulders, her mother pulled in tightly against his side, as he offered his protection.

Watching Scott's face, his love for them an intense fire, Kane finally understood. The man would fight to the death for Sarah and her daughter. Such devotion would not be easily overcome. The battle would be formidable, the cost too great. Kane's brief captivity made him vow. He would die by his own hand before being held prisoner again. That didn't mean he couldn't take Graham with him.

Hovering under the branches, shivering in the snow, Kane watched the little family—because that was the only thing one could call them. They formed a whole, meshing to the point of not being able to see where one ended and another began. Theirs was a bond that was almost tangible. He longed to reach out, grab hold, become a part of it. When they moved indoors, Kane pulled down a branch and began to whittle in order to occupy his mind. To steady himself. He worked diligently at his craft and imagined this place, woman, and child were his.

At nightfall, the trio returned to the truck, the little girl cradled in the ranger's arms. Sarah's love was a fierce shield, evident in the moonlight as she secured her daughter in the car seat, and they drove away. Kane was fooling himself if he ever thought Sarah and Lila could be his. He tried the garage, found a scrap of paper and pencil, and wrote a note to accompany his carving. A farewell and a warning, left behind on the deck overlooking the frozen expanse of the lake. Hard. Cold. Like his heart.

Gripping the railing, picturing what could be his, his anger became a firestorm. To escape capture or the possibility of unspeakable violence, Kane fled into the night. Bent on putting as much distance between himself and the little family on Pleasant Lake as possible, he moved on. Waited until authorities left *his* beloved home. Took what he could, unearthed his father's army jeep from beneath its concealing branches, and made his getaway. Deeper into the Adirondacks.

He never planned on going back but his nightmares dragging him into the past were beyond his control.

Slamming the door on the barely banked rage that threatened to overcome him with the raw memories of that desperate time, Kane fought his way back inside, making himself snug in his new home. He couldn't stop shaking from a bone deep chill. He stoked the fire, wrapped himself in his mother's quilt, and drank a cup of herbal tea from the pot already prepared and kept warm on the fire. He settled himself on the floor, as close as he could get to the flames, and fought to redirect his mind to more tranquil paths after his night terror.

He did not consciously returned to his time in prison and he shied away from thoughts of Sarah. She was not his, never would be, and did not belong as surely as Kane did not belong in the world outside the woods. There was no comfort in memories of his parents and sweet Caroga, his sister. Without his family home and familiar haunts, he was too grief-stricken, too lonely, and they were too…gone. The focus had to remain on the here and now.

The wind howled eerily outside as if alive. The walls of his tiny dwelling shook but they held. Daddy would be proud. Thanks to his teachings and innovation, Kane had turned an abandoned hunter's shack into something livable. The cracks in the walls were sealed tight, holding back the frosty chill of winter. The old stone fireplace did its job well, warming the tiny space while the smoke was funneled from the chimney to the forest floor to mimic nothing more than ground fog or a mist, another example of the ingenuity of Kane's father. Gathering his mother's blanket tightly around him, more for the comfort and reminder of her presence than out of necessity, Kane was grateful to be warm. Safe.

An involuntary tremor ran through his body, an aftereffect of the dream that had taken him back to that suffocating prison and the journey that followed. He closed his eyes, let the memories wash over him.

The weather had been much like this on the day he discovered the cabin. It had been treacherous, due in part to the Nor'easter that had the land in its mighty grasp but also because of Kane's mounting dread that he would be captured again.

After driving for hours, he found a seasonal road that would not be plowed. He fought his way in as far as his jeep could manage, and set about the backbreaking task of concealing it.

Taking down pine boughs, dragging felled trees, and muscling rocks, he left behind what looked like the remnants of a windstorm. The snow would finish the job. If Kane was lucky, he'd never need it again. His last encounter with civilization had soured him on having any part of it. The license plates were tucked inside his coat. He scratched out the vehicle identification number with vicious strokes of his hunting knife.

If anyone found the jeep, there would be no traces connected to Kane Johnson.

Two large duffels, courtesy of the US army and his father's sojourn into Viet Nam, weighed him down as he struggled deep within the forest's heart. Exhausted from his ordeal and heartsick at all he had lost, Kane's emotions threatened to crush him. He sought shelter, perhaps a large, uprooted tree or a cave, when he stumbled upon an abandoned cabin. Nothing more than a shack really, barely discernible in the blinding snow and wind.

His footsteps faltering, his body and spirit pushed to the limit, he managed to reach the building, collapsing on the small landing. The door was ajar, the windows uncovered by glass, allowing the snow to pile up on the floor. When he could move again, Kane entered with caution and closely examined the building.

The roof needed repairs; there were sizable gaps. Where the elements had not made their way inside, evidence of wildlife inhabitants was clear in the form of nests, droppings, and the remains of past meals. A sturdy fireplace, consisting of stones cemented together, had withstood the test of time. Something caught Kane's eye on the cornerstone; approaching to see more clearly, he saw a date: 1892.

Most likely, hunters had erected the cabin back before the strict regulations that protected the Adirondacks were in place. As time went by and the government enforced the preservation of the forest, many buildings were deemed illegal. It was also possible that a hermit, like Kane, had lived and died there. Whatever its history, the place was empty. As far as Kane was concerned, finders, keepers.

That first night, he cleared out the cubbyhole of a bedroom. Bundled up in the clothing and blankets he had salvaged, he slept like the dead. Kane did not know how long he was lost to the world. He awoke, stiff and shivering from the cold. The sun pricked at his eyelids, pulling at them until he squinted at the daylight and saw the snow had stopped.

As much as he was wont to remain secluded in his refuge and forget about the world, there were things that needed to be done in order to survive. If he was anything, like his father before him, Kane Johnson was a survivor.

The task of making his new home livable was no small undertaking. What might make others surrender only made him stronger—he was a Johnson and he would follow his father's tradition of forging his own way.

The outside of the shack was left basically untouched. Kane hung shutters over the windows to withstand the wind, but in a haphazard way that lent to a ramshackle appearance. The door was jammed shut. If anyone tried to enter, they would think the hinges no longer worked. The snows piled higher and higher until the building nearly disappeared.

A narrow, hidden path from a window in the rear would allow comings and goings unseen. Upon closer scrutiny of the *dilapidated building, perhaps from a curious hiker poking about or someone else on the wrong side of the law,—or the right side—a barren room would be the only thing to meet the eye.*

Kane's improvements were subtle, keeping his hands busy, his mind sane, holding him back from falling over the edge into a pit of despair. Using a lifetime of learning from his father, he closed the gaps in the ceilings and the walls, making the building as airtight as possible. Debris was cleared away, leaving a bare but clean space. The tiny bedroom, a mere closet of a hideaway, was out of the line of sight and windowless. The one place he could truly claim as his own.

Layers of fresh pine branches piled high with blankets made do as a bed. When the weather broke, Kane would take his ax, chopping and carving, until he formed a box-bed. Without the benefit of nails, a rare commodity, his forefathers' method of tongue and groove was the only option. In the spring, he could gather the tall, meadow grass to make a soft, sweet mattress. Pine boughs tended to prick his skin and crackle with each movement, but they were better than the hard ground, unforgiving in its coldness.

His few mementos of his parents—two photographs and Daddy's photo album, his mother's cross from her rosary, her hairbrush, and his father's tools—were stowed away neatly in a corner. His sole decor—his carvings and the glass cardinal he bought for Sarah—were arranged about the room, something to draw the eye and lift the spirit when it was sinking down.

Once the shack was made habitable, the most challenging work began: the simple act of daily living. He went on even though it felt as if his own world had ended. A body did what a body knew. The birds of the trees did not imitate the squirrels nor did the fox swim like the mallards unless he was planning to eat them. Living off the land, taking solace in the woods, Kane followed the example set by his parents. A comfort to him, it was all he had left of them. The wilderness would never grow old, even when Kane did.

Kane stared into the flames of his fireplace and pushed aside the memories of his mother, father, and sister that were salt to an open wound. Their absence hurt with a physical ache to the point that he cursed them for their lack of foresight. How could they have raised him in utter contentment only to abandon him? He had regained his freedom. There was no pleasure in it. His was a fearsome loneliness, a pit that threatened to swallow him whole.

A chill went straight through him every time he thought of the alternative. That time away from the wilderness—no less terrifying for its brevity—could be held at bay during the day when Kane refused to be idle. At night, when he closed his eyes and fought to sleep, he relived it over and over. His mouth would go dry, his stomach pitch, and his heart begin to pound in the same way as the fateful night he heard the crack of a rifle breaking the silence, the moment when there was no doubt. Whoever was out there was coming for him.

Watching the fire flicker and dance, he dug down for the gumption to get up and start his day. With a heavy sigh and limbs that dragged in a way they never had before, Kane dressed. He washed in the basin of water he'd warmed over the fire and ventured out into the strange, half-light, half-dark before dawn. He would hunt. Gathering sustenance was necessary. First, he would crest the nearby mountain.

The storm from the previous night had settled, draping the wilderness in white powder and plunging the temperature below zero. Kane's breath hovered in a cloud, coming in hearty huffs as he pushed himself to move when his body wanted nothing more than to burrow down into any warmth to be found; the critters had the right idea, snug in their dens. His father's snowshoes, purchased long ago from the store in Canada Lake, did their job well, carrying him up the slope to the top.

The whole world held its breath, filling Kane with an expectancy that was never disappointed, and the sky was on fire. The reds, pinks and oranges paved the way for the glory of a blazing sun. It didn't change his circumstances or take away his pain, but was enough to get him through another day, like Kane Mountain had for 45 years.

Peace was elusive. Kane's thoughts turned to Scott, as they often did, and he cursed him again. Everything had changed the moment the ranger breached his cabin and freed Sarah.

In an effort to escape the clamor in his mind, Kane headed in the direction of his shack. He used a roundabout route. It was vital to never go anywhere using the same trail, to leave no evidence of his passing. No one had crossed his path in the two months since his arrival. That didn't stop him from looking over his shoulder. He would always look over his shoulder. Another rumble in his stomach urged him to move quickly and a chill entered his bones when the bang of a shotgun disrupted the silence.

Ducking down behind a rock, he held his breath and waited. Another shot was fired, drawing closer to Kane's hiding spot. Remaining still and using every ounce of skill he possessed, he played the waiting game and willed himself to become one with his surroundings. Pressed low to the ground, in clothing worn pale with age, it was easy to blend with the stone and snow. After all, Kane's entire life had been about blending in.

The pounding of fleeting hooves and the wind of a doe's passing brushed by him. A trail of red painted a map for others to follow. With a sinking heart, Kane heard laughter, irreverence. Two men drank from a bottle they shared and fired recklessly into the air, talking of trophies and skins. They were foolish, hunting for sport, disgusting him. Kane hunted to live and sparingly because he knew the value of a life—any life.

Kane trailed behind them, their drunken, weaving path easy to discern. The noise alone would have given them away. The temptation was strong to leave them and fade into obscurity. At the same time, he could not stand by and be idle. He was uncertain of his plan of action until he saw the doe, a lifeless shell, her blood staining the snow beneath her in a brilliant crimson.

A wave of fury, equally bright, washed over him and he was upon them. Kane's was a daunting strength, honed by experience, fueled by anger. The hunters went down without a fight, taken unawares, their weapons yanked from their hands. A nightmare in a mantle of snow, crusted in hair, eyebrows, and winter beard, Kane rose above them and unleashed his wrath at their waste of life.

"Get the hell out of these woods and if ever I catch you poaching in these parts again, you can forget about the DEC. I'll deal with you myself." There was a clumsy scrambling and initial staggering in the snow until they gained their feet. The speed of their departure would have been comical if he wasn't sickened by the loss before him.

The body of the doe, beautiful in death as in life, brought him to his knees, emptied the contents of his stomach, and made his eyes wet with tears. Kane had witnessed and been an instrument of death for the animals of the wild too many times to count, for survival. Never as a senseless diversion. He honored all creatures that were sacrificed by his hand, never wasting their gifts. Their deaths were a necessity, not to boast or for a display.

Head throbbing and weary, he made the sign of the cross and said a prayer for the lost deer. When he could muster the strength, Kane hoisted the carcass up onto his shoulders and began the journey home. He stumbled several times and had to take pause to rest. He could not leave her behind. The animal's life would not be given in vain. Kane would make many meals and clothing to last him much of the winter.

He didn't know how much time had passed, only that the sun was low in the sky by the time he returned to his cabin. Sleep would be welcome after the deer had was cleaned and butchered. It was strenuous and ugly work, but eventually packs of meat, wrapped in hide, were buried in the snow beside his home.

Venturing indoors, he discovered his fire had gone out. Wood had to be hauled in and stacked, the fire built up again, and Kane needed to wash up before he could even think about food. His appetite was gone anyway.

Exhaustion should have taken the upper hand and sent him to bed. Instead, he was restless, unsettled after his encounter with the hunters. Hoping to restore his sense of equilibrium, Kane sat down on the floor before the fireplace.

Somehow, a stick and his pocket knife found their way to his hands and he was whittling. Working with wood, especially carving, always soothed him. Feeling the warmth and smoothness of the branch in his hand, his mind carried him back to his father and a time when Kane was a little boy with only happiness in his life.

He sat on his father's knee, an arm as sturdy as an oak wrapped around Kane's middle. Daddy held a branch and the pocket knife that would later become his son's. His father's hand moved freely, the form of a rabbit swiftly taking shape beneath his touch. The completed project was placed in his child's hands. Daddy laughed and it was a deep, rich sound, one that Kane hoped to have when he grew older.

Mama scooped up her little boy in one arm, making him whoop in delight, and pulled on Daddy's hand with the other. Daddy lit up when Mama was around, like a candle. They ran alongside a burbling creek, one of her favorite places. Once Caroga came along, his baby sister would join them. It was the place all three were laid to rest.

The stick and knife slipped from Kane's fingers as grief made his hands start to shake. His body finally gave in to fatigue. He slept and he dreamed. It was his family's cabin again.

Kane opened the door to the embrace of warmth with the fireplace crackling. The loving work of his father's hands and the comforting touches of his mother were everywhere that he looked, along with his sister's presence. Two shining heads with caps of golden hair sat in front of the fire. They turned and their smiles were for him and him alone. Kane smiled back.

127

Sarah and Lila had truly become his own. He stepped forward to take pleasure in their company when the door was yanked off its hinges and Graham Scott stood in the doorway. *"Hell hath no fury like mine!"*

Kane awoke with a start. He felt the familiar rush in his veins and ache in his head from an anger that threatened to consume him. He picked up his wood and knife, hoping for something to ease his mind. There was a bitter taste in his mouth and he realized he had bit down on his lip, making it bleed. Shapes took form quickly; Kane had inherited his father's talent.

He held the figure of a woman first, capturing Sarah to a tee. A little girl appeared next until the Lila of his dream was held in his hand. Last, Graham Scott was drawn in his mind then lived in the wood. With a fierce growl, Kane pitched the image of the ranger into the fire. He might understand why Scott did what he had to do. Still, Kane's loathing had not abated. It only grew in proportion until he feared he'd live with a flaming canker within for the rest of his days.

The ranger was with him, waking, sleeping…and each time Kane closed his eyes, he was ensnared in the steel teeth of visions. Of Sarah. In his home, in his arms. In his bed.

They would not leave him alone, would not give him peace…until they pushed him out, to venture back to Pleasant Lake. He took the journey on foot , trudging through the snow, foraging for two days. He hoped the treacherous conditions would be a purge, taking away the torment of Sarah…and worse yet, the all-consuming bonfire that burned inside, seeking to destroy Graham Scott.

Nearly starved, exhausted, so weary he could barely think, Kane staggered to his perch, the vantage point that gave him a clear view of the ranger's home once before and witnessed the unthinkable. Their wedding.

As Kane watched the gathering, saw the couple on the ice, shining brighter than the stars and moon above, a pain stabbed through his heart. He stumbled away, unable to breathe, certain of one thing. Sarah would *never* be his. As for the ranger and the hot rage that threatened to reduce Kane to cinders…he suspected those coals would burn deep in his heart until it stopped beating.

9

"*THIS IS MY SHOW AND TELL, MY DADDY.* He's a conversation officer. That's his job so that's why I brought him on 'What I Want to Be Day.' I want to be a conversation officer too. His real name is Graham Scott. Before he and Mommy got married, I'd call him Crackers. Get it? Graham Crackers?" The audience, consisting of forty kindergarten students, rewarded Lila and Graham with uproarious laughter.

Both classes had merged together in the gym for their special guests. Melissa Ashley and Sarah made quick work of restoring order, allowing Graham to speak. He smiled and tipped his hat while Lila sat next to him, obviously thrilled to be in a big chair like him. "Good morning, everyone. I'm Officer Graham Scott. Yes, my first name is Graham, just like the crackers you like for snack. I've even brought a few boxes for all of you to have later today so you can remember my name. Lila has a little trouble with saying the name of my job. I'm a *conservation* officer, not a conversation officer. Having a conversation means to talk with someone."

He had to wait for a wave of giggles to stop. "That means I work to conserve or protect the woods, the mountains, and the waters of New York, plus all the people that spend time there. I help put out forest fires. I take care of hurt animals and I help anyone that has been lost or hurt in the wilderness. Most of my time is spent in the Adirondacks. I also make sure people don't break the laws so I'm like a police officer too. When it's time to go home, your teachers are going to give you each a little Smokey the Bear from my office to remember me. Always take care of the outdoors! Maybe I'll see you one day when I'm out doing my job."

Graham gave Lila a hug and kiss, lifted his hand in a wave, and stepped off the stage. With so many visitors talking about their careers, there was no time for questions. It was just as well; in his experience, kindergarten children wouldn't stick to the topic. They'd be telling him about how they stuffed a Lego up their nose or what caused their newest boo-boos.

Sarah mouthed her thanks as he found a spot to sit down and watch the rest of the guests. There was no sense in leaving. When Mr. Vicenza discovered Graham would be there that day, he asked if it would be possible to present to the sixth graders for their career day as well. Graham had informed him it would be a pleasure. Visiting the schools to provide education and outreach services was another part of a forest ranger's job, one he enjoyed immensely.

After an hour passed, feeling more like an eternity for a man accustomed to the outdoors, Graham found himself on the stage in the auditorium. This time he preferred to stand, drawing himself to his full height that was considerable at 6' 2'', pacing back and forth as he looked out at fifty children that would be moving on to middle school in the fall.

Graham had their full attention, the room gone silent, when one of the students asked if he carried a gun. Lifting his jacket, he revealed the 357 pistol in its holster, always at his side. "It's not loaded right now, if that makes anyone feel better, but it's part of my uniform, just like a police officer or trooper, one I must always wear. I have the authority to uphold all of the laws of New York State, even though conservation is my specialty. Unlike other officers, I am not restricted to any one area either, so tell your parents not to speed if they see me parked at the side of the road."

There was a flurry of whispers. Graham waited until they'd quieted down. "I know a lot of you probably think it's a waste of time talking about careers when you're this young, but I can honestly tell you I was your age when this job chose me. That's right—it chose me. I've always been crazy about the outdoors, especially growing up in the Adirondacks. There is nothing I love better than spending my days taking care of the wilderness, animals, and people within its boundaries. It's like breathing to me. Keep that in mind when you're thinking about a job. Think about what really gets you excited, makes your blood start pumping, and go for it."

A boy in the front raised his hand for a question, calling out at Graham's nod. "Is it true that you rescued Mrs. Scott from some guy that took her into the woods? Are there a lot of crazy hermits like that?"

The question pulled Graham up short although it shouldn't have. These kids were old enough to watch the news and would certainly be aware of what happened to one of their teachers. He pulled himself together and gave consideration to his response. "Yes, I did rescue Mrs. Scott, near Kane Mountain, and no, there aren't a lot of crazy hermits out there. Our woods are really quite safe if you are careful, come prepared, and always have someone else with you."

Another hand shot up in the back. As Graham gestured for the girl to speak, the sight of Sarah beside her gave him a jolt. It must have been her lunch break and she was sitting in. He was glad to see her smiling face. At the same time, his stomach pitched at the turn in conversation.

The next question justified his discomfort. "Is it true that you found a dead girl in Rockwood Forest where Mrs. Scott was abducted?"

Every eye focused in on Graham. Whereas before there had been some whispering and fidgeting as was expected from a large group of kids, he had their undivided attention now. He felt his heart start to trip and a cold sweat broke out on his skin.

Caroline Richards was a topic he avoided at all costs, one that Graham still had a great deal of trouble accepting.

Sarah nodded to him, sympathy in her strong and steady gaze, giving him what he needed to go on. "Yes, a dead girl was found in the forest. Her name was Caroline Richards and I identified her. You need to understand that authorities believe what happened to her was an accident. In over twelve years as a conservation officer, I did not witness any crimes beyond poaching or trespassing. What happened to Caroline and Mrs. Scott are not the norm. The lakes, rivers, mountains, and wilderness are a treasure. Go out and enjoy them. Respect them. Remember: there is no reason for fear. Use them wisely, take care of them, and I guarantee you'll all find something to love. Good luck choosing your future careers. Your teachers have bags with pamphlets about the Adirondacks for all of you. I hope to see you out camping this summer."

Graham made a hasty retreat off the stage, unable to answer anything more that might take him someplace he'd rather not go.

Moving out the back stage door, he stepped out to find Sarah already leading her class back down the hall from the cafeteria. He managed to catch up and give her a quick kiss on the cheek. "Hey, babe, I'll talk to you later. Love you."

Graham could see that she was torn, wanting to comfort him, unable to leave her class. He gave her a big smile in reassurance and hit the door. Once in the privacy of his truck, he pressed his forehead to the steering wheel, let out a breath he didn't know he'd been holding, and began to shake. Sarah's abduction and Caroline's death still had that effect on him. Maybe they always would.

THE NIGHTMARE RIPPED HIM FROM SLEEP, pulled him out of the bed and warm covers, sending him out to the deck. He sat down on an unpadded metal chair, shivering uncontrollably more from the images that would not fade, rather than the frigid bite in the air. Graham welcomed the cold, hoping it would make his mind freeze. Sarah came out to join him, wrapped snugly in her bathrobe and heavy slippers. She pulled a quilt around his shoulders and tucked herself into his lap, just holding on until he stopped shaking.

"Better now?" She asked him, winding her arms around his body and holding on tight.

As long as she was with him, everything was better. No problem seemed too big, not even the memories he couldn't escape. If there was one thing Sarah could understand, it was the memories. She had a great many of her own. Graham was sure he had not even scratched the surface.

His body gave and he leaned his head on hers. "I was outside Kane's cabin and I could hear you inside. You were crying. I banged on the door until my hands bled, broke my way in through a window. When I finally reached the loft, you were lying face down on the bed. I turned you over and you were

Caroline Richards, staring up with no light in your eyes." A shudder took hold and he covered his eyes with his hand as if that could erase the pictures in his head.

Sarah ducked her head under his chin and tried to be a heater; he was so cold, like ice. "Hush. It's over now. You need to take me to her grave someday, to pay my respects. I could have so easily ended up like her, but I had you and God watching out for me. That's all I could think about when I listened to you talking to the kids at school. I'm sure it's their questions that triggered your dream. Come back to bed. You're really cold. Let me keep you warm."

He stood up with her soft body tucked in under his arm, the quilt sheltering them both. Her sweet scent and the simplicity of her presence eased the tightening inside his chest. He crawled back into bed and Sarah turned toward him, her legs and arms a tangle around him. His safety net.

"You know what? You're my best therapy," Graham whispered to her softly. It didn't seem possible that sleep would come for him after the nightmare, but Sarah managed to take him with her until they both were breathing softly and knew the mercy of nothingness for a little while.

The call came in at four a.m., making the reprieve a brief one. Two men on snowshoes were missing on Blue Mountain, the namesake of the town and lake below the peak. They had been expected back for dinner the previous night. It might not have been that great of concern in the summer; in

February, in the grip of a cold snap, it could mean life or death. When friends were unable to find the wayward travelers on their own, they called in reinforcements.

Lucky me, Graham thought to himself as he climbed out of his truck and did a final check of his pack. It was his first real case since he brought Sarah home. Upon returning to work, he had done routine patrols of the forests and parks in the area, watching for poachers and any other violations. The ranger that generally covered the Blue Mountain Lake region was on vacation and others were already occupied. That left Graham as the closest alternative.

He pulled on a heavy, knit cap and gloves in addition to his snow pants and insulated coat, his thoughts lingering on Sarah. It had been very hard to get out of his toasty bed for a second time that morning, especially since it was warmed by his bride. She'd owned that title for only a month and a half but it would be his name for her, a blessing and answer to fervent prayers, until the day he died.

It was a good thing Sarah was a saint; she accepted the call of duty for a conservation officer at all hours of the day or night, regardless of the season or the weather. She understood because she had made it through to the other side of terror thanks to Graham and his job. A note on the nightstand next to her promised to pick up where they had left off in the middle of the night. It took a conscious effort to pull his thoughts from her now and focus.

137

It was six o'clock and the skies were just turning to gray, a precursor to dawn's light. The wind was picking up and the temperature had dropped; not a good sign. A cold front was on the way in, bringing the potential for a severe, winter storm, perhaps the worst to date. All the more reason to kick it up a notch.

Graham strapped on a pair of snowshoes and began the trek up the marked trail. In normal conditions, it was a moderate hike of four miles to the peak and wasn't too strenuous. In severe, winter weather, for people unaccustomed to the environment and terrain, it could be disastrous. Unfortunately, all forecasts pointed toward a blizzard, increasing Graham's sense of urgency. His primary goal was to get the two young men, on winter break from college, off the mountain before the inclement weather settled in.

Daybreak arrived without much prospect of additional light. Storm clouds gathered on the horizon, great towering columns of white that turned a menacing gray. Snow began to fall around the first mile in, fat, fluffy, flakes that looked like the pale sky of winter was breaking apart and coming down to the ground.

Graham cursed how slow his pace was compared to other times of the year. He had to work his way through several feet; even with the benefit of snowshoes, he could not move as quickly as he would on bare ground in a good pair of boots.

By the time he made it through the third mile, the snow was pounding down on him in earnest, making visibility next to nil. The air was bitter and actually hurt to suck it in. Graham did his best to take shallow breaths which was becoming more challenging with exertion and the increased elevation. He didn't want to delay. As the conditions worsened, he was overcome by a heightened anxiety, pushing him to close the gap to the top.

Periodically, he called out for the lost hikers and scanned the woods without a glimpse of them. He didn't deal well with people vanishing. His personal hell brought on by Sarah's disappearance drove him on this case and would every time in the future. *No more bad news*, Graham vowed to himself as he pressed his way up the trail.

Physical strain, bitter cold, and walking the tightrope between panic and cool-headedness tampered with his judgment. Ignoring it all, he reached the top in a rush, about to take on the downward slope when the solid ground was replaced by air.

Graham slipped, lost his footing in a desperate scramble, and dropped over a ridge. There was the sickening sensation of a free-fall, his stomach plummeting to his toes and then the terrible thud of impact as his feet hit the ground, and he crumpled in a heap. A bloom of pain exploded in his lower back, stealing his breath away and the world went mercifully dark.

GRAHAM CAME TO UNDER A FINE BLANKET OF SNOW. He had landed on a sheet of rock, shielded from the brunt of the storm by an overhang above his head. A fierce gnawing in his back felt like something had a hold of him and wouldn't let go; then he remembered—the fall. He shifted and almost blacked out with the pain.

His back was on fire. The only blessing—his legs weren't numb. "Good going, Graham," he muttered out loud. "When you do something, you have to do it right." His back…he'd done something serious to his back.

How could he get out of this mess? There was only one way to find out. Steeling himself, he gritted his teeth and took a deep breath, slowly rolling over on to his stomach. The pain was so bad, Graham nearly threw up. Standing up wasn't happening. Staying put wasn't an option either. Otherwise, he'd freeze to death.

Think, think, think! What were his options? Glancing skyward, he could barely make out his backpack, dangling from a tree branch high above on the ridge where Graham had stepped off into space. It contained his phone, his first aid kit, food, water, all the of the necessities—and might as well be on the moon. There was no way he was going to make that upward journey.

That left only one other way out—Graham would have to crawl. Winging a desperate prayer to the heavens above, he rose up on his elbows and started to scoot forward. The movement set his head to swimming and he actually threw up a little. Forehead pressed to the snow, he waited until the worst of the pain had passed and started to do an army crawl, dragging his legs behind him. Pain stabbed through his body every time he attempted to use his feet for leverage.

The going was excruciating at a snail's pace. Graham didn't know how long he could keep it up, only that he had to find shelter of some sort to avoid dying of exposure. The elements were joining forces against him as the snow gained momentum and the temperature plummeted.

His teeth began to chatter with a chill that settled within his bones and he knew—it was more than just the cold. Shock and hypothermia were at war to take him out. Graham would be damned if he was going to let that happen.

"Sarah, I'm *not* giving up," he muttered with fierce determination. They had been through too much to be separated now by a fluke accident.

Pure nerve and pig headedness had carried him through the worst period of his life; Graham was counting on both to pull him through now. A glance up at the sky showed a growing dimness, on the downward slide into night. He clamped his jaw shut and shimmied forward, determined to find someplace to take refuge.

At least an hour later, the rocky area running along the ridge receded and the woods surrounded him. About twenty feet ahead was a fallen tree. Perhaps he could get underneath its branches and burrow into the snow for insulation. His head bowed down and he closed his eyes to make the distance seem shorter.

The torture continued until Graham hit something warm and solid. His eyes snapped open to find a pair of feet wrapped in thick, deerskin boots. Overwhelming relief flooded a system strained to the limit. Someone had come to him, an angel of mercy.

He looked up and reared back, his every instinct shouting at him to escape. His scream tore through the air as a knife of pain jabbed him in the back. Broken. It had to be, but that was nothing compared to his heart, and a mind about to come unhinged.

"WELL, IF IT ISN'T OFFICER SCOTT. Somehow I knew it was inevitable that we would meet again. Don't worry. I'm not happy to see you either." Kane Johnson dropped down on his haunches to peer closely at the face that had hounded his nightmares.

This man was responsible for handing him over to the law and taking away his life. That Kane had started the turn of events by stealing Sarah was irrelevant. Graham Scott had made his world come crashing down, something that was not easy to forget. In bringing Sarah home, the ranger had taken away Kane's chance of ever going back to his own home.

The Lord giveth and the Lord taketh away. Kane did not fail to see the irony in holding this man's life in his hands at this fateful moment. *An eye for an eye*, flashed through his mind from bible readings with his father when he was a child. Tempting, extremely tempting, but Kane wasn't sure he had it in him to be *that* ruthless.

Graham's jaw clenched and he reached for the pistol in his jacket, a move he must have regretted what with the agony written on his face. A moment's thought and he took pause. What was he going to do? Johnson was his only hope. Killing Kane certainly wouldn't help the situation. The ranger closed his eyes and bowed his head in defeat.

It gave Kane grim satisfaction to grasp Graham's situation. The ranger was in trouble. Deep trouble. "As much as we both don't want to be here in this time and place, we both know that you need me. And as much as I would prefer to leave you here to nature and the will of God, I can't do that…because of Sarah."

Graham stared up at him, long-simmering hatred warring with desperation in his eyes. He gave a slow nod then dropped his head to the snow. What choice did he have? His only other alternative was to take his chances with the elements. The odds were stacked against him.

Kane reached out and took hold of the injured man's arm, marveling at the tension running through his frame. "Let's get you up and to my place."

He rose to his feet in one fluid motion and brought Graham with him. The ranger swayed and his face went a terrible shade of gray, but he held onto consciousness. They began a difficult progress through the woods, with Kane as a support system when Graham's body was ready to give out. Every step was paid for in agony; even though Kane bore most of the burden, the torture must have been unbearable. By the time they stopped, the ranger was covered in a cold sweat and shaking uncontrollably.

A small building stood before them, surrounded by trees, nearly succumbing to the snow. Decrepit in appearance, outsiders would consider something like it nothing more than a nuisance and eyesore to be torn down.

Kane nodded his head with a bitter curl to his lip in place of a smile. "Home sweet home. Nice, isn't it?"

With jerk, he half dragged Graham along a concealed path to the back of the cabin. Kane climbed through a window and proceeded to pull the injured man in after him. Clamping down on his lip hard enough to make it bleed, the ranger barely held onto consciousness with the jarring of his back.

Grunting with exertion, Kane eased Scott down on his bed. It gave the woodsman a perverse satisfaction to provide Sarah's man with nothing more than blankets on pine branches in his cubbyhole of a room. It wasn't the best accommodations, but was a better alternative to sleeping outdoors.

Stripping out of snow encrusted outerwear, he built up the fireplace until the snug space was roasting and added water to the kettle hanging over the blaze. Glancing back, he could just make out Graham's face, turned to the fire from the adjoining room. The man was white as the falling snow with tremors running through his body. His torture was obvious. Kane didn't feel any sympathy.

*"YOU…YOU'VE OUTDONE YOURSELF…*your father would be proud." The chattering of Graham's teeth got in the way as he forced himself to make small talk, anything to keep from going out of his head with the pain. It was important to stay on Johnson's good side. The Lord only knew what the man would do if he became angry. The glare in Kane's eyes, lit by the reflection of the flames, only intensified Graham's apprehension and tied his stomach into knots.

"Thanks. It's nothing compared to what Daddy built. I didn't have the time or materials to do better." Kane's tone was hostile and he poked at the logs under the fire with a vicious thrust. "In all of my imaginings, I never pictured playing host to you." Showing remarkable restraint, the woodsman remained calm.

He poured tea into a cup and brought the steaming brew to his unwanted visitor. Kane put an arm around Graham's shoulders and held him up. "Drink this. You need fluids and you need to get warm." He held the cup while Graham sipped slowly, beating down the pain.

Graham slumped back against the blankets when the tea was gone and closed his eyes. Exhaustion was making his body heavy and his mind slow. What did it matter if he was out for a little while? Kane wasn't going anywhere, not in that weather, and what did he care?

There was a tugging on his snow pants and he was wide awake, trying not to scream against the unwelcome movement. "God, do you have to do that? You're killing me."

Kane shook his head, face grim. "I wish I didn't but your pants are soaked. You need to get dry or you could be done for."

He attempted to pull the snow pants down and Graham's head began to spin. Deeming it too difficult, the woodsmen went for the simple solution. He sliced them and yanked them off, covering Graham with a blanket.

Graham's hands dug into the quilt and he turned his head to the side, losing the tea he had just drunk. He nearly bit a hole through his lip each time his back was jarred. Grateful to be left alone, covered and warm, his body went slack. It was a losing battle, his eyes almost too heavy to stay open.

Kane built the fire up higher and prepared something in a kettle hanging over the flames. It must have been hot in the small shack, even though Graham couldn't feel it, because Sarah's abductor stripped off his flannel shirt, leaving only an

146

old, green t-shirt underneath. His forehead was covered in sweat, damp hair clinging to his skin. He stirred the pot and went to the window. Graham's every instinct made him want to grab the knife, used to slice off his snow gear, and run the woodsman through...except he couldn't move.

"Tell me about her. Tell me about Sarah." Kane turned away from the fire and met his reluctant patient's gaze.

Graham let out a hiss between clenched teeth and drew himself up until he was in a sitting position. He had forgotten himself and tried to stand. The pain nearly took him over the brink and his voice shook. "I owe you *nothing* about her. She does *not* belong to you."

Kane leaned against the wall, crossing his arms as he did, resentment clear in his stance. "You took her back. You stole my life from me. I am completely alone. Parents, gone. Sister, gone. Home, gone. The least you can do is tell me if she is well."

There was anger, but there also was hurt in eyes like golden honey, gleaming brightly, only visible for an instant. Kane had taken his hair out of its leather binding and it fell around his face in a sandy-colored shield streaked with white, hiding a storm brewing within that was almost as strong as the one that raged outside the cabin's four walls. Or within Graham's heart.

"You'll have to kill me before I give you anything that belongs to her. You stole over half a year of her life, from her daughter, her parents, and don't get me started about what you cost me. Let it rest, Kane. She was never yours. You had her body. You never had her soul." Graham spoke with steel in his voice, his fury making him forget his predicament, if only for a little while.

KANE PUSHED OFF FROM THE WALL and returned to the fire to settle himself. Even in his dire condition, the forest ranger was a formidable opponent. Confrontation was foreign to the woodsman. His parents had shown him by example how to live a peaceful life and the wilderness had taught him to master a calmness of spirit.

Everything changed when Graham Scott violated his childhood home, robbed him of the woman he loved, and sent him to jail. Whenever Kane's thoughts turned to the ranger in the months since his escape, a fearsome rage stirred within. It was a feeling he didn't relish and he fought to regain his equilibrium now. That he'd have to deal with the man in close quarters was unexpected and truly put his self-control to the test.

"Sleep now. We're not going anywhere until daybreak." Kane might as well have talked to his door; the ranger was out. He sat by the fire and began to whittle the form of an animal out of a tree branch, his mind going back to his days with Graham Scott's wife. The wood snapped in his shaking hands and he threw it into the flames. Kane's head dropped to his knees as the hopelessness of it all threatened to drown him.

10

SARAH TRIED TO GO BACK TO SLEEP after Graham left, but a sense of unease was nagging at the back of her mind while a queasy stomach had her hanging over the toilet. After a cup of tea and a few nibbles on some crackers, the discomfort eased until Sarah thought about the last time she'd felt this way early in the morning. She had picked up a pregnancy test a few days before. Holding her breath and crossing her fingers, Sarah took the test and set the timer.

Five minutes passed and her intuition was confirmed. Slightly shell-shocked, she sat down on the bed and stared at the little plastic stick with a plus sign. They hadn't wasted any time on this one; they'd only been married about seven weeks ago. Delight made Sarah bounce to her feet and start pacing.

Graham would be so excited! He'd told her often how he wanted more children with her, and Lila...she would be over the top! Her five-year-old had been begging for a little brother or sister for the past few years. They had been lonely before Graham came into their lives; Lila's father had died in the war in Iraq without ever meeting his daughter. Sarah was the only thing the little girl had. Then Graham came along, changing everything.

Sarah wished she was still next door to her parents' so she could run over to share the good news while Lila was there for another overnight. After living with them during her mother's absence, her Nana and Pop Pop enjoyed having the little girl come for sleepovers. Sarah was almost out the door, set to take the drive into town, when she stopped herself.

Graham should be the first to know. She debated calling him and decided he should hear the words in person. She wanted to see his face when he heard the news. He'd gone through hell without her. A little piece of heaven was well overdue.

When would he come home? The day dragged and as the hours wore on, Sarah's anticipation became tinged with anxiety. It wasn't like Graham not to check in with her. He'd been searching for six hours. Weather reports warned of brutal storms to the north. What if Graham was in trouble?

There was no reason to think he would be, both competent and a survivor, but Sarah couldn't shake the feeling. Something was wrong. She tried his phone and was sent directly to voice mail. There might not be service. Sarah didn't care. She was worried. She made another phone call.

JIM WAS ENJOYING the extreme pleasure of a lazy day at home, something that rarely happened. He sat on the couch with Jeanie's head in his lap while she stretched out. She had

151

made it to her sixth month of pregnancy, yet it continued to be a bumpy ride.

He would breathe easy again once this baby was safely here. Jim stroked her dark curls and watched her eyes droop shut. He couldn't help smiling to himself. His wife looked like an angel when she slept.

The phone rang and he silently cursed at the disruption. A glance at the number on the caller i.d. readjusted his attitude. "Hey, Scottie! Are you watching the game? It's a good one!"

"Jim, it's Sarah. I'm sorry to bother you. Graham went out on a call to Blue Mountain Lake at four this morning. There were two hikers in trouble. He said it would be routine, but it's been over six hours and he hasn't checked in. It's not like him. I can't get through to him and the regional office hasn't heard from him either. I know I'm being silly but,… I'm worried." There was a pause on the other end and Sarah's voice cracked, betraying her emotions.

"Give me a few minutes, I'll pick you up and we'll take a drive up there. We'll probably cross paths on the way and go for coffee, laugh about this. I'm sure he's fine. See you in a bit, Sarah." Jim hung up and stared off into space.

There was an uncomfortable twisting in his stomach. He knew Scottie could handle himself, but something about this time didn't feel right. If Jim had learned anything when it came to Graham, and his own line of work for that matter, it was to follow his instincts.

"What's wrong?" Jeanie stared up at him intently. She sat up and took his hand when he still didn't speak. "Jim, you're scaring me."

He shook his head, as if clearing away a cobweb, and smiled although the worry was still there. Jim couldn't keep secrets from his Italian wife. Like a gypsy, she saw all and knew all. "It's Graham. He went up to Blue Mountain Lake this morning to help some lost hikers and Sarah's afraid something's wrong. He hasn't checked in. He always checks in with Sarah, usually on the hour." He ran a hand through Jeanie's hair. "I'm going to take her up there. I hate to leave you."

Jeanie kissed his cheek. "Don't be silly! I haven't had any more contractions in a month. The medicine in the hospital during that stint last month must have done the trick. I'll probably be begging them to induce me. Go. You know he'd be there for you."

Jim stood up and kissed the top of her head. "Promise me you'll take it easy, got it?" He stared at her with an intensity that could burn its way to her heart. He wouldn't leave without complete assurance.

"All right! I'll be good. I'll hold this couch down and I won't let it go anywhere. Now get going!" She pulled him down for one last kiss, the kind of kiss that would keep him warm, safe, and eager to come back home.

"BUT I WANT TO GO TOO, MOMMY! Why can't I come?" Lila held on tight to her mother's arm. Ever since Sarah's return, the little girl had a hard time letting go or with any separation. Their counselor said to be patient with her and eventually Lila would adjust.

Sarah knelt down and gave Lila one of her best hugs ever, the kind that just about squished her insides because those were the only kind she knew how to give when it came to her daughter. "Honey, I want you to keep Nana and Pop Pop company. Jim and I just want to go see if Graham needs any help doing his job. He's way up north where it's snowing and I don't want you to catch a cold."

Lila's eyes were huge with fear when she looked up at Jim's face. He was trying to smile back at her, but wasn't convincing. "Is Daddy okay? He doesn't usually need help. Look at how he found you." She held on tightly to her mother and began to sniffle, tears close to the surface.

Jim reached down and scooped Lila up into his arms so he could spin her around. It was a tradition, one he would not think of forgetting now when she needed it most. "Don't worry that pretty head of yours. Everything will be all right. Mommy just wants to make sure for herself. You know how mommies are, taking care of everyone. Besides, it's only fair after all that your daddy did for your mommy. I'll take good care of her. You can count on me, kiddo." He kissed her cheek and put her down.

Lila hugged his legs and gave Jim a smile. "I know you will. We're really lucky to have a policeman friend. I won't worry because Mommy won't be alone this time and if Daddy is in trouble, you'll know exactly what to do. All policemen do, right, Nana?"

Sally Anderson lifted Lila up into her arms, tucking her little, shining head into her shoulder, and her granddaughter's arms wrapped tightly around her neck. It took every bit of a grandmother's skill to nod and sound reassuring. "Yes, sweetheart. You haven't a thing to worry about." Sarah's mother told a different story in the sea of trouble in her eyes.

JIM PULLED HIS SUV into the parking area at the trailhead on Blue Mountain Lake. The snow had picked up in force on the drive, now a curtain falling down around them, making it difficult to see more than a few feet ahead. It was three o'clock. They had called the regional office. Still no word from Graham. The lost hikers had found their own way out a few hours earlier.

Give it a couple more hours and their daylight would be gone. Sarah's heart fell at the sight of a green pick-up from the Department of Conservation. A bumper sticker from Lila clearly identified it as Graham's. She had been clinging to the hope that his truck would be gone. That he was on his way home and they would all make fun of how paranoid she was, like a mother hen.

She and Jim sat in utter stillness, staring at the truck. The full-blast of the heat washed over them while the windshield wipers swished back and forth, snowflakes dissolving as they hit the heated glass. "Now I know what it was like for Graham when he found my car and couldn't find me." Sarah's voice was small and broken.

Jim cleared his throat, his brown eyes shadowed with dark memories. "The way he looked that night you disappeared, when I came to help him search....I don't ever want to see him like that again. It was like a part of him died and he wasn't truly living again until he brought you out. Thank God for Lila. His weekends with her were the only thing that kept him sane and it was the thought of her that saved him when...."

He suddenly broke off and nervously drummed his fingers on the steering wheel. "Did Lila tell you about their special Sundays?"

Sarah laid her hand on his fingers until they stopped tapping. "She told me all about every one of their family days together. Lila never said anything about Graham needing to be saved." She peered closely at her husband's best friend, watching his skin begin to flush.

Jim's jaw tightened, mulling over a past that was best forgotten. "Did you hear about Caroline Richards?"

At Sarah's nod, he plowed on, but couldn't look at her. He stared ahead at the snow. "The night that Caroline's body was discovered, I brought Graham to identify her. For an instant, we both thought it was you, the resemblance was that strong. It shook Graham, to the core. Before he had a chance to recover, Lila turned up missing at school."

Sarah couldn't hold back a soft gasp. Jim turned to take her hand. "It wasn't long, maybe a half hour and Graham took charge of the situation, knew right away to go to the nature trail. He brought her home."

Sarah felt Jim's trembling and met his troubled gaze. "What is it you're not telling me? What happened to Graham?" She kept her voice soft and steady, encouraging him to bare his soul.

"I had a bad feeling. I'd never seen him brought that low before. Finding Caroline and almost losing Lila…it was too much. Jeanie and I decided to surprise him with dinner; he hadn't been eating well or sleeping well. He wasn't doing much of anything well just then. I had this feeling deep in my gut that something was wrong. We made it to the house after dark. I couldn't find him inside. Something made me look out front and that's when I saw him go under in the lake. He didn't come back up."

Sarah's fingers dug into Jim's hand until it hurt. Neither cared nor noticed. "Are you trying to tell me he…he tried to commit suicide?" She had known that her abduction had taken a toll on those who loved her. Only she and the Lord knew how much it had cost *her*. Sarah never imagined that it had nearly taken the life of the man she loved.

157

Jim shook his head. "I think it all got to him...the girl that he couldn't save, the not knowing where you were for so long, the thought of anything happening to Lila. I was there in an instant after he went in, fished around, and pulled him out. I gave him hell. Graham told me he snapped out of it the second he hit that icy water because of Lila."

Sarah began pulling on her gloves with hands that shook, brushing away tears as she yanked her hat down over her ears and jumped out into the snow. "Something's wrong, I just know it. Either he's hurt or he's lost. You and I both know that Graham *doesn't* get lost."

Jim was beside her in seconds, strapping on his pack and following her. He flanked her as they started up the trail. It was a struggle to see the yellow markers on the trees. Sarah could not miss the odd irony of their situation. It seemed that history really did repeat itself, except this time the roles were reversed and Sarah had come to Graham's rescue.

They didn't talk. The wind and the bitter cold made it difficult at best. It was necessary to concentrate on the simple task of putting one foot in front of another. After two hours, they made it to the top, both winded and fatigued with numbed toes under the straps of their snowshoes. There was no sign of Graham and even if he had made any marks of his passing, the elements had wiped them out long ago.

Jim was close behind Sarah when she almost lost her footing and nearly went down. "Look out!" he shouted and gripped her arm, pulling her back before she went off the ledge they could not see through the pelting sheet of white.

Sarah leaned against him, panting, heart hammering from her close call. Her eyes fell on something dark hanging from a branch. *"What on earth?"*

She inched forward, Jim still protectively holding on to one arm while she stretched out and made a grab for it. There was resistance until it finally came loose to settle in her lap as she dropped onto the ground. "It's Graham's pack! You don't think…." She glanced down below. The drop was considerable, sending a chill down her spine that had nothing to do with the weather.

Jim peered over the edge and shook his head. "He's not down there now. He either made his way out or someone helped him."

Jim pulled back from the ridge and helped Sarah to her feet. "Listen, it's going to be dark soon. We'll be no good to Graham if we freeze to death out here tonight. We are not trained in survival like he is. I bet he's found himself shelter or he might have already made his way out. We've got to turn back because the way forward is unfamiliar territory. We'll go get a motel room and come out first thing if he's not waiting for us, okay? It's our best shot, Sarah."

Her stomach was in a tangle at the thought of leaving without her husband. She didn't think Graham had made it out. She couldn't shake the image of him lying somewhere, helpless

159

and injured. Closing her eyes, she said a prayer. "All right. I don't like it, but you're right."

The storm around them was nothing compared to the one in Jim's eyes. "I don't like it either, but I know we'll find him and he'll be all right." Sarah hoped God was listening in because they needed all of the help that they could get.

11

THEY HAD TO WAIT UNTIL DAYLIGHT to go back up the mountain. It was the longest night of Sarah's life and she had thought nothing could be longer than the nights spent in Kane's cabin. Jim hit the road even though there were warnings to stay home. The weather had been officially upgraded to a blizzard. It didn't matter. They *had* to find Graham.

"What if….if he was out in the open, exposed in the cold and snow….will he still be…"Sarah broke off, unable to complete the words racing through her head. If she didn't say it out loud, it wouldn't be true.

Jim squinted through the windshield, wipers going on overdrive, and his hands tightened their grip on the wheel. "Don't even *think* it. Graham knows better than the rest of us what it takes to make it when you're in trouble in the wilderness. I'm sure he's figured something out. *I wish I could see better!*"

The snow was shooting at the windshield, giving the impression of driving through a tunnel of white. "I don't know if we're going to find anything in this," Sarah whispered brokenly.

Jim reached for her hand and gave it a squeeze. "I don't know *how* we'll do it, but I know we *will*."

GRAHAM WOKE WITH A START and cursed with the spike of pain skittering down his body, bursting at the base of his spine. Kane's hand was pressed to his forehead as he hovered next to the bed. Water was held to lips that had gone dry and Graham gulped it down with the thirst of a man in the desert.

"Is it morning?" His words were slurred and his head throbbed. It was dark in the cabin what with the shutters blocking the windows. The gale outside had not abated, the wind howling and shaking the tiny building.

Kane shook his head, forehead creased in concern. "No, it's the middle of the night. You were crying out in your sleep. When I came to check on you, I realized you were on fire with fever. We can't wait until morning. I've got to get you where someone can help you. If it were something minor, I could handle it. This," Kane gestured to Graham's prone body, "This is major." He turned away and began to dress for the elements.

Graham felt sick at the thought of going through that window again, or anywhere else for that matter. It was warm in the cabin. If he didn't move, didn't breathe, didn't think, he was in relative comfort. The will to go on was wavering. Staying here didn't sound so bad anymore. It was definitely preferable to the snow. "Can't you bring help to me?"

The woodsman wheeled on Graham so fast it made the his head begin to spin, the fury in Kane's eyes making him wish he had kept his mouth shut. "And take away *another* home? No thank you. We'll go and you'll be grateful for it. I don't have to help you at all, but my parents raised me to be a Christian and by God, I'll behave like one. Besides, I didn't get help for my sister. I'll regret that until I meet my maker. I won't have you weighing on my conscience too."

Fully dressed, he began to wrap layers of blankets around his patient. Another jolt, and blessed darkness came for Graham again.

KANE CONTINUED TO DRAG a makeshift stretcher through what had become the worst storm in at least a decade. Enemy he may well be, but his strength of body and character were considerable. Both were nearly exhausted after hours of fighting the weather. Setting Graham down to catch his breath, he propped himself against a tree.

Graham's eyes were heavy and he longed for the oblivion of sleep. The pain that had become his constant companion had no mercy. He'd swiftly regained consciousness the moment Kane wrestled him from the cabin. He shifted as little as possible and paid for it with what felt like a hot poker jabbing him in the middle of his back. Tears sprang to his eyes and he nearly bit through his lip again to keep quiet.

Since sleep was impossible, he watched Kane go about his business. The oddity of Graham's situation didn't escape him. Now he knew exactly how Sarah had felt, trapped and at the mercy of this man. However, the woodsman was not staying true to form, risking his freedom to help Graham, a fact he could not fail to appreciate.

Watching Kane as he leaned against a tree, hands on his knees, regaining his strength to continue, Graham tried to give him an out. "Leave me. Drag me under a tree, out of the wind and snow. Go back. You've done enough."

Kane shook his head in bewilderment and knelt down to feel Graham's forehead. "You must be delirious to suggest such a thing. You wouldn't stand a chance, not in your condition, not in this blizzard. They'd find your body, nothing more. I can't do that to Sarah. I know what I did to her was wrong. This is my way of trying to make it right."

He stood again, gathering his resolve when Graham's hand clamped down on his arm with what was left of his strength. "Sarah is doing all right. She has nightmares and she's afraid to be left alone, but she's happy to be home, so happy to be with Lila. I pray to God that I make her happy too, that I can make up for how she's been hurt. It will take a lifetime, everything I've got. Thank you for giving me a fighting chance to do that. I think Sarah would say thank you too."

Graham's voice shook and his hold loosened on Kane's arm. It had taken a great deal out of him to say those words, grudgingly at first, flowing more easily in the telling. He wasn't ready to forgive yet. Still, he owed the man his life and his gratitude.

Kane gave a nod, his response curt. "Thank you. Enough talk. Let's get you out of these woods." He picked up the stretcher and continued to combat the storm one tenacious step at a time.

It could not be denied. The trip was torturous for both men. Kane was nearly overcome with the struggle to keep the elements from having the upper hand. No matter. They'd gone too far to turn back. For Graham, the war with his own body threatened to do him in with the debilitating pain and fever. He felt so bad at this point, his body was screaming with an agony that nearly drove him out of his mind.

Both men were on the edge of surrender when the forest gave way to the road. Although it was buried under a mounting accumulation of snow, it gave a spark of hope in an otherwise grim situation. Kane set down the stretcher and dropped onto the ground next to Graham, both catching their breath as relief washed over them.

"It could be a while before somebody comes. All the sane people are tucked away at home." Graham fought against sinking into despair.

After the initial rush upon reaching their destination, he couldn't help but see the hopelessness that confronted them. Even the plow trucks would stay off the road until the storm blew over. It was a minor thoroughfare, supported by a small population with little traffic. The boondocks defined this particular region of the Adirondacks. *More like the outer limits,* Graham thought bitterly to himself.

"We'll wait." Kane used his words sparingly. If he felt any anxiety, the woodsman didn't show it. He removed his glove and felt Graham's forehead, cursing softly at the heat that was making the snow melt upon contact with his skin.

Timely help, that was what they needed. By the grace of God, it would surely come. Graham began to pray. *Please God. Don't do this to Sarah. Not again, not like Lee. Bring me home to her.*

They waited. Graham really had no idea how long, minutes or hours. Nothing was clear anymore except for the white-hot agony down low, in the center of his back. "You don't have to stay. If they find you with me, there will be questions, suspicions. They could bring you in."

His eyes closed, keeping out the snow bombarding his body, containing his desperation. There was the comfort of a human touch on his shoulder, firm and warm, pinning him down to earth when his spirit was ready to let loose.

"You let me worry about that. You just worry about hanging in there. Sarah's waiting for you. I'd give anything to

166

have a woman like her waiting at home for me." Kane's voice was gruff, but a grudging respect colored his words.

The sky gradually lightened, the night giving way to dawn although it was difficult to differentiate between the two in the midst of the squall. Kane stood and began to stomp back and forth in the snow in an effort to keep warm. "We've got to keep moving." Kane picked up the end of the stretcher and began trudging down the road when the faint glow of headlights announced the arrival of others.

"What are you doing?" Graham mumbled as the world tilted with the sudden movement. His eyes slammed shut while he fought down the nausea brought on by vertigo. He could feel himself being pulled and a coating of snow that brought some relief to a body on fire.

They came to an abrupt halt and Kane dropped him back onto the ground. Graham cracked an eye open to see the woodsman dart into the path of an oncoming SUV, arms raised high over his head. Covered in snow and bulky with all of his layers of clothing, he resembled the Abominable Snowman. In such a remote location, people would be bound to hit him and ask questions later.

"Kane, get out of the road!" Graham lifted himself up only to have his world turn black.

12

SARAH PEERED THROUGH THE BLINDING SNOW, trying to find the exit for the Blue Mountain Trail. They had decided their best chance was to come in from the opposite direction since it was most likely Graham had found shelter somewhere past the peak. *Past the point of no return,* came an insidious whisper in her mind. She ruthlessly pulled herself away from that train of thought.

Her fingers tightened on to the door handle, face pressed to the glass, while she prayed for a miracle. "I can't see anything. Did we miss it?" She turned toward Jim when a blur of movement caught her eye and a snow-encrusted monster rose in front of them on the road. "Watch out!" She shouted as Jim wrenched the steering wheel and sent them for a tumultuous spin until the vehicle careened to a stop on the opposite side of the road.

Jim continued to grip the wheel, the both of them gasping for breath. "You okay?" At her nod, he craned his neck to look behind them. "What the hell *was* that?"

Sarah grabbed hold of his arm. "I think it's a man and he's moving away." Her eyes squinted as she tried to see more clearly in the storm. "Jim, look over there, on the side of the road! There's something lying on the ground. I think it's a person!" Heart in her throat and hope fluttering in her stomach, she thrust open the door and dropped down into snow that almost reached her knees.

"Sarah, wait for me!" Jim climbed across the seat and tumbled out beside her. He patted his side, reflexively checking for his gun. Sarah shook her head. They'd already discussed the fact that he left his firearm at home.

In a strength born of determination, Sarah forged ahead through snow that threatened to pull her down like quicksand. The air stabbed at her lungs as she took in great gasps and she began to shiver after the warmth of the SUV, but she remained focused on one goal: reaching the other side of the road and whatever was lying before her.

With a desperate thrust forward, she closed the gap and dropped down beside a body that shook uncontrollably under a mountain of blankets, proving the victim was alive. Sarah crawled closer and gave a little cry. "Graham! Thank God, Graham, we've found you. It's Sarah and Jim. Graham, we're here!"

She peeled off one of her gloves and pressed a hand to his cheek, nearly pulling away with its scorching heat. Something tugged at her and made her glance up to see the snowy stranger from the road receding back into the forest. He turned once and the flash of eyes like honey hit her with a jolt.

169

Kane. The recognition was instant. He gave a nod of his head and he was gone.

Jim knelt across from Sarah, tempted to follow the mysterious Samaritan, but they had more pressing matters at hand. He burrowed through the layers that covered his best friend until he found his hand. "Graham, come on buddy! Wake up! It's Pete and your stubborn wife. Talk to me!" They could both feel the heat emanating off of his friend's body. Jim shook his head. *"Graham, snap out of it!"*

SOMEWHERE, THROUGH A DENSE FOG CLOUDING HIS MIND, Graham heard voices. He drifted toward them even though the pull of the darkness was powerful. It was the little things that he took notice of first. Someone with a firm hold of his hand. A soft touch on his face. The blessed coolness of the snow as it kissed his skin. He shifted, the slightest of movements. The fire that was his back made him regain consciousness with a ferocity that had him gritting his teeth.

He opened his eyes to see an angel beside him, *his* angel. "Hi, Babe," he told her in a voice gone hoarse as if from disuse.

"Gee, Scottie, I didn't know you felt that way about me." Jim hovered across from Sarah, eyes dark with worry. "You're burning up, Scottie," he said gruffly. "Where are you hurt?"

Graham's eyes drooped shut for a moment, a moment longer. He was so tired, so damned tired, but Jim's insistent grasp pulled him to awareness. "It's my back. Something's not right. It might be broken." Graham steered clear of the gory details; merely thinking about it made it hurt more. Incapable of moving on his own, he dreaded the inevitable moment when *they* would move him, like it or not.

Jim glanced at Sarah, quick to assess their options and take charge. Like Graham, he was a man of action, ready to jump in with both feet and worry about a safety net later. "All right. We have to get him medical attention, sooner rather than later. An ambulance isn't going to cut it under the current conditions. Med. Flight would be preferable, but I don't think they could get off the ground until this lets up. That leaves us."

Sarah nodded in agreement and Graham's heart plummeted; the nearest hospital was in Gloversville which meant at least two hours when the roads were clear. Why did it have to be so far?

Jim adjusted his position, slipping an arm beneath Graham's shoulders. "You take that arm while I take the other. Once we have him on his feet, I'll bear the brunt of his weight. Ready, on the count of three. One, two, three!"

Grunting in effort, Jim heaved Graham up off the ground with Sarah's help. Graham couldn't hold back a moan and his head dropped forward, his body nearly going limp in their arms as he was dragged forward.

171

It wasn't pretty and it wasn't easy, but they managed to reach the vehicle. Getting Graham settled inside had everyone sweating and white-faced from the ordeal. Sarah sat in the back seat with him, his head and shoulders in her lap while she held on tightly. She would not let go of him. "Try and rest now. It's going to be all right."

"Hang on to your hats. This could be a wild ride." Jim checked his four-wheel drive, and put it in gear. He made sure the road was clear which was actually quite laughable. A hastily muttered prayer and he began the harrowing journey home. Silently, Graham prayed too.

He couldn't stay still. The heat was on full blast yet a fine shivering continued to ripple through Graham's body and the slightest movement felt like he was being stabbed in the lower back with tiny knives, digging in deeper every time. Sarah pulled off his winter cap and ran her fingers through his sweat-soaked hair, giving him the simple reassurance of her presence.

Her hand came to a rest on the top of his head. He could feel it quiver. "Graham, what can I do? I feel so helpless."

"Just hold me and don't let go." An attempt at a smile was chased away by the throbbing in his body. It seemed to be in time with the beat of his heart and it was making him feel nauseous. Graham really didn't want to throw up on his wife.

Sarah bowed her head and her arms tightened around him, his lifeline. "Jim, what if we made it worse getting him in here?" She continued to stroke his hair, her touch soothing. Graham buried his head in her midsection, but not before she saw tears streaking down his face and a jaw clenched hard enough to make the tendons stand out on his neck. "I'm sorry, I'm so sorry."

GRIMLY STARING OUT INTO A WHITE WALL that only gave way a few feet ahead of them, Jim was at a loss. What they needed was a doctor, but that wasn't happening. The only resort left: push on. It did not escape his attention that they were crazy, stupid, or both, to be out in these conditions. None of that mattered. Graham was in bad shape and time was slipping through their hands. The longer his back went without treatment, the greater risk of permanent damage.

"We can't do anything except take one minute at a time and get there as soon as possible. I promise you I am doing the best that I can." His foot inched down a little further on the pedal, giving them a burst of speed. If they were fortunate, they would stay on the road and continue to have it to themselves.

There was an insistent beeping; it was his phone, providing an unwelcome distraction on a nightmare drive that required his full attention and then some. "This is Jim," he answered tersely over the speaker.

"Jim, it's Sally Anderson. Thank God I reached you. I wasn't sure you'd have service. Did you have any luck finding Graham?"

173

She was out of breath, as if flustered or worried. The tone made the hair on Jim's neck stand up, strong enough to make him sit up straighter. Tension built until he thought he would snap.

"Yes, we have him. He's been hurt. Sarah and I are on our way to Gloversville. We're over an hour away, but it's the closest thing we've got." He spared a quick glance at the clock before returning his focus to the road. They'd been driving for nearly that long already. It felt like a lifetime. Impatience prodded at him to make their destination *yesterday*.

"Please be careful and get here as soon as you can. I hate to add to your troubles, but Jeanie called me around six o'clock this morning. She was having contractions, thought it might be false labor, but they didn't go away and they were coming on hard. That's when she reached me and I brought her to the hospital right away. I'm with her now. They've given her Terbutaline to stop premature labor and it seems to be working." There was a brief pause. "She's been asking for you."

Jim's hands tightened on the wheel. If he had the power, he would take flight! Restricted to the ground, his foot came down hard on the accelerator, making them sprint forward and fishtail. Wrestling the vehicle back under control, but not doing as well with his heart, he cleared his throat and attempted to sound like he had it together.

"Please tell her that I'll be there as soon as I can." He started to pray like he had never prayed before—for his wife, his unborn child, and Graham.

SARAH'S HEART DROPPED AT HER MOTHER'S MESSAGE. More bad news heaped on top of a plate that was already full. Graham still trembled beneath her, his body taut, although he did not complain. She looked down to find him staring up at her through eyes clouded with pain.

Somehow, she put on a shaky smile. "Hanging in there?" At the slightest nod, she blurted out the question she had sworn she'd keep under her hat until a better time. "How did you meet up with Kane Johnson?"

Graham was too sick, in body and at heart, to get into it. He tried to brush it off with humor. "We're old hunting buddies. We go back forever."

Her piercing gaze and failure to laugh forced him to revise his answer. "I fell off the ridge when I was hiking. It was stupid, really stupid. Lo and behold, who shows up as my knight in shining armor?" He winced, his teeth clamping down on a lip worn raw. "I really don't want to talk about it anymore, not right now, okay? I'm really tired."

Not wishing to pry, Sarah continued to stroke his hair. She brought a water bottle to his lips, allowing him to drink, cradling his head when he couldn't hold it up any longer.

"That's all right. It will keep. Rest now. We'll be there soon. You can count on Jim."

Her eyes darted to the rearview mirror, caught by Jim's reflection and a nod of confidence that none of them felt. So this was living on a wing and a prayer. Where was that angel when they needed it?

JIM SLAMMED ON THE BRAKES, making the SUV skid until it came close, alarmingly so, to the entrance. He'd already called ahead and a team was ready when they pulled in, consisting of two strong paramedics with a gurney. Graham had been slipping in and out for the last half hour. He barely registered the fact that he was being moved, his body limp until someone shifted him in an exactly the wrong way and he screamed.

Sarah gripped his arm as her husband went even whiter if that was possible. She had to resist the overwhelming temptation to slap the guy. Jim's temper was hanging by a thread, making him snap, "I *told you* to be careful with his back! What are you trying to do—paralyze him or kill him?"

"Sorry, I slipped on the ice." The emergency medical technician, resembling a military man in build and haircut, pressed a hand to Graham's shoulder until he had eye contact. "I didn't mean to hurt you. When you're feeling better, you can punch me in the nose or kick me where it counts, whichever is preferable."

"I'll remember that." A ghost of a smile flitted across Graham's face and then it was gone. He raised a hand, searching the faces around him until he locked on to Sarah. "I love you. I'll see you in a little while. Sorry to be a pain in the butt."

The paramedics paused for a moment, allowing Sarah a chance to bend down close and press a lingering kiss to his lips. "You're not a pain. I'll be right here waiting for you and remember I love you more." She pulled back before he could see her cry, but not before Graham's palm cupped her cheek. It felt as if it was on fire.

Jim cleared his throat, eyes suspiciously moist, and squeezed Graham's arm in reassurance. "You'll be all right now. You're in the best of hands." His voice was gruff with emotion and he started to turn away. Graham grabbed his arm, forcing him to meet his gaze.

"No, you're wrong. I already was in the best of hands. Thanks for coming to get me." Graham gave them his crooked smile before his eyes closed and they wheeled him away. Sarah and Jim stood in the hallway, staring at the doors after they swung shut, feeling helpless.

Sarah felt as if her heart had been wrenched from her chest with an aching that was nearly physical. How could she let him go it alone? She should be in that room with him. Fighting the urge to run after the gurney and throw herself on top of him, she turned to Jim. He stood with his hands on his hips, staring down at the floor. He held himself together, just barely.

When she touched his arm, it was like grabbing hold of a livewire. "You've done all you can. Go. Jeanie needs you now."

Jim reached back to rest a hand on his neck, absently kneading the muscles that had become painfully tight. Looking up at Sarah, there was no doubt that he was torn, wanting to be everywhere at once. "Are you sure, Sarah? I hate to leave you alone. I could wait until Graham is out."

Sarah wrapped her arms around him and kissed his cheek, motionless for the first time since they'd gone on their desperate search. "You sweet, sweet man. It's no wonder you've had my husband's back all these years. He couldn't do better for a best friend. You go ahead and take care of your wife. I'll be all right, I'm a big girl." She stood up on tiptoe and whispered in his ear. "Thank you so much, Jim. I couldn't have done it without you."

JIM STEPPED INTO A DARKENED ROOM, lit dimly by the monitor beside Jeanie's bed and the sunlight creeping through the shades. Sarah's mother sat in a chair by the bed, keeping watch for the sake of her daughter's good friends; Jeanie's parents were in Long Island.

Sally rose when Jim entered the room and gave him a hug. "She's been resting peacefully for some time now. I'll leave you two alone. Is Sarah in the waiting room?" At his nod, she quietly slipped out.

Jim pulled the chair up to the bed and dropped down into it. He studied the monitor blipping beside his wife, but could not make heads or tails of it. It wasn't shrieking an alarm; he assumed that meant all was well. The same could not be said about Jeanie.

She looked impossibly small in the large, white bed. At only five feet tall, it seemed to swallow her up. Her face was washed of color, lashes and hair a dark contrast, while her forehead was furrowed as if from fretting. *Fragile,* floated to the surface of his mind.

It was the best way to describe her. His wife looked as if she might shatter at the slightest touch. He picked up her hand with great care and pressed his forehead to it. He would wait, for however long she needed, and let her sleep. He would pray and worry some more, because that was the only thing Jim *could* do.

There was a shifting of the covers, sheets sighing against skin, and Jeanie ran her fingers through his hair. His heart lifted at her touch. That alone was enough to make the situation bearable. "Hey you."

Her hand was cold. Jim sat up and kissed it before pressing it against his cheek. "Hey yourself. How are you feeling?"

He held his breath, in anticipation of her answer. No one had mentioned the baby. Jim didn't think it was too late. *Please, God. Don't let it be too late. Not again. Please.*

His fingers found their way to her wisps of dark hair, adorable in its pixie cut. That was how he thought of her, a fairy of a creature with a fiery streak. There was no way, no how he'd let anything bring her down.

"I'm okay now. The baby's all right too. They did an ultrasound and I heard the heartbeat. I made them run the tests and wouldn't stop badgering them until they did. The nurses were afraid of upsetting me so they hopped to it." There was a feisty gleam in her dark eyes until the tears rose to the surface and overflowed. "I was scared, Jim, really scared. I thought I was going to lose this one too." Her voice broke and her face crumpled in on itself.

Jim pushed the covers aside and climbed in next to her, careful of wires and the i.v. tube before he wrapped his arms around her. "You didn't. That little bugger is a tough cookie and she isn't going anywhere. I have it from a reliable source."

There was a sniffling against his chest. Jeanie gave him a wobbly smile. "Oh, yeah? Who's that and what's this about 'she'? It could be a boy." She tucked herself in close and waited. There was a slow, easy unraveling of all of the knots that had tied Jim up since they saw his best friend's truck at the base of Blue Mountain.

"The source is none other than Graham Scott and when he says something is so, it's so. As for being a girl, that's what the munchkin is, no doubt about it. Only a girl like you would be in such a hurry to get here. We'd better start planning names." He started rattling off a few, like Hildegard and Bertha, extracting the giggle he was waiting to hear. Listening to her laughter, he could finally breathe.

Jeanie's mirth ended as she looked up at him, serious again. "What about Graham? Is he okay? Sally said he'd been hurt, but she didn't know the details." The room grew quiet, the monitors making the only sound as his wife studied him closely. "Jim, tell me about Graham."

He shook his head, still haunted by their journey to the hospital. "He fell off a ridge and did something to his back. It's pretty serious. It gives me the shakes just thinking about being hurt like that, dragging himself through the snow in search of shelter, burning with fever. I don't know if he would have made it if we didn't go looking. He's in surgery right now. We'll have to wait and see how he makes out."

With a nod, Jeanie snuggled in close. "Why don't we sleep on it? Everything will look better if we give it time." Jim couldn't argue with that. They drew up the covers, turned away from the blinds, and let sleep take them. United, there was no problem too big.

13

SARAH PACED UNTIL A HAND SQUEEZED HER SHOULDER. She'd know that touch anywhere. She turned to her mother and let herself be gathered in. "Oh Mom, I'm so glad you're here. How's Jeanie?"

If she directed her thoughts to someone else, Sarah could make it through the next minute. It would give her a fighting chance of surviving the next hour or however long it took until she was with Graham again.

Her mother looked tired. Hospitals and drama tended to take it out of a body. Sally gestured to two chairs tucked in a corner and they settled themselves. "The doctor thinks she's all right now. They're going to keep her overnight for observation and she'll be on bed rest for the remainder of her pregnancy. It's been a rough road for that girl. She was so frightened when I picked her up this morning."

Her mother shook her head at the memory before she took her daughter's hand. "How is Graham and whatever happened to him out there?"

Sarah kept her eyes trained on the floor; otherwise she'd start to cry and she wouldn't be able to stop. "He's in surgery right now. He fell and broke his back, had burst fractures or something in several of the vertebrae in the lower back. They're dealing with bone splinters and compression. There's a high fever too which probably means an infection, or just his body fighting because it's gone haywire. One of the nurses just filled me in after an initial battery of tests. Graham wasn't well enough to tell me what happened." She broke off, her voice starting to shake and her vision to blur.

Her mother pulled her in close, tucking Sarah's head under her chin like she was a child again. "He'll be all right. If there's one thing we've all learned from experience, Graham is a fighter. Now you sit tight and I'm going to call your father. He and Lila have been near crazy with worry." She pulled her cell phone out of her purse and went off to a more private area.

Alone with only unwelcome thoughts for a companion, Sarah rested her elbows on her knees and bowed her head to her hands. The thin hold on her composure threatened to come undone, leaving her vulnerable when she had fought so hard to be strong.

The rift in her soul, first formed when her husband, Lee, died in the Iraqi war, widened once again. Time had brought healing, time and the wonder of Lila. The blessing of Graham in her life pulled the edges closer together until only a fine line remained, barely noticeable except in rare moments of weakness. It had been blasted open again when Kane Johnson nearly destroyed her life. In the three months since her return, friends and family had helped her to close the gap, but Lila and Graham were the main reasons that she considered herself whole.

Now, Kane Johnson had interfered in their lives again. Laying eyes on him, coming to the realization that he might be responsible for her husband's condition, shook her to the core. If she lost Graham, the chasm within would be irreparable. Any speck of compassion or mercy for her abductor had been stamped out the instant she found Graham lying helpless and hurt at the side of the road. Anger, hot and consuming, replaced any hopes of leniency. She focused on that rather than the fears that circled her mind like sharks.

Desperation tiptoed on the tail of her rage, tendrils snaking their way in, ready to drag her over the brink. She teetered on the edge of a pit with no end in sight, staring into a darkness and fear she had not felt since she'd left Kane. Sarah almost stepped into that black hole when the sound of footsteps and a voice she loved more than anything, with the exception of Graham, pulled her back.

"Mommy! Mommy! You're back and you found Daddy. I knew you could do it!" A little ball of energy in the form of her daughter flung herself at her mother with a force strong enough to knock the wind out of her.

Sarah wrapped her arms around Lila and rocked her, tears burning at the back of her eyes. She looked up to see her father wearing a wobbly smile, but smiling nonetheless. He bowed down to give his girl a hug; perhaps the world could be set right again if given half a chance and a few more of Dad's hugs.

Sarah wiped at her eyes and stroked her daughter's hair. "Ladybug, what are you doing here?"

Lila looked up at her mother with eyes like saucers and her bottom lip poked out, on the verge of trembling. "I had to come when I found out Daddy was in the hospital, I just had to, Mommy! Plus, Jeanie's here and everyone else. Pop Pop and I were just bursting, waiting at home. It's okay, isn't it, Mommy?"

Sarah gazed down at a face that mirrored her own as a child; Lila would always carry that resemblance along with a big piece of her mother's heart. "Yes, of course, honey-pie. We have to wait right now. Daddy hurt his back and the doctor is fixing it. Nana told me that Jeanie and the baby are okay. I'm sure everything is under control. It might be boring while you're waiting. Are you sure you want to stay?"

Steve cleared his throat from the chair beside her, wearing an expression of long suffering. "Don't even *think* about sending her back home. Wild horses couldn't drag us away, could they, girlie?" He patted his knee and Lila crawled up on to her grandfather's lap. A grandpa and granddaughter always had the perfect fit.

"No way, Jose. Have you ever seen any wild horses, Pop Pop?" That set everyone to snorting and giggling, a badly needed diversion on a day that had stressed everyone to the limit. Lila looked at each member of her family, confusion written all over her face. "What's so funny? Maybe Pop Pop used to be a cowboy. I'd like to be a cowgirl. We had cowboy and Indian day, actually Native American day, at school."

The conversation flowed into the next topic with the ease known only to a five-year-old. While everyone listened to her rattle on, a nurse passed through and saw the little, busy bee. A supply of paper, coloring books, and crayons found their way to the little girl, occupying hands while minds continued to roam.

Sarah's head was bent over her daughter, admiring Lila's drawing of their family, when she felt the strong urge to look up. A young doctor, a recent addition to the staff, approached with a purposeful stride. Strands of golden hair poked out stubbornly from his surgical cap while green eyes flashed behind wire frames.

He caught her eye and didn't break contact, giving a nod of assurance on the way. "I'm Dr. Joshua Jones and you must be Mrs. Scott. Your husband told me to look for the girl with sunshine in her hair and the sky in her eyes. He made me come right away, was quite insistent—stubborn, I might add. He's in recovery and doing well."

Something inside of Sarah broke loose and she let out the breath she didn't know she'd been holding. "Thank God. How bad was it?"

The presence of her parents, blanketing her in their love, pressed close while Lila became motionless in her arms. Sarah's hold on her daughter tightened. How frightening this had to be for the little girl after her mother's disappearance.

"The break was a serious one, several vertebrae damaged by the impact from the fall, causing burst fractures; we had to take great care with bone fragments in a delicate area that could have led to paralysis, given its severity and location. Once he's healed adequately from the surgery, Graham will need to wear a rigid, form-fitting back brace for 6 to 12 weeks and require physical therapy for at least an additional 6 weeks. The other concern is a fever of some sort and a pretty, wicked one at that, probably his body's defense mechanism to his injury or the result of a bone infection."

Something in Sarah's face made the surgeon gesture to the chairs beside them. He took her hand in his, offering her strength and comfort. "What with the circumstances of your husband's injury, his exposure to the elements, and delay in care, an infection of some sort is likely with his weakened immune system. We have him on a strong cocktail of antibiotics and a powerful painkiller. His temperature is already coming down, which is a good sign. We should have him on the mend and out of here in a week or so. He'll be in recovery for another hour or two. Once he's in his regular room, you can see him." Dr. Jones leaned forward, applied a little bit of pressure to her shoulder with a smile, and was on his way.

Sarah sagged in relief, sending up a prayer of gratitude. One hurdle down. Now to play the waiting game before they could get him home. *One thing at a time*, she reminded herself. She gave Lila a little squeeze. "Hey, Ladybug, what do you say we take a walk and get a treat out of the vending machine?"

THE INSTANT SHE WALKED IN THE ROOM, SHE WAS HOME. Sarah didn't need four walls or a special place, only Graham. "You're mother really did pick the right name for you. You *are* a homecoming, every time I see you." There was a catch in her voice and her eyes blurred with tears, but she held it together. Only a few steps to his bed and she was beside him, the only place Sarah belonged.

Everything was a little fuzzy. The light filtering in the room through closed blinds was creeping under his eyelids, his thoughts were a jumble, and the pain in his back was a dull throb that almost felt like it didn't even belong to him. The mattress gave as Sarah's weight bore down beside him.

Graham cleared his throat that had become like sandpaper and opened his eyes to the welcome sight of his wife's smile. "I bet that the Scottish warrior I was named after never did anything like this. What are you up to, Beautiful?"

"Oh, just hanging around. How do you feel?" She leaned forward to drop a butterfly of a kiss on his forehead, his nose, and his lips.

"Like an idiot. I'm the expert and I went in there alone, in a rush, and made a royal mess of things. Did they hear anything about those college kids?" Her fingers brushed hair from his eyes, pleasantly cool to the touch. He caught her scent, apple shampoo and a blend of perfume and that which belonged to her alone. Relief flooded through him. She was here.

At Sarah's lack of response, he swallowed hard, suddenly feeling sick to his stomach. "Please don't tell me they didn't make it." In the act of survival and dealing with Kane, Graham had lost sight of his duty.

"Unbelievable. You nearly died and all you can think about is someone else." Sarah tilted his chin until she could stare him directly in the eye with that brilliant bolt of blue that always shot straight to his heart. "Look at me and listen. Those kids found their way out only a few hours after you went in. It looks like they had all of the good luck and you made up for it with the worst luck ever."

She hesitated, allowing silence to settle between them. "Tell me about Kane."

Kane Johnson. Graham wanted to take all that was within him, every scrap that belonged to that man, and lock it away. He pictured a strong box, hefty and black, padlocked several times over and wrapped in chains. If only Graham could raise it in his hands and heave everything into the deepest, darkest waters never to be seen again, that would give him satisfaction. Give it time, fifty years or so, and maybe then he'd be ready to open the box.

It was a heavy weight on his chest, the box filled with Kane, pressing down until he could barely breathe. Talking to his wife, because she was the only person who could truly understand, was the only remedy. Graham knew she would not be denied. Sarah would be patient. She would not poke or prod; that was not her way. Rather, there was a calmness in her, the eye of the storm. He grabbed hold like a man being swept away by a hurricane.

"After I fell—it was a stupid mistake, not taking precautions, racing blindly into disaster—I knew I had to take cover. I crawled to the forest; it felt like forever. I had almost made it to the trees, when I bumped into a pair of boots. Speak of the devil. They belonged to our friend, Kane. He brought me back to his cabin, took care of me, and carried me out when he saw how bad I was. The only reason I'm alive, and it's *killing* me to say it, is Kane Johnson."

Graham's face darkened at the memory until a hint of a smile brought back a little light. "Actually, he told me the only reason he helped me was because of you and the debt he owed, so really, I'm here because of you."

Sarah leaned forward and rested her head on his chest. He could feel her heart fluttering and her trembling. When she spoke, her voice trembled as well. "I don't care who brought you back to me, just that you are alive. I was so scared and after what happened to Lee…I don't want to feel that way again. Losing you, that would be more than I could take."

Graham rested a hand on her shining head and closed his eyes, grateful to be with his girl. He managed to shove Kane's box to the back of his mind and didn't plan on opening it for a while. Sleep was coming for him until the door opened and brought a whirlwind in.

"Daddy! I was so worried about you!" Lila shouted out and shot across the room, in spite of her grandparents' efforts to restrain her and keep her quiet. She pulled up short upon seeing his still form. Standing by his head, she set her small hand on his cheek. "Daddy, are you all right? You're white like a clown before he paints his face like we saw at the circus."

Soft laughter, from everyone, filled the room while Sarah sat up and wiped her eyes. Graham turned toward his little girl and reached out for her, pulling her snug against his side. "I'll be right as rain in no time, Lila my lovely. I'm a little sick right now and I'll have to wear a brace on my back for a while. That's all. There's nothing for you to be worried about."

Lila's face lit and she touched his cheek. "Can I help take care of you? I can be a really good nurse. When are you coming home? I won't go until you and Mommy can go too."

She turned and looked at each member of her family, waiting for an answer that no one knew.

Sally walked around the bed and wrapped an arm around the little girl's shoulders. "We have to let Daddy rest right now. See how droopy his eyes are getting, just like the times you try and stay up late to watch TV? Why don't we walk down to the cafeteria and you can pick out whatever you want for lunch." She let go and gave her son-in-law a kiss. "We're so glad you're going to be all right, Graham. Don't give us such a scare again."

Lila wouldn't leave until she had delivered hugs and kisses of her own; Steve had his turn next, giving Graham a little hell along with his love. "You're too important to us, son. Don't take such risks again. Too many people are counting on you." The older man gave him a nod, scooped his granddaughter up for a piggy back ride, and escorted his wife out the door.

Graham felt a heaviness settle over his body to the point that breathing was work. His eyes couldn't stay open anymore and he gave up the fight. There was that cool, soft touch on his face again, a slight shifting beside him, and Sarah was stretched out on the bed.

She nestled in as close as she could get and whispered in his ear, "Sleep now. We'll be here when you wake up."

14

JIM LIE AWAKE, STARING AT THE CEILING,
listening intently to a rapid flurry of beeps from the monitor
beside them. It had to be the baby's heartbeat. Jeanie's was slow
and steady against his chest. That tiny rhythm became his whole
world, and he found himself trying to count every beat. He
began to second-guess himself, unsure if he'd lost the beat. That
was it. Jim had to take a break or he would lose his mind.

Moving with care, he slid out of bed. The medicine that
relaxed his wife's uterus must have gone to work on her whole
body because she didn't even stir. He kissed the top of her head,
and quietly slipped out of the room.

A trip to the rest room was in order, to splash his face
with cold water, lean on the sink, and catch his breath again.
When he was steady, he walked out to the nurse's station. "Can
you tell me where Graham Scott is located? Also, if Jeanie
Pedersen is looking for me, please tell her I went to see him."

Room number obtained, Jim wandered the hallways,
hoping to make his trip brief. He hated hospitals. The smells.
The drab colors. The fear and suffering that clung to the air

itself. There had been too many trips here and none of them were good. Graham's father's surgery and death sentence. Waiting on reports for his own mother's health. The D and C after Jeanie's miscarriage. If he never had to set foot here again, that would be too soon. Jim found Graham's door and nearly knocked it down in his haste to get in, like demons were after him.

Sarah lifted her head at the sound of Jim's entrance, saw how shaken he was, and went to him. "Is Jeanie all right? Jim, you're scaring me." She took his hand and squeezed hard. A moment too long passed until he relaxed.

"Sorry. It's just this place. It gets to me. Jeanie's good. I can take her home tomorrow and watch her like a hawk. How's my buddy?" He glanced over at the bed. Graham had not shown any signs of waking. Everything appeared to be in order. Jim's stomach untangled again.

"He's doing well. The doctor said the surgery was a success. They took care of the damage to his vertebrae from the fall. He was lucky—there was no nerve damage, but it was a near thing. They must have him on some pretty strong drugs because his fever has already broken. He's nice and cool now. He should go home in a few days." Sarah's eyes lingered on her sleeping husband and she wore the gentle smile of a mother hen content that her brood was well.

"Do you mind if I sit with him a little while? Jeanie's out and I couldn't sleep. I had to move around a bit." Jim shifted his weight from each foot, illustrating his point. He scanned the room and couldn't find anything to settle on. Sarah's hand on his arm drew his attention back to her.

"Go ahead. I'm going to check on Lila and my parents, maybe get a little something to eat. Do you want me to bring you something? You haven't had anything in quite a while." At his pause, she shook her head. "I'm not taking no for an answer. I'll choose something that I think you need." She left before Jim could argue.

"She's a hard-headed woman, like all of the best of them." The words were spoken so softly that they could barely be heard, slurred by medication and exhaustion. "But God love her, I wouldn't have it any other way." Graham raised a hand in salute to his best friend.

Jim pulled up a chair and clasped his friend's fingers in a fierce hold. "What are you doing awake? Pulling the wool over her eyes? Trust me, my friend. The womenfolk know our moves before we even think about them." He glanced at the monitor beside Graham. All appeared to be as it should be. His temperature read normal. The rhythm of his heart was steady and strong.

There was a shifting of the covers and a hiss. "My back is complaining and I have to go to the bathroom. I am *not* using a bed pan. You might as well just shoot me." Graham gave him his signature, crooked smile. "Help an old man to cross the road?"

Jim shook his head. "You really are an idiot." Assessing the situation, he threw back the covers, pulled the I.V. pole with monitors attached flush against the bed, and held out his arm. "This is stupid. It wouldn't be the first time we've been stupid. Let's do this."

Leaning heavily on Jim and hanging onto the pole, Graham made it to the bathroom, a sturdy back brace—and the pain—forcing him to move stiffly. He was a little whiter and a little shakier upon reaching his destination, but his eyes glowed with success. "Just wait for me out there. I'll only be a minute." He held on to the bar next to the toilet and waited for the door to close.

There was no sense in arguing. Jim had learned from the time they banded together in middle school that Graham Scott would do whatever he set his mind to doing. If his best friend said he'd move Mt. Everest, call the press and get ready to take photos. Jim leaned back against the wall and waited. He prayed Sarah wouldn't get back yet. She would kill him.

The door opened and Graham gripped the door handle until the bones of his knuckles stood out. "What do you say I lie back down before I fall down?" He started to sway, his balance precarious. The I.V. pole was wobbling and the blips, that could only be for his heartbeat, started to go crazy.

Jim ducked under his arm in the nick of time. "We'd better get you in bed before the cavalry arrives." If he could have carried his best friend, he would have. He half-dragged

Graham to the bed and pulled up the covers, when a nurse came in. Sarah was close on her heels.

The nurse checked the monitors and studied Graham's still form. He had closed his eyes and appeared to be sleeping again. "At the nurse's station, we noticed Mr. Scott's heart rate went up considerably. Are you aware of what might have caused this change?" She directed a suspicious gaze to Jim in a disconcerting manner, as if she could read his mind.

"He said the pain was worse and fell back to sleep. Maybe he needs more painkillers." Jim stepped out of the way, allowing Sarah to take his place next to the bed. She laid her hand on Graham's and got a squeeze in response. Jim gave her a wink. "I'm going to go back to see Jeanie. We're in room 204 if you need anything, all right, Sarah?"

She blew him a kiss. "We'll be fine, isn't that right, Sleeping Beauty?" She turned back to her husband and gave him the once over. "Remember, I'm a teacher with eyes in the back of my head. I know all and see all so you might as well tell me what you two were up to." Graham looked up at his wife. He was about to face the music.

Jim saw the nurse standing with arms crossed, the determination on Sarah's face, and knew it was time to get out of Dodge. He took the muffin she had pressed into his hands and debated on a cup of coffee. Considering that choice unwise what with the precarious state of his stomach, the water bottle in the hall would suffice. He returned to Jeanie's room to find her sound asleep, allowing him to relax long enough to eat his muffin and wait for her.

"*I WANT YOU TO GO HOME.* I'm out of danger. There's no reason for you and Lila to stay here tonight." It was evening; Sarah and Lila had eaten in the cafeteria. The Andersons had already headed home. Lila was coloring at the foot of the bed while Sarah sat beside Graham to keep him company.

The day had been one of the longer days in any of their experiences and everyone was tired. Graham looked absolutely miserable. "I really appreciate the fact that you want to be here, but they have me so drugged up, all I'm going to do is sleep. I'll feel better if I know you two are home in your own beds."

Sarah tried to argue. Lila gave him her best puppy dog eyes. They joined forces and pleaded. Adamant, nothing would make Graham budge. In the end, they kissed him goodnight with a promise to come back first thing in the morning.

IT WAS A GIRLS' NIGHT. DOING HAIR, MAKEUP, AND NAILS. A movie and popcorn followed, anything to keep their minds busy. Bedtime was another story; Sarah was staring into the darkness with eyes gone dry, when Lila climbed in next to her. They snuggled in close and finally fell asleep, trying to fill the empty space that belonged to Graham.

There was a ringing in her mind. Sarah thought she heard the whistle of the tea kettle at first. When it wouldn't stop no matter how many times she turned off the knob, Sarah realized it wasn't a dream. Opening her eyes, she stared at the clock on the nightstand. The red numbers announced that it was eight A.M. The click of the answering machine finally cleared the haze in her mind and she picked up the phone. "Hello?"

"Good morning, Mrs. Scott. It's Joshua Johnson at the hospital." His voice was laced with what could only be described as exasperation on top of a layer of weariness. Sarah's heart jumped, fearful something was wrong, until the surgeon put her fears to rest. "Do you realize your husband is as stubborn as all get out?"

Relief bloomed inside and made laughter bubble up to the surface. "Yes, I've heard that before." Sarah wrapped the cord around her fingers, playing with it as she would her hair if it wasn't pulled up in a ponytail. Lila moved in close next to her and curled up against her side like a little, wooly bear.

"That's probably one of the main reasons he was successful in bringing you home. I know it has to be a sensitive topic, but I remember your story from the news. The reason I'm calling is your husband demands to go home. *Today*. Mr. Scott told me in no uncertain terms that he would find his way home using whatever resources he has available, which he assures me are considerable. Otherwise, I can make life easier on all of us by signing his release and calling you. Your husband has also informed me that I cannot keep a patient against his will and he can lie in bed at home more comfortably than he can here."

There was a long expelling of breath. "So, I am choosing the easy way."

Sarah found herself staring into Graham's summer-green eyes in a picture from their wedding. She shook her head. What a man! "Are you sure it's all right for him to come home? I'm nearly as stubborn as he is. Graham will do just about anything for me. If you want me to talk him into staying, I will give it my best shot."

Laughter met her on the other end. "Somehow, I don't find that hard to imagine. I think he can go. I'd prefer to have him here where I can check in on him and make sure he behaves, but your husband probably will rest better at home. When the pain gets to be too much, he'll need medication. I'll have antibiotics and pain relievers ready for you when you get here. Hot and cold compresses could provide some relief as well. You'll have to make sure he wears his back brace, at *all* times. Sitting should only last for brief periods and he should take short walks. Otherwise, I prescribe plenty of rest and Mrs. Scott, *please*. Get here soon." The line disconnected.

Sarah looked down at Lila to see her staring up with eyes and ears wide open. She gave her daughter a big smile and a hug. "Guess what? That was Dr. Jones and he said that Daddy can come home today. We'd better get ready!"

She might as well have let a cyclone into the room. Lila gave a whoop, threw back the covers, and jumped out of bed. She raced down the hallway, yelling, "Daddy's coming home! I'm getting dressed, Mommy! I'll be ready right away, I promise!"

Sarah felt as excited as her daughter, so excited she actually did a little dance. She pulled out clothes for herself and started rummaging for something for Graham to wear. Fiddling with his sock and underwear drawer, something poked her hand. She pushed everything aside and pulled out a wooden carving of three deer. Sarah dropped it as if it was a flaming, hot coal.

The workmanship was extremely familiar. For nearly seven months, Kane Johnson had made carvings for her as a way of courting her. Here he was again, insinuating himself into their lives. This time, the woodsman made it as far as the bedroom.

Lila came bounding in, dressed in her favorite, ladybug dress. She did a little twirl. "Do I look okay, Mommy? I thought Daddy could use a little good luck." She waited expectantly, tugging on her mother's arm.

Sarah pushed her discovery to the back of her mind and gave Lila a hug. "You look perfect. Let me get dressed, we'll have a quick breakfast, and it will be time to go."

Lila skipped off, mumbling something about a card, while Sarah put on fresh clothes for the day, something Graham would like, and slipped the carving into her pocket. This wasn't over yet.

GRAHAM SAT IN A WHEELCHAIR, trying to find a comfortable position and failing miserably. The medication, although necessary, was making him sick to his stomach and he had a headache to beat the band. Jim and Jeanie waited with him, Jeanie in a wheelchair of her own, per hospital regulations. They had tried to talk him into staying. He would not budge. Graham would not leave his girls home alone another night, not with Kane Johnson hovering in the background. He didn't trust him, not for a second, no matter what passed between them on Blue Mountain. The man had been to his home at least once. It could happen again.

The door opened and Sarah walked in with Lila, her eyes drawn immediately to Graham. He sat rigid in the chair, unable to slouch thanks to his temporary brace and the pain. Soon, his molded brace would arrive and he'd be locked in, 24/7. His girls made the rounds of hugs and kisses, first to Graham, then Jeanie and Jim. Graham focused on them to hold the fierce throbbing at bay.

Sarah rested her hand lightly on Jeanie's belly. "Hey, little one in there, give your mommy a break and stay put. It's the best place on earth. A little more time to perk and then you can come out."

They talked for a few minutes, Graham notably left out of the conversation until Sarah asked Jim and Jeanie if they could take Lila for a walk, only for few minutes while she spoke to her husband. Jeanie pretended she was a race car, pulling Lila on to her lap, while Jim revved up and they took off down the hall.

Sarah knelt down beside Graham and placed the carving in his hand. "We made a promise to one another before we married. No secrets. This looks like a nasty, little secret."

Graham sucked in sharply, his stomach tightening into a knot. He wanted to look away, but this was his wife. His fingers closed over the woodland image and he swallowed hard. "Christmas Eve, when you came back to my house…I walked out on the deck and found this. There was a note—'Leave me to the Adirondacks and I'll leave her to you. Kane.' There was no way in hell I was letting him ruin that night and if I told you about this, that's exactly what would have happened. I meant to burn it, but something wouldn't let me. I stuck it in the back of my drawer, hoping to forget about it, yet it was always there like the bad feeling in the pit of my stomach that never quite goes away. I'm sorry, Sarah." He closed his eyes tightly.

Sarah cupped his face in both hands, her voice choked. "Graham Dylan Scott, *look at me*. I understand why you didn't tell me. I even forgive you. Starting now, *we* have to let him go. He did us a terrible wrong, but Kane started to make amends

203

when he saved you. Let's forgive him. Maybe that bad feeling will finally go away."

She wouldn't look away, her eyes holding the promise of the sky, clear and deep enough for him to see forever. To see a future free from the shadow of Kane Johnson.

Graham shook his head. "I don't know if I can do that. I don't think I'm strong enough. Isn't it enough that I no longer want to kill him? Live and let live. I can do that. I don't know about the rest."

Sarah pressed a kiss to his lips. "We'll be strong enough together. We survived what Kane did to us. The hate and resentment has festered long enough, eating us up inside. Let's finish this, Graham, and be whole again."

He was shaking and his eyes started to burn. Reaching out like a blind man, Graham pulled Sarah on to his lap and wrapped his arms tightly around her. He buried his head in her sweet-smelling hair. "I can't promise you anything when it comes to Kane, but I'll try." When the others returned, they found the couple holding on to one another with the carving clenched in Graham's hand. He wasn't ready to let go yet.

15

WAKING UP IN HIS OWN BED FELT LIKE HEAVEN.
The smell of the sheets. The comfort of flannel. His favorite
pillow with all of the lumps. Opening his eyes to find his wife
by his side. She was better than any medicine that money could
buy. Graham stretched his arm out and felt an empty space
beside him.

The sound of retching was faint, muffled under the
sound of running water. Graham's eyes snapped open. Sarah
was sick? He fumbled with the covers, worked his way to his
feet, and carefully hitched himself up to a standing position,
breathing out in a hiss.

The door was slightly ajar. Moving at an infuriatingly
slow pace, he made his way across the room and pushed the
door open all the way. Sarah was on her knees, holding on to
the toilet. She was pale and there was a fine sheen of sweat on
her forehead.

Cursing his clumsiness, he inched his way in and held
on to her shoulder. "Baby, are you okay?"

Sarah blew her hair out of her eyes with a shaky smile.
"You've got that part right."

She stood up and looked him in the eye, waiting. When the light of comprehension dawned on his face, she ducked under his shoulder to give Graham support because he was starting to sway. "You're happy, right?"

When he could remember how to breathe again, Graham gave her a smile to mirror hers. "Are you kidding? If I could dance you around the room, I would. I want to go out and shout it to the world. I thought I already had it all, but this…this is amazing."

LEAVING THE HOSPITAL WAS THE RIGHT MOVE. Over the remainder of the winter break, Graham slept and ate well. He was the model patient, taking his medicine, short trips around the house, and resting. Sarah and Lila were the perfect nurses and company while he went between the bedroom and the living room.

Sarah felt he was well enough to be left alone on the Monday they were due back to school. She didn't like it, but knew he'd be all right. Lila was another matter. She woke up, feigning sickness, and climbed into bed beside her Crackers.

"Lila says she doesn't feel good. I think she really wants to be your nurse today." Sarah whispered to Graham as she bent over the bed, ready to head out to school. She didn't have the heart to fight with her little girl. Lila squeezed her eyes shut and breathed in deeply, pretending she was asleep.

Graham smiled and his hand drifted up to stroke Sarah's hair. "Let her stay and take care of me for one more day. I'll convince her I'm okay and she can go back tomorrow. Drive safely, have a good day, and remember—somebody loves you." He pulled her down and stole a kiss.

Sarah nodded and kissed the top of Lila's head. "I love you and Ladybug too. Take it easy and I'll call at lunch."

She walked away, resisting the urge to look back, slipped on her coat, and headed out the door. It was hard to leave them, harder still to get in the car and pull out. She hadn't gone anywhere alone since the day Kane stole her.

It felt foolish, but Sarah locked the doors while sitting in her driveway, something she had never done before. With a flick of the wrist, she cranked the radio up high and held on to the steering wheel as if for life. Her eyes darted from side to side, to the rearview mirror, half expecting Kane to be lurking. How ridiculous since they had undeniable proof that he now lived hours away in Blue Mountain Lake. A cold sweat broke out all over her body. Her heart began to hammer and she was hyperventilating. Sarah hadn't even left home.

You can do this. You can do this! The voice in Sarah's head was fierce.

If she lingered any longer, Graham would come to the window and see her losing it. There was *no way* she was dragging him outside. Remembering the advice of their counselor from the few sessions they had attended, she took a deep breath and let it out slowly.

A count to ten sounded through her head, her hand went to the shifter, and she made it out of the driveway. *One small step for woman, one giant step for Sarah Waters Scott.*

The road stretched before her, impossibly long in its twists and turns. The half hour journey became eternity as endless calamities played through her mind.

Think happy thoughts. Happy thoughts far outweighed the bad ones in her life's story. Sarah reconstructed the best of the best: the day she married Lee, when Lila was born, and her wedding day with Graham. The images unfolded in her mind, clear as a movie on the screen.

There was an awareness of the pavement before her, the glory of the sunrise, and the grace of deer in a meadow of white. The warmth inside her car enveloped her in a protective bubble and the radio played the first song Sarah and Graham had danced to at their wedding. The vivid reel of her imagination played on until she pulled into her parking spot at school.

Sarah closed her eyes and wiped at her wet cheeks. *Thank you, God.* She stepped out into the early morning sunlight and tipped her head to the sky. Soaking it all in, she celebrated her accomplishment—her first solo flight.

"*COME ON, LILA MY LOVELY.* Let's move to the living room. We can camp out for the day, but let's have breakfast first." Graham's little helper was getting restless.

She'd been still for about fifteen minutes after her mother left before she started to toss and turn. A trip to the bathroom was followed by a another run for water. The puppies, aroused by Lila's movements, scampered in and jumped on the bed. Exuberant in their morning kisses, they made the mattress bounce up and down, giving Graham's back a jolt every time. It might be immobile in its brace, but ached something fierce when disturbed. Tight-lipped, Graham asked Lila to let the dogs out in the fenced area in the backyard, giving himself a chance to regain his composure by the time she returned.

"Okay, Daddy. I'll get breakfast." She stood before him with her pale hair falling down her back.

Her cheeks were rosy from her playtime with the dogs and her blue eyes as bright as her mother's. It hit Graham how lucky he was. Not only did he have the blessing of Sarah in his life, but this adorable child that was everything he could ask for and more. *Will the baby be like Lila?* The thrill of anticipation made him smile.

Graham patted the bed once he could breathe again. "Come over here and give Daddy a good morning hug. I think I really need one."

He opened his arms wide and Lila climbed up, looping her arms around his neck and holding on tight. They remained still while he wished the moment could last forever.

"How's that feel, Daddy? Are you ready now because my tummy is getting rumbly." Lila touched her nose to his and gave his an Eskimo kiss before getting down.

"Let's go." She held out her hands and planted her feet. Tongue poked out in concentration, she let Graham hike himself up to a sitting position, allowing him to stand when he was ready. She dutifully waited for his shuffling steps to catch up to her as they slowly made their way downstairs, never rushing too far ahead in case he needed her.

"You go ahead, Ladybug. I have to go to the bathroom. Why don't you put something on TV?" Graham made his way in, awkward since he couldn't bend, but he managed.

Washing up involved leaning on the sink when he became wobbly. He took care to maintain his balance; the first day, he fell, crashing to the floor and had Sarah in a panic. Scraping a hand through his hair, he shook his head once again at the predicament he had caused.

Stupid, Graham. You were plain stupid. He choked down his antibiotics and pain medication which resembled horse pills, took a long swallow of cold water to wash out the bitter aftertaste, and joined Lila in the living room.

A steaming cup of coffee and a homemade bun, fresh baked with her mother's help, waited on the end table by the couch. Lila had arranged the pillow and stood at the ready with Graham's favorite blanket.

It was too much and staggered him, the sweetness of it all. He took a minute to control his emotions as he arranged himself on the couch. Graham laid down inch by inch, moving at a snail's pace, and she covered him.

He gathered his little one in close, eyes burning. "You're too good to me, Lila. I might need to find more excuses to keep you home."

She giggled and danced her way to the recliner because Lila never simply walked anywhere. The little girl was constantly in motion, brimming with the energy of a five–year-old, good to see after her candle had almost been snuffed out by Sarah's disappearance. "I can't wait until summer vacation, Daddy! Then we can go camping lots and maybe I can go to work with you sometime. Could I do that, Daddy?"

Lila took a big bite of her own sticky bun while she waited for an answer, covering her face in sugary goo. A sip of milk followed, giving her the most endearing mustache made of milk.

"I would like nothing better." He sipped his coffee while Lila blew bubbles in her milk. Graham licked the tips of his fingers after he polished off his pastry; Lila tried to wash her face with her tongue.

The sight started them both to laughing, something they hadn't done enough of in the last year. They were making up for it now. Graham made room on the couch, inviting his little firefly of a girl to snuggle in. The choice of what to watch was up to her; he didn't care. Graham spent his time watching her.

Their morning was a lazy one as they enjoyed the simple pleasure of being together. Graham even dozed off again, the warm weight of Lila a comfort that overrode the constant ache in his back. When he awoke, Lila was stretched out on a blanket on the floor, tongue clamped between her teeth as she drew on her jumbo pad of paper. She hummed as the images flowed from her pencil. She was washed in sunlight, her blonde hair gleaming. It almost hurt to look at her, she was so beautiful.

His breath caught as he made another memory when the creepy sensation of being watched set the hair on his neck standing up. A shadow, in the shape of a man, fell across Lila. Mouth gone dry, Graham glanced up at the window and swung his legs off the couch. He was ready to gain his feet, desperately looking for a weapon if he had to defend her. There was nothing there.

He stood too fast, his back screaming, and made his way to the large, picture window that looked out over the lake. There was nothing out of the ordinary. The deck had been cleared and he saw nothing in the snow. With a shake of his head, Graham went to the door, made sure it was locked, and checked the back door as well. A scan from each window revealed nothing.

There was a tugging on his hand as he stood in the kitchen, staring out at the lake. "Daddy, what's the matter? I can get you anything you want. 'Member, I'm your helper and Mommy wants you to lie down. Come back to watch 'Pink Panther.' It's your favorite." Lila stood next to him, serious about her job as nurse.

Graham laid a hand on top of her head to ground himself again, waiting for the painful thudding of his heart to return to normal. "Okay, Ladybug. I just needed to stretch a minute. I'll lie down again, but only if you'll keep me company."

He reinstated himself on the couch with Lila and drew the blanket up around them. His arm tightened around the little girl and he swallowed hard, trying to shake the unease that wouldn't let go. It must have been his imagination or his medication. Real or not, Graham didn't let down his guard the rest of that day, unable to breathe easy until Sarah walked in the door.

16

"*JIM! WHAT ARE YOU DOING?* Put me down! I am not an invalid!" Jeanie beat on her husband's back. She might as well have pounded on a brick wall. He had scooped her out of bed and was carrying her down the stairs, ignoring her protests. Her caped crusader had arrived.

He gave her a devilish grin, mischief written all over his face. "I just can't get enough of you, Jeanie-girl! What can I say? You drive me crazy." He closed the gap to the living room and set her down on the couch. She crossed her arms and glared at him, but Jim knew his Jeanie couldn't stay angry.

The doctor had ordered bed rest for the duration of her pregnancy. Jim prayed, at the opening and close of each day, that it would be long enough. He took those orders very seriously and waited attentively on his wife. Occasionally, she managed to walk into another room if he was occupied. Otherwise, he insisted upon carrying her. Since no family members lived nearby, Jim had to take a leave to ensure his wife did as she was told. Being as stubborn as his wife, he'd do whatever had to be done.

Her lunch waited on the coffee table and her favorite soap opera was about to begin. Jim took himself off to the kitchen to avoid being drawn into the drama. At moments of weakness, when he was idle, he found himself sucked in along with her. The instant Jim found himself following the storyline and caring about the characters, he vacated.

The dishes were taken care of and a pot of sauce bubbled on the stove. He took a taste, scowling in exasperation. Why was it that it never came out quite right even though he followed his wife's recipe to the letter? Jeanie had magic in those Italian fingers.

"Jimmy, come sit with me. I'm all alone out here."

It was hard on her, being restricted to as little activity as possible. Jeanie usually didn't mind being alone because she was a whirlwind around their home. There was always a project, a masterpiece in the kitchen, home improvements in the form of paint or wall paper, or she was cleaning the place like a madwoman. Everything had changed since the last trip to the hospital. The doctor's orders meant being still. For someone like Jeanie, it was a prison sentence.

Jim carried a plate with a sandwich in one hand, a beer in the other. He sat down on the end of the couch and set his Jeanie's feet in his lap. His hands were skillful, massaging each foot until she actually groaned in pleasure.

"That feels amazing. Maybe you chose the wrong line of work." Her eyes began to droop and her head fell back, sleep taking her with ease.

He shook his head, smiling at the wonder that was his wife. Jeanie was tired these days even though she did little. Boredom was mainly to blame, but a nagging concern pricked at the back of Jim's mind. Sometimes, he had the feeling that the effort to support that little life growing inside of her was taking everything out of his Jeanie-girl. His appetite gone, he set the plate down and simply watched her.

What else could he do to make this easier? The house was under control, passing Jeanie's meticulous standards. His cooking was improving. He tried to fill each day for her, with movies, books, board games, word searches, and conversation. Regardless of his efforts, there was never enough to make them forget the anxiety, hardest on Jeanie because that tiny, question mark's life depended on her.

Jeanie had close friends to help see her through. Jim did his best as her husband; he'd damned well better for a girl like her. Neither could stop up the hole made by missing family. If only they lived nearby.

Jim's parents had chosen Florida when his father, Tony, retired from the police force. After Claire's close call with cancer, he had decided to take her someplace warm and mild to make the most out of every second. Jeanie was from Long Island. Her father, Rudy, ran a successful, Italian restaurant while his wife, Marlene, managed the adjoining pizzeria and bakery. The San Giorgios embodied the Italian spirit with over-the-top personalities, loud mouths, and big hearts. If they thought their little Giovanna was in trouble, they'd be there in a blink. Jeanie didn't tell them because she didn't want to disrupt their lives. Without siblings, there was no one else to help carry the load.

Jim carefully moved his wife's feet, stood up, and stretched out the kinks from sitting too long. He covered her with a blanket from the back of the couch and took care of the lunch dishes. Another taste of sauce proved this batch was tolerable after adding a dab of this and that. The laundry had to be brought up from the basement, but took little time to get squared away. Chores complete, Jim stood by the kitchen window. He stared at a light snow, tumbling pell-mell, like his insides.

"Jim, go out for a while. You've been cooped up long enough. Why don't you see Graham?" Jeanie made him start, padding up to him on silent feet.

She wrapped her arms around his waist and pressed her head to the middle of his back. Her belly, round and hard, was a tangible reminder of their worries until the little bugger gave a hearty kick, making them both laugh.

Jim turned around and set his chin on the top of his bride's head, arms encircling her and drawing her closer. "I don't trust you. You might do something you're not supposed to do, say get up and walk around." Jim teased with good humor, but the edge beneath his words was obvious—he meant business.

Hanging her head in defeat, Jeanie went back to the couch and put her feet up with a sigh. She was going stir-crazy, Jim could tell. He would take her for a drive, anything to provide a diversion, except that was not bed rest. Kneeling down by her head, he stared into her eyes and saw a storm brewing. She looked away.

"I hate this. It's like I'm trapped in my own home and so are you. It's my fault. There's something wrong with me that I can't do this like normal people." The tears spilled over and Jeanie wiped them away angrily.

"Hey, hey, hey. Stop talking about my wife that way. Nothing is your fault and I can think of nowhere else I'd want to be than right here with you. Every bit will be worth it when little Whatchamacallit gets here." Jim reached out and began to massage the warm, roundness of her middle until she went loose.

Jeanie reached up and ran her fingers through his hair which had grown a little longer what with time off from work. Lately, it tended to fall in his face. She brushed it away, making him shiver. "I know you're right. That still doesn't mean you should be prisoner here. Sarah called earlier and told me Graham is going crazy. He knows exactly how this feels. Get out of here and give him a break."

Jim visualized the baby, continuing circular strokes. He found himself lulled by the motion and leaned his head against her belly. He didn't move until a kick or jab of an elbow pressed against his cheek. "Take it easy in there, Whozywhatzit. Your mother is not a playground." He let out a gust of air. "I don't want to leave you alone."

Jeanie fumbled with the blanket and spoke so softly he could barely hear her. "It's all right. I won't be alone."

There was the sound of the door opening and closing, followed by a shouted greeting in a voice he knew too well, one with a strong, Long Island accent.

Jim closed his eyes. "You didn't...*Please* tell me that your dad is here too."

Rudy San Giorgio was a big bear of a man with wild black hair and a growl in his voice. He had a heart large enough to hold the world and welcomed the man his daughter chose as long as he was a good man. His father-in-law loved his son-in-law and Jim felt the same.

His mother-in-law, Marlene, was another story. She had the same stature as her daughter, more ample from indulging in the sweets she loved and baked so well. Her dark hair, streaked with pure white, was always in a tight bun, revealing facial features very like Jeanie's. Their similarities ended there.

Marlene had high standards with no room for compromise when it came to everything—her business, her household, the expensive clothes she wore, or anyone that was

219

involved with her only daughter. Jim had the sneaking suspicion she had wanted better for her only child, a doctor or a lawyer, and nothing he did was good enough.

"I didn't do anything, I swear. She pried it out of me the last time we talked. Her mother antenna went up or something. I told her we had everything under control, but you know my mother. Pop is too busy at the restaurant. I'm sorry, Jimmy." Jeanie sounded so contrite that he couldn't be mad.

"It's okay. I just wish I'd been prepared so I could dig out my Superman cape." He gave her a wink and turned around to face his mother-in-law who had just entered the room. "Mom, it's good to see you!" He opened his arms wide. She stepped in and gave him a poor excuse for hug, barely skimming his cheek with a kiss.

Marlene stepped back, giving him a critical once over. "I wish I could say the same about you. You're looking a little rough around the edges and that hair is getting shaggy. I'll trim it before I go. Jitterbug, you are just glowing!"

She turned to Jeanie and gave her a real hug, her eyes glistening. They all knew it was a lie. Jeanie was pale with dark circles under her eyes. Her characteristic zing was missing.

Marlene threw a dagger of a glance at her son-in-law then returned her attention to her daughter. "I hope you're getting plenty of rest."

Be careful what you wish for or you might get it. Jim left the room, fighting to swallow bitter words, and took their visitor's suitcase to her room. His regret for lack of family did not mean submitting himself to the torture of a solo stay with his mother-in-law. Small doses, that was about all he could take. With advance preparation.

Taking a deep breath to steel himself, Jim went to the kitchen and began brewing a pot of coffee. "Hey, Mom, would you like some?"

"You know caffeine isn't good for the baby or Jeanie, especially in her precarious condition. How can you tease her that way?" Marlene stood in the doorway, leaning against the frame.

Her arms were crossed and she wore a scowl of disapproval. Her eyes scanned the room and she noticed the pot of sauce on the stove. She walked over, gave it a stir, and took a taste. "This sauce needs more oregano. Jeanie must have been distracted when she made it." She proceeded to add spices and take over as was her habit.

Jim's hold on the counter tightened until his knuckles stood out. "The coffee is decaffeinated and *I* made the sauce. Is there something else I can get you, maybe some tea?" Or some alcohol. Sleeping pills. Valium. Anything to soften the edges.

Marlene shrugged. "Since the coffee is decaffeinated, I guess it will do. Make sure you bring some to my Jeanie as well. Don't bother with something to eat. I have pastries from the bakery. You can join us if you'd like." She walked out of the kitchen, nose high in the air.

Jim's hold on control was slipping, heading toward an eruption. He prepared a cup for everyone, spoon banging loudly against the china, and carried everything out on a tray. Fluffing a pillow behind Jeanie's back, he gave her the first cup, followed by Marlene's, ending with his own. He swallowed the steaming brew fast and scalded his tongue, which only added to his misery. His stomach began to burn. He drank on anyway. Jim reached out for a pastry only to have his hand slapped.

"No, no, no. The mother gets to choose first. What did you do to this coffee, Jim? It's bitter as can be." Marlene tossed the remark over her shoulder, extending the box of pastries to her daughter. "Take your pick, honey, anything to soften the bite in that coffee." She barely let that jab settle before stabbing him with the next. "After we're done, you can take a rest and I'll do some housework around here. You can tell it *needs* a woman's attention."

"*Mother*! Jim has done a wonderful job. I couldn't do better myself. Will you please stop picking on him?" Jeanie's cheeks were streaked with red, her eyes bright with agitation. The baby gave a hearty kick, as seen by the rise and fall of her blanket. She winced and rubbed the offended spot, biting down on her lip.

Jim left the room before he said something he'd regret. He went to the kitchen and took down a bottle of pills to relieve heartburn, even though his problem was worse than that. With shaking hands, he poured them out and swallowed them down with coffee. Bad choice. The cup went down the drain, along with the rest of the pot. Finally, he rested his hands on the sink, closed his eyes, and began to count to ten.

"You really shouldn't be taking those, a man your age." Jim slowly turned around to find his mother-in-law hovering in the doorway, watching him closely. She stepped forward and handed him her empty coffee cup. "Those pills aren't good for you." Her hands went to her hips to drive her point home.

Jim stared down at his feet because he didn't trust himself to look at Marlene yet. *She's Jeanie's mother and your elder. Remember that.* When he finally met her gaze, his voice dropped with the intensity of emotions that churned almost as badly as his gut. It was a struggle to keep the volume down, but Jim was bound and determined to keep the peace for his wife's sake.

"My ulcer isn't doing me much good either. It started the moment Jeanie was in trouble with this pregnancy. Listen Mom, I'm glad you're here. Jeanie needs everyone in her corner and she loves to spend time with you. If she's happy, I'm happy. I have a problem with one thing—you and I seem to butt heads whenever you visit. I'm asking you to please lay off in front of Jeanie. It upsets her when you poke at me and she can't afford to be upset. She came really close to losing another baby and I am doing everything in my power to make sure that doesn't happen again. What do you say—truce?" Jim held out his hand, palm up, and waited.

For an instant, Jim thought she was going to turn him down. Marlene was a stubborn woman, but she placed her well-manicured hand in his and gave it a tentative shake. "Truce. I am who I am, Jim. It's hard for me to keep my mouth shut, deserve it or no." The words were said begrudgingly and the closest thing to an apology that he was ever likely to receive.

"Thank you." He gave her a nod and slipped past her to the living room.

Jeanie sat, cupping her coffee mug in two hands, her expression apprehensive. Jim bent over her and gave her a kiss, keeping his voice light. "Everything is all right. Your mother and I have come to an agreement to get along. I'm taking you up on your offer to go to Graham's so you two can have some alone time. Make sure you behave yourself. I love you."

He lingered, reluctant to leave her, until his mother-in-law returned and sat down in the recliner. "Don't let her get away with anything, Mom. She tries to bend the rules if you don't watch her with the eyes of a hawk. The doctor said bed rest and I take that to the letter. If she isn't in bed, she's lying down somewhere else. Call me on my cell if you need anything." One more kiss for his wife and Jim hit the door nearly at a run.

17

JIM CRANKED THE ENGINE ON HIS SUV and resisted the urge to peel out. He craved a drink, something long, tall, and cold, but he was strong. Besides, his job had taught him—drinking didn't solve anything.

Thirty minutes, with the heat blasting and the blare of the radio, went a long way toward restoring Jim's good humor. The Adirondacks worked their way in, smoothing the rough edges, as they always did. He just might survive his mother-in-law. A visit from Marlene hadn't killed him yet. A man could do worse than tolerate a sharp tongue if it helped his wife and unborn child.

He was tapping his fingers to one of his favorite songs when he pulled into Graham's driveway. An environmental conservation truck was parked in the driveway; Graham's was in the garage. Jim hopped out and approached the unfamiliar vehicle when someone in a green uniform walked out the Scotts' door.

Jim raised a hand in greeting. "Hello, fellow officer." They might not be from the same branch, but each upheld the laws of New York State. Showing respect was customary.

The man was tall, with dark hair and intense blue eyes. He carried himself in a way that gave Jim the feeling of déjà vu. "Hey Pete, how are you?"

The visitor held out a hand and gave Jim's a hearty shake. His smile was wide, eyes bright. Propping himself against the truck, he waited for a spark of recognition.

It was like an optical illusion, viewing the image of the present while Jim's mind shifted to the past. "Danny? Danny Rogers! Man, it has been a long time, but you haven't changed much. Graham told me about you coming aboard the Department of Environmental Conservation. How's it going?"

"Good, really good. I have to tell you, Graham turned my life around. I was about to go over the edge with nowhere to turn when he caught me. He told you the story?" At Jim's nod, he continued. "He must have been a God-send. I love my job, my family has food on the table, and my wife is happy. I'm proud to be a man again. Right now, I'm glad I can return the favor by covering Scottie's territory until he's on his feet again. Let's stop and have a drink sometime, catch up, okay?"

Jim gave him a pat on the back. "Sounds good. I'll talk to you soon, Danny." Danny pulled out as Jim climbed the steps. Leave it to Graham. That's what he did, lending a hand whenever necessary with no thought for himself.

A good rap on the door and a pixie pulled it open, dancing in the entryway at the sight of her father's best friend. "Mommy, Daddy, Jim's here. I just knew it was you! Two visitors in one day—that's exciting!" She was forced to stop when Jim pressed a finger to her lip.

"Whoa Nelly! You've got my head spinning, you're talking so fast. How about I give you a ride and you can fill me in on all of the news, okay?"

He didn't even wait for a response. In one easy move, Lila was up in the air and perched on his shoulders. She squealed in delight as Jim galloped through the house.

Sarah stepped out of the kitchen, hand raised like a crossing guard. "Whoa Nelly is right! What do you think this is, the Kentucky Derby? I'll kindly remind you that we are in a civilized household." The scolding was directed at Jim, the supposed adult.

"Aw, that's no fun. Let me give you a ride and you'll see." He wiggled his eyebrows and received a laugh in response. "What, you think you're too old? You are never too old for a pony ride. Ask Graham to give you one when he's better." Jim became serious as thoughts turned to his best friend. "How's Scottie doing?"

Sarah's forehead creased and she let out a deep breath. "I think he's healing well. Still, his back aches all of the time. The cold this time of year doesn't help. It's the being cooped up that's driving him crazy. He's out in the living room. Go on out and I'll bring you something in a few minutes."

Graham was stretched out on the couch, propped up on pillows, arms crossed while he stared into the flickering flames in the fireplace. He looked miserable. Being forced to stay put was torture for someone that was constantly in motion. Jeanie could be part of his support group.

At the sight of Jim, Graham brightened visibly. "Pete! Have you come to spring me? I'll go anywhere. Just get me off of this couch!"

Jim gave him a quick hug and dropped down in the recliner that faced Graham. "Sorry bud, no can do. Besides, I've run away from home. Mind if I stay in your spare room?"

He thanked Sarah when she placed a cold beer in his hand. Jim would be having that drink after all. His eyes closed in ecstasy with the first swallow, opening at the clink of Graham's bottle against his.

"What did you do?" Graham waited patiently.

He shifted in an effort to get comfortable. His brace encased his back from his waist to his shoulders and had to feel like a cage, yet he didn't complain. The beer went down and a smile stayed on his face.

"I have one word for you: Marlene." Jim finished off the bottle, tempted to get another. "I don't know why, but the woman has it out for me. I must have done something terrible to her in a past life." A sigh of long-suffering came from the

228

region of his toes. "I don't think I can go back home until she leaves. We're talking months." He looked up at Graham, his tone bleak. "Save me. Please."

Graham handed his bottle to Jim. "Here. You need this more than I do. I've witnessed a tongue-lashing from that woman. I'm lucky. She likes *me*. How's Jeanie doing?" Typical Graham. There was no time to talk about himself when his friend had more pressing problems.

"She's holding her own, but I think the baby is taking everything out of her. She's tired all of the time and her appetite isn't good. I don't like it. I wish I could do something." Jim drank the second bottle down and felt a bit of a head rush. It didn't ease the pain in his gut.

"You're there for her, one hundred percent. There's nothing more anyone can do. Hang on, Pete. You two will get through this and soon." Graham reached out to him, steady. Always rock steady.

AN AFTERNOON AT GRAHAM'S, keeping his best friend occupied with cards and a game on TV, put Jim in a much better frame of mind. He walked in his house to be met by an incredible smell from the kitchen. Marlene had been baking. His stomach growled and made him follow his nose.

One look and he groaned in pleasure. "I must have died and gone to heaven. Cannolis are my favorite and yours are the best ever."

"I know. Don't touch. You need room for your dinner." It was uncertain if Marlene was acknowledging how much he liked the heavenly pastries or the fact that hers were the best.

The table was set, a tossed salad was prepared, and noodles bubbled on the stove. "I hope it's all right I set for three. Jeanie said she could be up for short periods of time. I thought she'd like to join us at the table." His mother-in-law didn't turn around, continuing to stir the pot of sauce.

Jim had to admit that she had a point. What difference did it make if she was sitting up in bed, on the couch, or in a kitchen chair? "That's a good idea." He stepped forward and dipped his finger in the sauce, his eyes widening at the improved taste. "You dumped my sauce, didn't you? This is too amazing to be mine."

Marlene raised her hands in protest before stirring up any resentment. "I most certainly did not. You had a good base. You just needed a little of this and that. I'll show you sometime. Jitterbug, dinner's ready!" She called out to the living room, her voice carrying easily.

"I'll get her." Jim walked into the next room as Jeanie was rising from the couch, belly protruding. It was encouraging to see her getting bigger with the passing of time.

He wagged a finger at her when he saw her guilty expression. "You were close, but you won't get away with it." He scooped her up and carried her to the kitchen. "Enjoy the moment. You're living in a romance novel."

Jeanie's eyes flashed and her tongue was sharp. "Some romance novel! None of the girls in those stories have stomachs out to here or feel as big as a house." She breathed through her nose, glanced at her mother, and cooled off when she could look at her husband again. "All right. It's not so bad. I *do* like how you spoil me."

To prove her words, she gave her husband a kiss. Her mother said grace and they spent a pleasant hour. Talking. Eating. Laughing. Everyone lived.

OVER THE COURSE OF THE NEXT WEEK, Jim maintained his normal routine. If he didn't, he would go completely insane. He was up early, handling household chores before his mother-in-law could take over or complain. It was easier to run errands knowing someone was with Jeanie. Marlene stayed out of his way and he steered clear of her, giving Jeanie a chance to catch up and have all the girl talk she could want.

The evening of the fifth day arrived an eternity later. Jeanie was in the shower, taking advantage of the hot water to soothe an aching back and feet. Jim leaned against the door, listening to her sing. His eyes closed and he let himself get lost in the sound of her voice until the water turned off. "Prepare yourself, Madame. I'm coming in."

He grabbed a thick towel off the shelf and made his way through the steam. "Jeanie-girl, where are you?" His tone was playful. "Are you in here or do I have to send in the dogs?" He reached the curtain and pulled back the thin material.

"I'm in here, all right. You can't miss me!" Jeanie gestured to her growing belly, eyes widening at a particularly strong kick, clearly visible in her naked state. "Easy in there, Junior! You can't come out that way!"

Jim laid his hand on her stomach and was rewarded with another kick. He leaned forward and kissed the spot, his hair becoming damp in the warm mist. Love welled up inside of him, near to overflowing. "I can't wait to meet her."

Jim stood and handed Jeanie the towel before he broke down with feelings that were always close to the surface these days. Her robe was next before he swept her off her feet again.

"Jimmy, this is ridiculous! I'm going to forget how to walk and I'll break your back!" Jeanie scolded. Both were laughing as he carried her to the bedroom. Neither noticed Marlene standing in her doorway, watching them intently.

Once Jim had his wife settled, he went downstairs to get a bedtime snack. They had a tradition to drink chocolate milk and have something sweet. With the arrival of Jeanie's mother, the pickings were better than ever. He pulled up short at the sight of Marlene sitting at the kitchen table. A steaming cup of coffee sat in front of her. Another waited across the table.

"Hi Mom. Is everything all right?" There was something about her that felt strange.

232

"Sit down, Jimmy. Have a drink with me. I made it just the way you like it, heavy on the cream and sugar, light on the coffee." She gestured to the opposite chair and pushed a plate of Italian cookies his way.

Her eyes glistened when she looked up at him and Jim had the horrifying thought that Marlene might cry. "I owe you an apology. I came here, convinced that my Jeanie was having problems with this pregnancy because of you. Forgive me, but I thought it had to be the dangerous line of work that you do. When I realized you had taken time off from work, I figured you weren't taking care of her or the house."

Marlene raised a hand, pushing back the hurt he couldn't hide. "I have never been more wrong in my life and when I'm wrong, I say so. I have never seen someone more devoted. You're housekeeping is amazing; Jeanie *couldn't* do better and she learned from me. The cooking..." She gave a little laugh. "That's not as good as my girl's but for a man, you're pretty good."

She laid her hand on his and this time, the tears did fall. "How you take care of my daughter is unbelievable. I could not ask for more if I talked to God. You two don't need me because you have each other. I've already told Jeanie that I'm heading home tomorrow. I hope our truce can be permanent."

Jim swallowed hard, his voice rough. "I think that's a possibility." He stood and walked around to her side of the table. "How about we seal it with a hug?"

His arms opened wide and she stepped in. It wasn't so hard after all.

"I CAN'T STAND IT ANYMORE!" Jim winced at the sound of his wife's voice carrying throughout the house. He wouldn't be surprised if his neighbors heard her as well.

He stood in the hallway, back pressed against the wall outside their bedroom, reluctant to enter. Jeanie had been confined to bed rest for over two weeks and she was ready to climb the walls. Her mother had left a few days before and the "same ol' same ol'" wasn't cutting it. Drastic times required drastic measures. Jim had brought in the reinforcements. He gave a little nod and sent them in.

"Me neither, Slim. Slide over." Graham walked gingerly to the bed, as if on egg shells, his crooked grin and wicked eyes making Jeanie smile in a way that only he could manage. Slim? She looked like she'd swallowed a small watermelon!

He sat down slowly, breath coming out in a rush, and swung his legs up on the bed. "I don't know about you, but I say let's ditch our jailors and head for the beach!" Sarah was behind him in a flash, propping pillows up against his back. Graham winced as he leaned against them and gave her a wink.

Jeanie gave him a fierce hug and kiss on the cheek, more animated than she'd been in days. "Graham! Thank God, someone who really understands! Let's go to Vegas, the

Bahamas, or around the block. I don't care as long as I'm out of this house! Can you spring me?"

Graham gestured pointedly at his brace. "I'm at a slight disadvantage at the moment. However, I heard that misery loves company, so here I am. I have a little help too. Lila brought the movies and Sarah has the refreshments. Let's make room for everyone and turn this into a bed party!"

Lila flitted into the room and climbed up next, wriggling her way in between the two adults. She tucked herself in under Jeanie's arm and gave her a big grin. "I'm ready for a party! We should have brought balloons. Come on, Mommy, let's start the movie!"

The covers moved over Jeanie's stomach and Lila's eyes opened wide. "Jeanie, I think the baby is trying to come out! There was a movie on TV once where that was about to happen to some girl and Mommy changed the channel except I don't think that was a baby. I think that was an alien. Are you having an alien?" Everyone was overcome with an attack of the giggles.

Jeanie gave the little pixie a squeeze when she could catch her breath. "No sweetie, this is definitely a baby. It's not trying to get out, it's moving around. Put your hand right here and you'll feel it again. The tiny tot is having a workout in there." Sure enough, her stomach rose and fell again, several times, making Lila's eyes get even bigger.

"Whoa! Mommy, you've got to come feel this! I can't wait to meet whoever is in there because it's someone that will want to play!" Lila kept her hand on Jeanie's belly and was joined by Sarah, who climbed over Graham.

She laid her hand next to her daughter's and waited, soon to be rewarded with another strong kick, making her face glow. Touching a mother's stomach while that new life was growing was like catching a little bit of heaven and holding it in your hand.

"Jeanie, if I were you, I'd enjoy the rest right now. With moves like that going on in there, you are going to be on the go, non-stop. That's the way Lila was and she's kept us busy ever since." Sarah gave her daughter a wink and took her friend's hand in her own. "I know it's hard waiting right now, but you'll be so happy when you get through this. You'll see."

Jeanie leaned her dark head against Sarah's light one, creating a striking contrast. "I know. I just can't stand staying put! I only hope I'm not stuck in bed much longer."

Jim arrived then with a tray of tall milkshakes and a jumbo bowl of popcorn. "All right, let's get started!"

He passed out the drinks first, handed the popcorn to Lila, since she was in the middle, and put a Disney movie in the DVD player. Thankful he'd had the foresight to buy a king-size bed, he found himself a spot next to his wife. "Did I do good?"

"You did better than good. You did great. Thank you, Jimmy." Jeanie kissed him, leaving his lips cold with the flavor of chocolate ice cream while his insides began to melt.

He looked forward to the question mark's arrival in order to have more of his wife's favors. Of course, they'd be too tired for anything once the baby made it to the outside world. He didn't care. The only thing that mattered was keeping his wife happy and their baby safe. Thank God for the miracle of good friends and family to help them along the way.

They watched two movies, ordered in pizza, and ate until everyone was groaning. There was the added entertainment of Jim carrying Jeanie to the bathroom and Graham taking a turn, nearly toppling over in the process. It was Jim's turn to give his buddy a strong shoulder on the way back to bed. Lila had to get in on the act, expecting a piggy back ride. In the end, everyone was full, exhausted, and had hearts that had grown lighter in the course of an evening.

Jim stood at the door, watching Sarah carry a sleeping Lila out to the car. Graham was shrugging into his coat, no small task with the restrictive brace that turned everything into a procedure. "Well, I think our work is done here. Thanks for calling us, Pete. I was driving everyone nuts at our house. If I helped to make Jeanie feel better, I've served my purpose."

"You guys made her night. I thought I was going to have to tie her down. Sarah's ready for you. Be careful on the walk and I'll stop by soon, maybe bring Jeanie there for a change of scenery." Jim gave his friend a pat on the back and waited until he was in the car. He gave a wave and shut the door, leaving winter's chill and the night outside.

The house felt strangely quiet after all of the excitement. Feeling a little bit of a letdown, Jim dragged his feet as he went through the routine of checking the locks and turning off the lights. He stepped into his bedroom and became still, mesmerized by the sight of his sleeping wife.

She still had him under her spell after all of these years. Her, dark lashes fanned against her cheek. Her tousled hair. Her lips curved in a small smile. His wife drew him to her like the moon pulled on the tides. He changed into pajamas, shut off the light, and slid under the covers, the urge to get close to her was too strong to resist.

There was a rustling of blankets and her arm came up around him. "Thank you, Jimmy, for everything. I love you." Her voice was heavy with sleep, her arm already limp. It had been a long day for her.

"Love you too. Sweet dreams, Jeanie." Jim set hand on his wife's belly, rewarded with a nudge from the life growing inside of her. He would never grow tired of the thrill of that touch. "I love you too, little Whatchamacallit."

18

HIS MIND KEPT CARRYING HIM BACK TO THAT NIGHT, in the snowstorm, with Graham Scott. In his dreams and in his waking hours, the images replayed like the pictures on the screen at the drive-in he'd visited once as a child. They gave Kane no rest, filling him with an unease that he could not shake.

It had been like hitting a wall upon his encounter with the ranger, a wall of anger and resentment. Insurmountable. Kane couldn't climb it or tear the blasted stones down. He almost walked away, his every instinct screaming at him to leave the man, let the wilderness have him, and finish him off. In Kane's nightmares, he found Scott's bones in the spring.

The memory of his mother gave him pause; she had taught him compassion and forgiveness. That peaceful woman, a comfort in all storms, merged with Sarah. Both were similar in appearance. That likeness had drawn Kane to the lone figure in the parking area outside the Rockwood Forest. Sarah had been a flame of hope, wearing a sweater of fiery red and a halo from the sunset over her blonde head; he had been a moth, unable to resist. Knowing his sister was desperately ill back at home, the stranger seemed a God-send.

Once Kane brought her home, he discovered that Sarah shared many of his mother's qualities. She was a teacher. She had a love for beauty. Family meant everything to her. Kane could not turn his back on Graham Scott for her sake. On that fateful morning when he dashed into the road to help the ranger, it took even more courage to walk away from Sarah than anything else that came before.

Her eyes haunted Kane. Made even more brilliant against the falling snow, they briefly flashed his way before focusing on her husband's prone body. Kane carried that image with him the entire walk home. He stared into his fireplace for hours, but only saw Sarah's piercing, blue gaze. When he closed his eyes, hers were the only thing that he could see.

Echoes of reproach, hurt, and despair came back to Kane from Sarah's time in his cabin. No matter how he tried to ignore them, he could not escape them. He could not forget her pain, her pleading, her silence. His own personal experience in captivity made him understand in a way he could not before. It was against the laws of nature to take a living creature and withhold its freedom. Such was a fate worse than death.

Kane tried to forget, immersing himself in the daily tasks of survival. There was always the hunt to keep him occupied, but he had no heart for it. He worked on animal skins, supplementing his meager selection of clothing and bedding. He dragged and chopped trees until he could barely move. When those efforts failed, he took to the wilderness for days at a time, losing himself in the beauty of winter's finery. He made his daily trek to the top of Blue Mountain and stood by the shores of Blue Mountain Lake, praying for absolution. Nothing worked.

The combination of solitude, guilt, and doubts about Graham Scott's survival became too much to bear. Kane had to know if his attempt at rescue had been successful or in vain—for Sarah's sake—and his own. He had to see for himself if the ranger lived.

Desperation drove him on a journey that lasted three days, the elements working against him what with the bitter wind, accumulating snows, and the falling temperatures at night. He traveled by night and slept in fitful spurts after daybreak, taking shelter beneath fallen trees, inside caves, and within the occasional hunting shack like his own.

Snow had to suffice for lack of water. The streams and lakes were frozen. Food was limited to what he had been able to cure. Gone was the abundance found in his childhood home where they had grown vegetables, collected wild plants throughout the year, and made the occasional purchase at the store in Pine Lake.

Kane would not risk a venture to town nor could he stomach being around others. Taking great care to remain hidden, he finally emerged on the quiet stretch of road that wound around Pleasant Lake, the Scott residence awaiting him, tucked behind a stand of pines. The last time he had traveled to the ranger's home, Kane had never intended to return. Life had other plans.

Kane spent a day and night, concealed in the trees, watching. At first, he only saw Sarah and the little girl through a large window that pulled him into their living room. There was light, warmth, and comfort, but no sign of Graham. Kane drew closer at night, waiting apprehensively. Sarah and the little one ate together and snuggled on the sofa.

Eventually, Sarah's daughter fell asleep and she was gathered into her mother's arms to be carried to her bedroom. Sarah's face tilted toward the window and Kane saw love burning there, fierce and bright. It was so strong. If he could, he would reach in, grab hold, and never let go. They left the room. Shortly after, the house was left in darkness. He still did not know what became of Graham.

After a restless night huddled under the trees, Kane watched Sarah walk out of the house in the pale light of morning. She was white and trembling, her eyes darting furtively as she moved briskly to her car. Once inside, she huddled with her hands gripping the steering wheel. He could taste her fear. Kane knew that her anxiety was because of him and shame washed over him. The longing to go to her, to make amends was strong, but he didn't budge.

The car pulled out of the driveway, proving once again how strong Sarah was. Lila was not with her. Someone had to be home with the little girl. Kane crept around to the deck and another large picture window. The wait was not long. Lila dashed into the room with two puppies at her heels and let them outside. She brought out a mug and plate of food, reminding his stomach he hadn't eaten in a long time.

The dogs came in and Lila stood by the couch, at the ready with a blanket when Graham Scott slowly and painfully worked his way into the room. He looked worse for the wear, pale with dark circles under his eyes, tired from his brief journey through the house.

Alive. Relief made Kane sag and lean against the support of the house. He gave thanks.

Clouds passed across the sun and made him feel safe to linger. Watching the two together, Kane saw their love for one another. Graham wore his on his face for all to see. It was magic. The woodsman had watched something special pass between Sarah and her daughter, but Graham and Lila also shared an unshakeable bond. Kane understood the power of its spell because he had experienced the same when his parents and sister were alive.

This was the reason Sarah could never be happy, why Graham would stop at nothing short of dying in his efforts to bring her home. Kane knew—if he had a family like theirs, he would do anything to stay with them, to keep them safe.

Longing to be a part of such a bond made him take a step closer. The clouds shifted, casting his shadow across the little girl, and he ducked out of sight.

Kane stumbled away and did not look back. They did not belong to him and he did not belong to them or their world. The wilderness drew him back into the fold, shielding him from outsiders. It could not protect him from the pain within.

He did not make a conscious decision on what to do next. His feet carried him of their own accord. Hours later, he found himself standing before the home his father had built. No signs of life stirred and the place had already fallen into disrepair. Time and nature would take it back. Kane went inside although he did not know what good coming home again would do.

When he was very young, before his sister had been born, his father brought him on a hunting trip. Kane had been bursting with eagerness because he was going to shoot his father's rifle for the first time. It had been winter, their breath making clouds and his snowshoes leaving huge prints behind them. They ate jerky and drank coffee from Daddy's army canteen. Kane felt like a grown-up.

His father chose a concealed spot where they could watch and wait. Silence fell around them and Kane caught the creatures of the forest in action. Squirrels scurried through the branches, rabbits took pause before hopping by, and birds filled the air with their chatter. Kane could have watched the show all day when his father squeezed his arm and pointed to a small clearing. A deer cautiously made its way closer, stopping to nibble on the sweet bark of a birch tree.

Kane could barely contain his excitement as he picked up his father's gun and readied the heavy rifle the way he had been shown. He raised it and took aim. Heedless of Daddy's sudden protest, he fired, and hit his target. Dead-on. His father shook his head, eyes filled with sadness, and gestured to the clearing again.

Kane looked up to see a fawn slip out from behind the trees. It nosed the body of its fallen mother and began to bleat. Horrified, Kane ran to the doe and dropped down beside her. He pressed his hands to her chest, trying to stop the red river that was already flowing. The blood continued to pump, the life running out under his fingers, and there was nothing that he could do to save her.

He sobbed, heart-broken, while his father stood beside him with a steadying hand on his shoulder. They took the deer home that day, both of them. Kane carried the quivering fawn and Daddy slung the doe over his shoulders; there was no sense in wasting good meat. Mama helped in the task of butchering while Kane was given the job of caring for the baby.

She would become his pet, too tame to live on her own. Caring for the fawn, preserving her life, helped Kane to overcome the death of her mother. It would be a long time before he could hunt again and he would never forget that day.

Standing in his dead, childhood home now, the sense of loss—of his family, Sarah, his home and his way of life—welled up inside of him and overflowed like the blood that ran from the fallen doe. Robbed of his strength, he was brought him to his knees in the hollow emptiness. Kane began to sob in a way he had never done before. What he wouldn't give to turn back time to the days with his family when all was as it should be. Darkness fell, bringing despair, and still he did not get up off the floor.

Countless memories weighed him down through the night hours. His parents were teachers, the wilderness his school and constant companion until his world became a little bigger when Caroga was born. Kane knew only happiness, all of his needs fulfilled by loving parents, his little sister, and the bounty of the Adirondacks.

Climbing Kane Mountain brought him as close to heaven as a man could get without crossing over. Kane longed to step into one of his happiest memories, with Mama, Daddy, his sister and the woods, and never come back.

Shortly after dawn, he roused himself from a wakeful state like daydreaming. He was stiff and shivering from the cold, barely able to move, but rose unsteadily to his feet. One last look at the place where he had been born, loved, and learned to live, and he walked out. He did not look back nor would he return. There was nothing left here for Kane Johnson.

There was one more place he had to go. The trek through the woods was difficult, grief ensnaring him, blinding him with tears. Within the space of three months, he had taken this path to bury each of his parents. Ben Johnson had been a survivor until the death of his wife, Mary, took away his desire to live. A little over a year later, a wasting illness accompanied by an incessant cough stole Caroga away as well.

Kane found himself kneeling before their stones, fingers tracing the lettering. Overcome with sorrow, he lay down in the snow, on top of their graves, arms outstretched as if to embrace them. "Mama, Daddy, Little Sister…I don't want to go on anymore. It's too hard being alone."

The shivering took him first, making his teeth chatter. Pain began in his extremities until it became unbearable. Still, Kane not move. A numbness followed and his eyes began to droop. He was so tired. Sleep would come for him soon and he would never wake up. It would be so much easier to give in. His family would be waiting for him and that was a comfort.

Snow was falling, dancing in the air and brushing against his skin. Kane could no longer feel the cold and the sky was filled with a light that was brighter than the sun. *That's strange. I've never seen the sun shine so bright.* There was pressure on his shoulder, warm and steady.

He looked up to see his mother and father standing beside him. Caroga knelt on the ground, her hand resting on his head. They looked the same as they had in his best memories of

247

when they were alive. "Mama! Daddy! Caroga, too! Am I in heaven?"

His mother smiled at him, in that sweet and gentle way that could always make him feel better. "We're in your dream. You're freezing to death. You *must* get up." She touched his cheek and her hand was warm, alive. "It's too soon for you to join us."

"Kane, we're sorry you're alone but you have to go on. You're strong enough. We've given you everything you need to survive. Don't give up. Show me what you've learned as my son." Ben Johnson took his boy and held him by the shoulders, forcing Kane to look him in the eye. He gave a nod of assurance.

" Daddy, I'm so lonely. I can't go on this way forever. I'm not strong enough." He dropped his head and would not look up again, filled with shame for letting them down. The loneliness was a blade, piercing him through the heart. Kane didn't know how he could possibly endure the pain anymore.

"We'll be strong enough for you until you are ready." Caroga's voice was the way he remembered it, like the music of birdsong. She wrapped him in a hug that stole his breath away. His father and mother rested a hand on his shoulders and they formed a circle that could not be broken, except by death. Kane's grip tightened until he thought their bones would crack, but they would not let go.

His eyes snapped open, snow drifting across his line of vision. He was shaking violently; his toes and fingers were numb. He grabbed hold of his parents' crosses and pulled himself up, pressing a kiss to each. "I'll try, Mama and Daddy, for you."

The last kiss was reserved for Caroga's and the tears came unchecked. Her death was still so fresh. "Miss you, Little Sister."

Kane began to stamp his feet and clap his hands together until a painful burning sensation replaced the numbness, proving he was still in the land of the living.

He didn't hesitate in turning in the direction of his new home. Like his father before him, Kane would take what life had thrown at him and make something good come out of it. If Kane had been the promise born out of his father's tragedy, he had to be his living legacy.

THE SUNRISE WORKED ITS WAY IN AGAIN. Bringing light to all of his dark places. Giving Kane peace and pleasure in his surroundings. At daybreak, he stood on the ridge where Graham Scott had taken his fateful fall, contemplating the drop. Amazing that the man had survived, that he hadn't been killed instantly. It only proved how hard-headed the ranger was.

How simple of a matter for Kane to step out into nothingness, meet his end. He shied away from those thoughts.

Mama and Daddy didn't give him the gift of life so that he could throw it away. One of the laws of survival in the wilderness meant nothing went to waste. That included Kane, the only one left of their legacy.

"I've never seen anything so beautiful." The voice caught him completely unaware, he had been immersed so deeply in thought.

Kane turned to see a young woman with small, lightweight snowshoes of some type of metal on her feet and a carved walking stick in her hand. Where Sarah had been fair, the stranger's hair was black as the bears in the forest. A riot of curls fought to escape her wool cap while her eyes, a russet brown like the fall leaves, stared back at him with the warmth of his hearth fire's flicker. She was tall and lean, almost equal in height. She was nothing like any woman he'd known before.

Somehow he found his voice, rusty from disuse, and used the lessons taught him long ago by his father. *Stay calm. Be polite. Make eye contact and smile. Give her no reason to be suspicious.* "I know. That's why I can't start my day without a trip out here. Once I've met the dawn, I can get back to work."

He glanced down at his clothes and let out a long, slow breath. Thank God he had worn something that could pass for normal. His father's old jeans were patched and frayed but acceptable, as was his worn jacket from the army. It was exceptionally cold, forcing Kane to tuck his long hair inside a knit cap. Hopefully, there was nothing questionable, or familiar, about him.

"I'd love to live here year round. I've come with a friend on vacation. She couldn't drag herself out of bed so here I am. There's only one problem. I can't remember the way back to my car." She pouted a little and Kane felt his heart give a twist.

He'd been down this road once before with a quiet woman who captured the sun in her hair and the sky in her eyes. Kane would not make the same mistakes again. The stranger's company might be tempting, but not enough to lose the gains he had made. Besides, Kane was strong enough to care for himself.

He cleared his throat and attempted to portray an unruffled, outward appearance. "I have a little time before I have to get back to my woodworking shop. I'd be glad to show you the way. Did you come in by the parking area next to the trailhead?" He kept his voice even and low, giving no cause for alarm. It was done with ease. Kane was a peaceful man by nature.

Her smile was bright enough to make his pulse race. "Yes, that's exactly where I am. Thank you so much. My name is Jillian Martin but I prefer Jill. To whom do I owe the pleasure of meeting as my tour guide?" She paused beside him and waited expectantly. Her eyes were intense, her manner forthright. Kane was blindsided by her openness.

"John Benson. I'm pleased to meet you." He offered his hand, recalling his mother's lessons on manners from his childhood.

Mary Johnson was determined that her son would be civilized, even though their interactions with others were far and few between. Kane suspected she hoped they would return to the outside world again one day. It never happened in her lifetime. On the contrary, the outside world kept finding its way to Kane.

They took their time traveling down the mountain. Kane truly was the stranger's guide, pointing out animal tracks, naming the birds, and showing Jill features of the land that would help to mark her way. How ironic that this woman appeared to be captivated by a woodsman and his knowledge. She was from the big city in New York and he was a novelty.

They emerged from the woods to find Jill's car waiting for her. She laughed and gave Kane's hand a shake, making a warm tingling travel through his body. "Thank you again, John. Would you care to share a cup of coffee with me in town? I'll buy. It's the least I can do."

Kane tried to picture himself getting into her car and walking into the local diner. To sit at a table, drink and perhaps eat with this woman, to feel companionship. Inviting, but he was not ready to get that close to civilization. "No thank you, that's not necessary. I really do have to get back to work."

He stood with his hand raised in a wave and *this time*, the girl drove away. Kane slipped back into the woods. He would probably never see Jill Martin again and wasn't bothered. That brief moment of normalcy was enough.

The walk back to his cabin gave Kane plenty of time to think. He did not see the scenery around him. A memory of Sarah played in his mind's eye instead. They had gone to bury his grief. Kane had been distraught and Sarah more so, desperate to return to the life she had known. She told him time would heal his loneliness and he might find a companion. The right way. Like normal people.

Perhaps, someday, someone would choose Kane. However unlikely it might be for a woman to willingly take to the woods, there could be someone drawn to the wilderness and its tranquility, someone looking for a man like Kane. That chance, even if slim to none, gave him hope. If his past would allow him to have a future.

19

"*REMEMBER TO ALWAYS HAVE RESPECT FOR THE ADIRONDACKS*. They can break the best of us." Graham gave his audience a rueful smile and tapped his cane on the floor, emitting sympathetic laughter in response.

"If possible, use the buddy system. It saves lives. There may be situations when you have to go it alone. In my line of work, the environmental conservation officers are spread out over a large territory, far and few between. We often work on our own unless there is a need to band together. If you find yourself going solo, remember not to take unnecessary risks. Learn from my mistakes. I hope we'll have the opportunity to work together in the near future. Thank you."

Graham levered himself up off the stool and walked with slow, measured steps off the platform. The cane helped him to keep his balance and bore the brunt of his weight, making the pain…bearable. He really missed being able to move freely.

Today's session had involved a group of local volunteer firefighters and rescue workers. A few came forward with questions, his host thanked him, and it was time to leave. His brief escape from home was a welcome escape, but he could only take short doses of freedom. Graham's back was already talking to him.

Danny Rogers waited for him in his trademark, green DEC truck. Graham had to grit his teeth when he climbed in to be the passenger, rather than the driver. Once again, he was reminded of his stupidity on Blue Mountain. Accidents happened all the time. They were made all the more aggravating when it was his own fault.

"Thanks for being my chauffeur. I know I'm a pain in the butt." Graham turned his face to the window and watched the scenery go by.

After one month of captivity, he'd finally been given medical release to do brief speaking engagements involving rescues, forest fires, poaching, and care for the wilderness. There were also public awareness and educational meetings. His superior had him lined up with many lectures in the coming weeks. Graham's first discussion group had gone well. That didn't stop him from itching to get back to the woods.

"Hey, everything all right? You're not looking too happy." Danny's eyes darted his way, quickly returning to the road.

Graham's fingers tapped the arm rest and he turned away from the window. "I just miss being on the job. I thought it would help, getting out of the house. It's a big tease. I've got two more weeks in this brace and at least a six weeks of physical therapy. I'm going crazy!" He ran a hand through his hair, dug his fingers in, and gave a tug out of frustration.

"I get it. That's how I felt when I lost my job and had no place to go but home. I sat and stared at the walls for days. Hang in there, man. There's a light at the end of the tunnel and here's 'Home Sweet Home.' Do you need any help?" Danny eyed the walkway, wary of icy spots or deep snow.

Graham gave his old classmate a crooked grin, some of his good humor restored. "No thanks. You've done enough, carting me around and listening to me mouth off. I'll see you in a few days for the next one."

He held on to the door with one hand, his cane in the other, until he could situate himself. Danny reached across to close the door and give a wave, on his way to do the job Graham loved more than any other line of work. It was like breathing to him, almost a shame to pay him for something he loved that much.

With a sigh, Graham watched the truck pull out and went inside. It had felt good to put on the uniform again, a sturdy, serviceable green that was a reminder of the forest. Too bad there was no need to keep it on. It was only noon. The girls wouldn't be home for hours. He might as well be comfortable.

Graham sat down on the bed and fought to remove his pants. By the time he tugged a loose pair of jeans up to his waist, he was sweating and cursing with the effort. His white t-shirt, beneath his button-down, would be good enough. Besides, it wasn't like he expected company.

A trip to the kitchen to forage in the fridge revealed exactly what he needed—a cold beer. Graham sucked it down while leaning on his cane and closed his eyes. He waited for the dull throbbing at the base of his spine to die down. Being out and about had taken a toll. He was hurting.

Grabbing one more can, he decided to move out to the living room. Graham wasn't prepared for an attack by the throw rug. The cane caught the edge, making it slide, and sent him in an untidy sprawl, flat on his back. The beer rolled away, walking stick clattering to the floor, the wind out of him. He closed his eyes to catch his breath. When he opened them, another pair of eyes, a taste of honey, stared back at him from the deck. A curse slipped out between Graham's gritted teeth.

Kane Johnson stood outside and raised a hand in greeting. He exuded no menace, waiting patiently for an invitation. The woodsman was the last person Graham expected to see.

His heart kicked it up a notch, threat or no, and a head rush made his vision go black for an instant. Not now. Passing out was not a good thing. Counting slowly to ten, breathing deeply in and out, Graham raised his own hand in greeting and pointed to the unlocked door.

Kane stepped in, bringing a rush of cold air and dusting of snow with him. He stomped his feet and removed his boots.

A creature of habit. Slowly and methodically, he hung his father's army coat on a hook by the door and brushed off his hair before approaching the prone man before him.

"I seem to be in a habit of getting you back on your feet these days." The words were said with a ghost of a smile as the woodsman offered his hand.

Graham wouldn't look a gift horse in the mouth. He set his hand in Kane's and found himself at eye level in no time. He gestured to the beer that had rolled across the floor. "Would you like a drink?"

At his surprise visitor's nod, Graham returned to the kitchen for another beer, making a wide path around the offending throw rug. He stood at the sink for a moment, gripping the counter, struggling to maintain his cool. When he returned, Kane had retrieved the other can and stood on the other side of the room.

The woodsman paused to study the pictures on the wall and pointed to one in particular. "Your wedding day?"

He would not meet Graham's eyes; perhaps his envy was too strong. Standing in Sarah's house, seeing her in her gown of white, was like rubbing salt in a wound. Or maybe his guilt was eating at him.

Graham nodded in affirmation. The photo was taken in the arbor down by the lake, under the glowing lights and stand of pines that were coated in white like a benediction. Sarah and Graham were side by side with Lila's arms looped around their necks while they held her. All three were laughing, their faces lit with joy as if from candles burning within. Jim had taken the picture and sent it as a gift to capture their day.

"Won't you sit? It's hard for me to stand for long." He waited until Kane dropped down on the opposite end of the sofa, looking uncomfortable, as if he might break.

Graham understood the feeling. He popped the top of his beer, watched it foam, and kicked it back in an effort to settle himself. *Guess who's coming to dinner?* Indeed. He almost snorted in his beer. This was not his first choice for a house guest, but the woodsman saved his life. Graham owed him a few minutes of his time.

Kane watched him closely, his expression perplexed. He picked up the can, fumbled with the tab, and pulled so hard that the small piece of metal ripped off. The woodsman took a sip and made a slight grimace. He took a longer gulp and shook his head at its bitterness.

"Daddy told me about this drink but we never had it." Kane set the can on the table. "You take pleasure in beer? It is like urine."

Graham's mouthful shot out in a spray and he nearly choked. He swiped at his face with his arm until he could speak again. "It's an acquired taste. Trust me. The more you drink, the better it gets." He took another gulp, nearly draining the can in one, long swallow, finding his nerve. "You didn't come here for a beer."

Kane looked uncomfortable, shifting in his seat. Graham's aggravation flared and his jaw tightened. "You've come before, that day soon after I came home, when I saw your shadow. I don't appreciate being spied on. Your note said 'Leave me to the Adirondacks and I'll leave her to you.' I've kept my end of the bargain. Being here today—*or at my wedding*— is not part of the deal."

Kane picked up his beer and slugged the brew down. He paused, as if steeling himself, and turned to face Graham with his hands pressed to his knees. His knuckles were white. This visit wasn't easy for him either.

"When I came here the first time, I thought that would be the end of it, that I could shut the door on my past. Funny thing about the past. It won't let go and it drove me back to the day you married. I thought that cured me of ever coming here again. Then we met on Blue Mountain. After you were rescued, I had to come, had to know if you survived. Because of Sarah. Today I am here so that all of us can finally let go of the past. To set us free."

Graham fought the urge to shoot to his feet. That simple movement would make the pain spike in his lower back and he would not give Kane the satisfaction of getting under his skin. "You want us to *let go*? How do you to propose to do that? It may be water under the bridge, but it's really deep and the current is strong enough to carry all of us away."

Kane raised his hands in protest. "I spent a long time being angry, resenting you for all that you took away from me."

" *You* stole Sarah, Kane. You brought this all on yourself. When will you get it through your skull?"

Graham clenched his jaw and his fingers curled into fists, anger simmering beneath the surface. This was a mistake. Letting this man in. Allowing him to get one step closer.

Kane bowed his head. When he spoke, Graham could barely hear him. "I know now, even knew then, that what I did to Sarah was wrong. I was *so* lonely after my parents died and your wife…she's an amazing woman, as you well know. Hard to let go."

He paused. Finally, the words spilled from his mouth. "I know that my penalty was just. That didn't make it any easier."

The silence in the room was heavy, broken only by the sound of their breathing. Kane took another drink to bolster his courage. "My brief time in prison showed me the horror of what it means to be held against one's will. With understanding, came guilt. I had to repay my debt to Sarah in some way. I believe that is why God brought me to you on the mountain."

Kane's mouth twisted in a smile that did not soften his expression. "It certainly was not for our love of one another, no? On that night, I looked inside of my enemy and gained respect. When you refused my aid in order to protect me, you earned my undying gratitude."

261

The woodsman stood, approached, and dropped down on his knees. Graham was mortified. "Kane, get up off the floor. This isn't necessary. You're sorry and you're thankful. I get it. *Stand up*."

No one had been subservient to Graham Scott before and he wouldn't allow it now. Funny, before Blue Mountain, he'd wanted nothing more than to bring this man down.

Kane looked up, his golden eyes full. A calm settled between them, if only fleeting. "I will always be grateful. You let me go when others would have locked me away. You could have hunted me down after my escape. I've not doubt that you would have found me. When you were suffering that night, you would not save yourself at my expense. I am here now to let you know that I deeply regret the hurts I have caused this family. I beg forgiveness from you, Sarah, and her little girl. Are you able to give it?" He extended a hand and waited.

Graham was like a balloon and all the air had been let out, leaving him sucked dry. He was suddenly tired, almost too tired to continue, but he had to get this done and over with. He took Kane's hand and jerked his head toward the couch. "I'm not going to say it again—sit next to me, not below me." He waited until his visitor's weight sank down beside him and let his breath out in a rush.

"Kane, forgiveness is something that is too big for me to bite off and chew right now. One day, I pray I can do it. I'm not there yet. I owe you my life and for that you have *my* gratitude.

That will have to be enough from me. As for Sarah, I cannot speak for her and Lila is too young to really understand this. They will have to come to forgiveness on their own terms…or they won't. That's a possibility you have to accept."

Kane's head dropped again, lines of weariness digging deeper into his face. It must have been hard, facing Graham again, bearing his soul. He rose to his feet and offered his hand once more. "I understand. Thank you. One day we might meet again. Not here. I promise. Do we have a truce?"

Graham picked up a tissue from the table and waved it. "White flag. Good luck, Kane."

It was a dismissal and the woodsman took it as such. He shrugged into his outer gear and stepped through the door. Graham saw him raise a hand once more in farewell and then Kane was gone, merging with the wilderness, making him doubt his senses—except for the extra beer on the coffee table.

At first, after Kane left, Graham couldn't move. His mind was too full, but his stillness didn't last. He gained his feet and traveled the lengths of the rooms in his house. While his progress was clumsy and didn't constitute pacing, it was close enough. It wasn't every day that the man who turned his life upside down made a peace offering. The question remained: how to handle it?

Another trip through empty rooms and Graham couldn't take the silence or his circling thoughts anymore. He picked up the phone and dialed. *Please pick up, please pick up.* There were a few rings and an answer on the other end.

"Hey, Scottie! Tell me you've got some excitement because I am going crazy here."

Graham almost choked on his words, they were that hard to get out. "Oh I've got some excitement, more than I can take. I don't want to talk about it over the phone. Can you come get me? I'll have Sarah and Lila pick me up so you don't have to leave Jeanie again." He waited for an answer and thought he might climb the walls if Jim said no.

"Sure. Jeanie's doing fine and she usually takes a nap about now anyway. I'll be there as soon as I can. Hang tight." The line disconnected.

Graham was sitting outside on his steps when Jim arrived, sucking in some fresh air, unable to stay inside a minute longer. The walls felt like they were closing in on him. He settled in his best friend's SUV and let out a sigh of relief.

"Thanks for coming, bud. I'm about ready to go out of my skull." He leaned back and closed his eyes.

"What happened? Last night, you were pretty revved up about doing that training today. Did they throw tomatoes at you or something?" Jim's typical humor relieved some of the tension. Not all of it.

"It's nothing a few years of therapy won't cure. Let me get my wind back and a beer under my belt, okay? Then I can tell you everything."

They were quiet for the rest of the ride. The radio created a buffer and a distraction. Slowly, Graham relaxed and his insides unraveled, untying the knots that had entangled him the instant Kane Johnson appeared at his door.

20

THE DRIVE TO JOHNSTOWN WENT A LONG WAY toward restoring Graham's equilibrium. The perilous journey upstairs to Jeanie's bedroom finished the job. Stairs were torture, best taken at a snail's pace.

He stood in her doorway, a little short of breath, and gave her his best happy face. "Hello Jeanie-girl. You're looking…"She cut him off with an upraised hand.

"Don't you dare say good, beautiful, wonderful, glowing or any of the other colorful adjectives visitors have been using when we all know it's a big lie. I look like a whale or a house, I'm not sure which. I'm tired, miserable, and cranky, Graham Scott. If you've come here to try and be cheerful, you can forget about it! You can turn yourself around and leave." She crossed her arms and scowled.

Jim slipped in beside him and gave him a jab in the ribs. "She's a bit of a grouch these days. She thought they'd finally spring her for good behavior, but the doctor decided to play it safe and keep her on bed rest. Talk about cabin fever!"

He went to his wife's side, kissed her on the forehead, and was rewarded with a reluctant grin. "I'll have you laughing yet. I'm going downstairs for a beer with Graham. Do you need anything?" In anticipation, he plumped her pillows, moved the remote within reach, and refilled her water.

"Freedom, but that's out of the question. I hate to say it but...I need to go to the bathroom *again*." Jeanie gave him such a pitiful pout that he started to laugh and it was contagious. She held up her arms and her husband scooped her out of bed, waited outside the bathroom, and reinstated her in her substitute for a throne once again.

"Okay, Queenie? That's her new nickname by the way." She waved him off, giving Jim the signal to clear out. He didn't have to be told twice. "I'll meet you downstairs." Jim scooted, allowing Jeanie and Graham a moment of privacy.

Jeanie took note of her husband's best friend, propped against the wall, and spread her arms wide. "You didn't think you'd get away with no hug and kiss, did you? I'm not that scary, am I?"

She waited. There was fear lurking in her eyes, that what she said was true. This baby had better make it safe and sound, for all of their sakes.

"Are you kidding? I need all the help I can get! I haven't been an angel myself lately. Maybe some of your sweetness will rub off on me." Graham left his post by the door and joined Jeanie.

He sat down beside her and rested a hand on her growing belly. "Hmm...I think you're almost ripe. You should pop any day now and I don't care what you say. You look pretty as a picture." He gave her a hug and a kiss, happy to bring back a little spark in her eyes.

Jeanie patted his hand, her face becoming flushed. "You're a charmer, Mr. Scott." She suddenly grew serious at something she saw in his gaze. Her hand tightened on his, holding him still. "Graham, what's wrong? You don't look right."

"You ought to know—too much time on my hands, stuck indoors. If you need anything, give us a holler, okay?" He left before she could press.

Jim sat in the living room with beer, pretzels, and a football game on TV. He motioned to the recliner across the room and put his feet up. "Come on, Scottie. Kick back, relax. Enjoy getting out for a while. Maybe I'll bring Jeanie to your place next to give *her* a change of scenery. She's really sick of this house."

"What about you? It's got to be hard on you, not being able to come and go as you please. What if Sarah comes over once a week to give you a break?"

Jim took a long drink of beer and let out a contented sigh. "That *is* good going down. Jeanie would love to have Sarah come over, you know that." Silence stretched between him as his eyes became troubled. He visibly had to shake himself out of it. "Enough about my wife. What about you?"

It took two beers and a good dent in the pretzels before Graham could rehash his visit with Kane. After all that had happened between the two men, it was not easy to deal up close and personal. Maybe in a few more years—say twenty or thirty— they'd forget everything.

Not now. Whenever Graham thought back to Sarah's disappearance, it felt like yesterday. The memories of his living nightmare had the power to bring on a full-blown panic attack. Kane Johnson was responsible. True, the woodsman had rescued Graham, his saving grace. That didn't make letting go of the past any easier.

"Let me get this straight. He came to *you* looking for forgiveness? Is the guy on something?" Jim ran a hand through his hair in frustration. "Maybe we should put some surveillance out on your place. I don't like it. The guy's been there at least three times now, like a stalker. We can catch him and put him away."

Graham stared down into his empty beer bottle. "No, I don't want to put him away. The man saved my life, dammit! He says this is it, he's not coming back." He closed his eyes, weary of the conversation. Why couldn't they erase everything that involved Kane Johnson?

There was the sound of the opening and closing of the door. "Hello? I know the pregnant woman is upstairs. Where are the lazy men?" Sarah's voice sounded through the house followed by the patter of sock feet.

A whirlwind in the form of a little girl flew into the room. She caught sight of Graham and launched herself into his lap, knocking the breath out of him.

"Lila my lovely! How was your day?" Graham buried his nose in her hair and breathed in the scent of the crisp, winter air, baby powder, and a hint of her favorite bubble bath.

The little girl was a welcome diversion, full of tidbits from her day with a tongue that ran at full speed. She hopped down from her father's lap, flitted to Jim to give him a greeting, then scampered off to Jeanie's room to visit with her.

Graham's arms and lap filled with another woman he loved next, her blonde hair catching the light of the sun as it fell against his face. "Hi, Handsome. How was your day?"

There was no way Graham was telling her about Kane, not yet. "I enjoyed talking to them. I'm just frustrated that I can't get out there yet. Telling others about my work gave me the itch! That's why I called Jim. I needed some company."

"The one who can really use it most is Jeanie. Head on up to see her, Sarah." Jim slung an arm around her shoulders. "She won't be Oscar the Grouch if you're here. Why don't you guys stay for dinner?"

Sarah nodded and the pair climbed the stairs. Lila's squeals carried all the way to the living room. Jim was either tickling her or giving her a piggy back ride. Graham found himself smiling at the sweet sound of a child's laughter. Strong medicine.

"WHOA! WHEN I INVITED YOU TO DINNER, I didn't mean you had to do the work. I *can* cook. Did Jeanie put you up to this? She said I was getting better."

Jim stood in the doorway of the kitchen, hands on his hips while Sarah chopped vegetables for a salad. She put all of the ingredients in a large bowl and tossed them vigorously, using more energy than a salad required.

"What happened to Graham today? Something is bothering him." Sarah was clearly agitated. She opened and closed the oven, stirred pots on the stove, and repeated the process all over again. She only stopped when Jim touched her arm.

"He's had enough of being cooped up. Graham's at his best when he's taking care of others. If there's anything else going on, it's up to him to talk. You're my friend, but he's my best friend and I don't take that title lightly."

Jim ducked out of the kitchen to set the table, avoiding further conversation. He brought Jeanie down and set her in a chair. Usually, she ate in bed or on the couch. She didn't want to be left out tonight.

"All hail her majesty!" Graham teased, setting his cane down so he could bow to a very exasperated, pregnant woman. She poked him in the stomach and pointed imperiously to the seat next to her. Sarah and Lila carried out the last of the dishes and Jim poured the drinks.

Jeanie's cheeks were streaked with red, whether from embarrassment or anger, and she shook her finger at everyone. "All right you guys, enough! I know that I'm being spoiled beyond belief, but it's not my fault." She bowed her head and for one instant, everyone thought she was going to cry.

She kept herself together and gave them a tremulous smile. "You're all too good to me. Thank you from the both of us. Jimmy needs this too." Her eyes met his and he leaned in close. His hand cupped the back of her neck and he whispered something that made her laugh.

They shared a simple meal of spaghetti, meatballs, salad, and Italian bread. It didn't matter what they ate. Spending time in each other's company worked more wonders than anything else possibly could. They laughed, joked, ate their fill, went to the living room to watch TV, and found room for dessert. The Scotts left with everyone's hearts a little lighter than they had been earlier that day. When Jim counted his blessings that night, his good friends ranked high on the list.

GRAHAM WAS QUIET AND KEPT TO HIMSELF the rest of the evening. He crashed on the couch. His legs were outstretched, his eyes staring at the flickering images on the TV without seeing any of them. If he could, he would go outside and start to run as the snow fell around him. Graham longed to move, to be free of the jumble of his thoughts, to not think at all, tiring out his body and his mind.

Sarah sat down on the edge beside him and brushed a strand of hair out of his eyes. "What's going on with you tonight? Remember—no secrets."

"I don't want to talk about it, no, I *can't* talk about it now. It will keep until Lila's in bed, okay?" His hand found his way to hers.

Sarah pressed her palm to his face. It was cool and soft. Graham closed his eyes and lost himself in the feel of her. She was trembling and so was he, on the inside.

"Okay. I'll be out in a little while." She left him to tuck in her little girl and read her a story.

The sound of her voice rose and fell, lulling Graham to that place in between sleep and wakefulness. He hovered there, but forced himself to his feet when the reading stopped. He took his cane and went to Lila's room to find both of his girls curled around each other like a bud about to open.

"'Night, Ladybug. I love you." Graham bent over the bed and pressed a kiss to her golden hair. She turned and reached up to give him a hug. She pulled him down until he sat on the edge of the bed beside them both.

"Next time, you need to read to me, Daddy. I love you. Sweet dreams." Her eyes were already drooping shut. She turned over and burrowed in close to Sarah. Her mother stroked her hair and turned out the lights. Graham left to give her a moment alone with Lila.

He sat at the table with a cup of coffee. Something stronger would be better, but he'd had too many beers earlier in the day. Alcohol had not been enough to take the edge off Kane's visit. Graham could see the images clearly as if they were being played on a video and still felt raw every time he watched.

He didn't look up when Sarah sat down across from him with her own coffee cup. "Please tell me what's wrong. I can't stand it, seeing something eating at you."

He told her everything, all of it spilling out like a purge. Graham tried to get the words right, to make her understand why the woodsman had come, and fought to keep his cool. That night on Blue Mountain had changed his opinion of Kane. That didn't mean he was ready to call the man his friend. Graham went into a tailspin each time they met.

Sarah stood and went to the window, staring out into the night as if she expected Kane to be out there. "I wish I had been home. There are some things I would like to tell him too. I want to thank him for your life, tell him we're going to be okay now, but I don't want to make it too easy either. I don't know if I can say I forgive him, not yet."

She turned back and sat down on Graham's lap, placing both hands on his cheeks so that he would have to look at her. "We'll find out together."

TWO WEEKS UNTIL FREEDOM. It wasn't so bad when Graham was out at the schools, talking to the kids, or meeting with the local fire department. Anything to get out of the house and his head. Being at home with time on his hands left him trying to sort out the muddle of emotions Kane had left behind.

Way down at the bottom, there was anger, burning low and slow, like the red embers beneath the ashes of a campfire. Stirring the flames again would be easy. All Graham had to do was think back to that evening in Rockwood, nearly a year ago, and finding Sarah's empty car.

He still woke up many a night, heart pounding with the fear of never finding her. Until he reached across the bed and found her sleeping at his side. Graham tried not to fan that fire. Let it be and it would put itself out.

Layered over the anger was gratitude, strong and unyielding, for the night on Blue Mountain when Kane saved his life. Like the wash of colors across the sky with every sunrise and sunset, Graham opened and closed each day with a prayer of thanksgiving. He was alive.

Finally, there was hope, close to the surface. *Hope floats*, he reflected, remembering the name of a movie he had watched with Sarah. It was rising, lifting a body up along the way like a pair of Canadian geese winging across the sky, bringing the return of spring. The encounter with the woodsman and his message brought Graham's family a step closer to a new beginning.

It left him no choice. He had to take out the box in his mind, of all things Kane, and put everything inside. He closed the lid, turned the key, and put it back. This time, the load wasn't as heavy and he didn't have to push as far. The key was in his hand, not thrown away. Graham came to the realization— it might not be that hard to look inside again. When he was ready.

"IT'S BRACE OFF DAY! IT'S BRACE OFF DAY! Did you know that's what they say when a boat is untied from the dock? I found that out when Ms. Ashley read us a story. Do you think we could go in a boat this summer?" Lila pounced on the bed, filling her mother's empty spot and making sure Graham was wide awake.

The faint sound of retching could be heard from the bathroom over the sound of running water. Lila's excitement dampened and her smile turned to a frown. "Is Mommy sick? Should she go see the doctor when you go to the hospital?"

Graham pushed himself up into a sitting position and pulled the little girl close to him, keeping his tone light. "No, no, Mommy's okay. She just has a little bit of an upset tummy. I think she might be a little nervous about going to the hospital. It wasn't much fun when I was there, was it?"

That was an understatement. Bad memories of his father's time in the hospital would always overshadow all other visits. He wished they had a separate building for mothers and new babies.

Sarah walked out of the bathroom, looking a little pale and shaky. "I didn't eat the crackers soon enough...Ladybug! I didn't know you were up, honey. Are you excited about going to Nana and Pop Pop's?" She joined her family on the bed and wrapped an arm around her daughter.

"I can't wait, Mommy. Are you okay? Daddy says he thinks you're nervous about the hospital. Do you have butterflies in your tummy? I'll get you one of those tummy chewies if you want to help you feel better." Lila's eagerness to help her mother made Graham's eyes sting.

Sarah pressed a kiss to her daughter's forehead. "Baby, that is so nice of you. I'm feeling better now. My butterflies are all gone. Why don't we go to the kitchen and make some breakfast?" She made sure to give Graham a kiss too and whispered, "Thank you," before joining her daughter.

They were not ready to tell Lila the news yet. Sarah's next doctor's appointment would mark the end of the first trimester. If she was given the all clear, they would tell everyone. Lila would be the first to hear the news.

Graham couldn't lie in bed any longer, too restless to be still. The anchor that had been holding him down for six weeks was coming off. He went to the bathroom, turned on the shower, nudging the knob as hot as he could take it. The warm water felt good, the anticipation of freedom even better.

By the time he dressed and made his way to the kitchen, his girls were ready for him with pancakes, sausage, eggs, and fresh fruit. "Wow! You two went all out! What's all of this for?"

"It's a celebration, Daddy! Just think—only a little while longer and you can go back to the woods again! Dig in! I made the eggs and Mommy let me flip the pancakes." Lila was already covered in syrup because she couldn't wait. She passed the food to Graham and continued the serious business of polishing off her plate.

Graham felt only sympathy for Sarah, nibbling on toast and nursing a cup of tea. "You outdid yourselves. This is the best breakfast ever."

He ate every bit and insisted on doing the clean-up while Sarah and Lila took their showers. He was sitting in the living room, tapping his fingers on the arm of his chair when they finally came out. "Ready?" He asked, impatient to end his captivity. At last.

"ALL RIGHT GRAHAM. TAKE IT EASY WHEN YOU STAND UP. Your back hasn't had to hold your weight without any support for a long time and won't have its normal strength." The molded jacket brace, custom made to fit his body and his constant companion day and night, sat on the table beside him.

Dr. Jones stood at the ready in case his patient needed assistance. In the excitement of losing the brace, people often tried to do too much, too soon.

Graham held on to the edge of the table and carefully lowered himself to the floor. He eased himself to his feet, testing himself. His back ached, but freedom was too sweet. He took a cautious, first step forward and almost caved. Sweat broke out on his forehead as he began to tremble and the throbbing kicked it up to protest more.

"You weren't kidding." He took a deep breath and tried again, held steady. Graham opened his arms wide, his smile wider. "Come here, baby. Lay one on me!"

Sarah ducked under his arms and gave him the best bear hug she had. He quivered with the effort to remain on his feet, but wouldn't give in. "Is it better now? Are you done going crazy?" She turned to roll her eyes at the doctor. "It's not easy keeping a forest ranger out of the woods."

Dr. Jones pointed a finger in warning. "Don't forget— you can't go back to work yet. You'll need physical therapy to strengthen those muscles and gain a better range of motion before I can give clearance. You'll have to wear this lumbosacral belt and continue with therapy for at least six weeks. Be sure to take it easy. You overdo it and you'll end up in here again or worse yet, on my surgical table."

He patted Graham on the shoulder. "Keep being a model patient. You two have a good day." An encouraging smile, a wave, and he was on his way.

"Thanks, Doc." Graham pulled Sarah close, burying his face in the sunshine of her hair. "Let's get out of here."

He put an arm around her shoulders. Sarah hugged his waist and they walked out. Together. Their progress was slow, steady, and by the power of his own feet—with a little help from Sarah's. They reached the car and he went to the driver's seat, a mischievous glint to his eye. "This time, *I'm* driving."

Sarah hesitated, her face clouded with doubt. "Are you sure you're up to it? You've only had that brace off for about fifteen minutes. Remember what Dr. Jones said about doing too much."

She should have known better than to argue. Graham leaned up against the car and held out his hand. Sighing in exasperation, she handed over the keys. "Stubborn man! Promise you'll stop if you're too sore or tired, okay?"

"No problem. I can handle this, really. I'm using my feet, not my back. Relax!" He sat down in the driver's seat and closed his eyes in obvious pleasure. "This feels so much better." Once Sarah set his new, lightweight brace in the back and was seated, he turned up the heat, put the radio on, and they pulled out of the parking lot. "So, it's early and we've got the whole afternoon while Lila's at your parents. Where do you want to go for a drive?"

Graham was met by silence. He turned to see his wife with her eyes trained on the passing scenery. She avoided looking at him as she answered in a low voice, "Blue Mountain Lake."

21

"HAVEN'T YOU HAD ENOUGH?" Graham's fingers tightened on the steering wheel. He unconsciously pressed down on the accelerator, putting on an unexpected burst of speed, the tension crackling in the air between them. Blue Mountain Lake was a reminder of where he had almost lost his life. It was also home to someone he'd rather not see.

Sarah gathered her resolve and turned to face her husband. She reached out and took hold of his arm. "Going there will help us to put the past behind us. Besides, what are the odds of seeing Kane? He keeps to himself."

"Why take that chance?" The drive was long, made longer by Graham's silence. He disapproved yet he abided by her wishes because that was who he was. His fingers drummed on the steering wheel, his body tensed as if prepared for battle. Sarah knew he was facing demons of his own.

His hand grew still. It found hers and held on tight. Whatever they faced would be as a united front. They were partners—in good times and in bad. "Don't be surprised if he turns up. Kane has a way of doing that when you least expect it. Are you ready for that possibility?"

"I'll cross that bridge when we come to it." A small part of Sarah wanted to see her captor, to put a period on that part of her life in place of a question mark. Otherwise, eternity would not be long enough before she laid eyes on the woodsman again.

The Adirondacks were in their glory, capped with snow, the pines dusted in white. Everything sparkled and looked like something out of a fairy tale, but Sarah saw none of it. She was reliving the past when the forest that had always been a friend became her foe, holding her prisoner with no way of setting her free.

She had been buried alive in her time with Kane. The wilderness, like an army of soldiers standing watch, closed ranks around her. Sarah never saw her way in, didn't know where she was, and couldn't find a way out.

The walls of the cabin drew in around her while her memories smothered her with their intensity. Kane was an impenetrable force, barring her escape without mercy. Sarah had prayed, pleaded, tried to run. The only reason she was free was because Graham never gave up on her.

She pushed Kane to the back of her mind and focused on the man sitting beside her. He sat straight and tall, his eyes trained on the road, his jaw clenched. After six weeks enclosed in that restrictive brace, he was placing strain on himself. His back had to ache...but he wouldn't cave.

That was Graham—don't tell him there was something he couldn't do. He'd find a way, no matter what. If he needed to walk on water, he'd have a talk with the Lord and figure a way to get the job done.

Sarah slid closer and slid a hand behind him to massage his lower back until he gave a small groan. "Does that help?"

"Don't stop. That feels so good. You've got it." He rested his hand on hers and some of the tension died out with the smile that tipped her way. "You always help me, simply by being there. I hope that I do the same for you. If that means taking you anywhere near Kane, as much as it kills me, I'll do whatever it takes. That doesn't mean I'll like it, but I'll do it." A companionable silence fell between them and they let the road take over for a while.

Two hours passed and Blue Mountain Lake spread out beside them, the light glancing off the smooth surface of the ice. The mountain rose above, a steadfast guardian and companion, lulling them into a sense of security. Sarah felt her lungs fill for the first time since she breathed the words, 'Blue Mountain Lake,' and her body sagged against the seat.

Until they passed a small road stand. Outside of town, on an isolated stretch of road. With no one around except a man sitting on the steps of a tiny porch. Surrounded by an extensive collection of intricately carved figures whittled out of wood. Sarah's hand tightened on Graham's thigh and he slowed to a stop, allowing them to study the stranger.

284

His hair, falling in waves to brush his collar, was sandy, streaked with white, lightened by exposure to the sun and weather. His face was clean shaven and expressive, but it was his eyes that were unforgettable. Pale, golden-brown, like a jar of honey glowing in the sun.

Sarah and Graham had seen eyes of that color on only one person and she knew them exceedingly well. "Graham, pull off the road."

His instinct must have been to keep the car in drive. Put the pedal to the floor. Never look back. Devotion to Sarah made him stop.

Graham visibly steeled himself, taking a deep breath before he squared his shoulders to step out of the car. A moment's hesitation and Sarah's door opened. Graham held his hand out for her. "You're *sure* you want to do this?"

In answer, she took his hand and rose on legs gone weak. Her heart began a wild dance and she swallowed hard, but didn't back down. Together, they approached the tiny building. The man was standing, leaning against a post as if it was the only thing holding him up, eyes burning in their intensity.

"Sarah?" If there had been any doubt, mention of her name confirmed her suspicions. Kane stood before them, younger with his hair cut short and his face made bare, familiar in his army jacket and frayed jeans, bearing his soul with one word.

Graham's hold was a steel vice. He would not let go. Sarah looked up at him; he had gone white and was limping, hard, back stiff and straight. His focus was on Kane and Kane alone. Sarah knew she was protected.

She tightened her grip on her husband's hand and nodded at the man before them. "Kane. What are you doing here?"

The woodsman dropped down on the step, running trembling fingers through his hair, his eyes clamped shut. The ghost of a smile curved his lips even as the color ran away from his face. "I'm taking your advice. Trying to get out some. Meet people. Join the human race. This tourist stand was the perfect spot. No one comes here except to fill the pamphlets."

His eyes snapped open and his gaze traveled from Graham, shifting to Sarah. "No one will recognize me now. I come a few times a week. That's about all I can manage. It's hard for me being around people…but *I'm so alone*. I'm always on guard, afraid they might take me back. You're not going to…" His voice trailed off and he looked away.

Sarah felt Graham stiffen beside her and glanced up. His gaze was formidable. No wonder Kane didn't say more. She spoke quickly before her husband did. "No, we're not here to interfere. We didn't even expect to find you, although I'm glad we did. Graham told me about your visit and I've wanted to talk to you." She extended her hand. Her husband's grip on her fingers began to hurt. "Thank you for saving his life."

286

Kane rose to his feet and took her hand in his own, gently as if she might break. Sarah thought Graham would snap in two. " It was the only thing I could do. I'm sorry for what I did to you. I couldn't help myself at the time. I was so lonely and afraid for Caroga that I was crazed. I'm better now. I know that doesn't fix what happened, but I will regret what I did for the rest of my life, Sarah." His eyes filled, his voice shook, and his head bowed down.

Sarah felt the sting of her own tears and cleared her throat, determined that this man would *not* make her cry. "You're right—you can't fix it. You can't give me back seven months of my life or erase the pain you caused my family. Only time can heal us. I don't think enough time has passed for me to forgive you. I don't know if it ever will, but you have my gratitude. That's the best I can do."

Kane nodded, let go of her, and turned to a shelf beside him. He chose two carvings and pressed them into her hand. "A lucky ladybug for your girl and a pair of loons to bless your marriage." He paused and picked up one more item. "For Graham, a walking stick. I think he might need it."

Graham didn't say a word, simply gave a curt nod and took the gift. The two men stared at one another, a look of understanding passing between them.

"Thank you, Kane. Good bye." Sarah took Graham's hand and they walked away, neither looking back or saying a word. She wondered if this would be the last time they met, finally closing a dark chapter in their lives.

They reached the car and this time, Graham chose the passenger side. The drive, *and* their encounter, had taken more out of him than he cared to admit. Sarah started the car and they pulled away, hopefully putting Kane Johnson behind them once and for all.

"ARE YOU ALL RIGHT?" Sarah stepped into the bathroom where Graham was immersed in a tub of steaming water, bubbles up to his chest.

He'd been in such pain by the time they came home with Lila, he'd been white-lipped with the walk to the house. Definitely too much, too soon. Four extra-strength Tylenols and a hot soak were in order. Sarah sat on the edge and took his hand. His eyes were closed, head up against the wall.

He didn't complain, never complained, but she knew. He hurt. "What else can I do?"

Graham gave her a smile, his eyes dark with the aching, but the smile was real. "Be you." At her pout, he took her hand. "You could get into the tub with me…no? How about running some more water, as hot as it can get? Let me soak a little longer and then I'll lie down with a heating pad, okay? I'll be fine. Go look after Lila." He kissed her hand, sighed in pleasure with the addition of heat, and closed his eyes again.

Sarah dropped a kiss on his forehead and went in search of her daughter. Lila was on the living room floor, coloring in a giant coloring book that was a gift from her grandparents. "Mommy, come color with me." She slid over and made room for her mother. The two stretched out together, warmed by the sun shining through the glass door and each other's company, until the picture was done.

"I'm going to check on Daddy. I'll be right back." Sarah stood up and stretched while Lila moved on to a new page.

A glance in the bathroom proved it to be empty. Graham was in bed, pressing a heating pad to the base of his spine; his other hand was tightened into a fist, clinging to the covers.

Sarah sat down beside him. "Honey, you're in pain. Let me call the doctor. Maybe he can prescribe something stronger."

He let go of the blankets and took her hand instead. "No, I'll be all right, really. Just have to let the medicine kick in. Why don't you send in Lila? We can put on a movie, have some popcorn. What do you say?"

Keep occupied, don't think about it, stay focused on others—that was how Graham had made it this far. He would make it the rest of the way.

Lila didn't have to be asked twice. She climbed up next to her daddy and started babbling away. Sarah brought in popcorn and ice cream sodas, they put in the funniest movie they had on hand, and unwound together. Eventually, she looked over to see Graham and Lila both sound asleep. Shaking her head, she closed her eyes and wrapped an arm around them. *If you can't beat them, join them.*

Sarah found herself somewhere she had been before, deep in the heart of the forest by a babbling brook. Two trees stood before her with branches that touched to form a heart. Kane knelt beneath it by two simple crosses made of wood, carved by his hands and the hands of his father. They read, "Beloved Wife" and "Father of My Heart." A third stood in the middle, "Beloved Sister."

She was drawn closer by the sight of another tiny cross in front of Caroga's; it hadn't been there when Kane brought her the first time. Coated with snow, the writing was unclear. Sarah dropped down and dusted off the simple marker made from pine. It read, "Here lies my anger, resentment, and pain. Let it die so I may live again."

Sarah opened her eyes back in her own bedroom. The television had been turned off and a blanket was pulled up over all three of them. She felt her heart slow and took a deep breath. "Are you awake?" Graham's voice was a whisper in the darkness.

She rolled over and reached across Lila's sleeping form to touch her husband, stiff and still beside them. "Yes. Did I wake you? I'm sorry." She found his shoulder and drew herself closer to set her head against him. "Are you all right?"

"I'm fine, just a little sore. I woke up to get a drink and couldn't fall back to sleep. You made a little sound, not quite a cry. You had another dream about him, didn't you?" Graham sounded so tired all of a sudden, as if he'd finally had enough.

Sarah deliberated, choosing her words carefully. "It wasn't really about him this time. It was about me. I was at his family's graves and I had a message that told me to let go. I think it's time, Graham. Seeing Kane today wasn't a bad thing. I'm ready to put him behind me."

Graham shifted so that he could put a hand on her waist. He let out a long, slow breath, taking his time before he spoke. "I don't know…I can't get him out of my head, Sarah. Was I wrong, letting him go the night he rescued me or the other times? I could have went after him. I think I could find his place now if I had to. Should I send someone out there? You say you want to put this behind you, but I don't know if I ever can, Sarah. *Seven months*! He stole seven months from all of us. How are we supposed to forget about it?!" He bit off his words before he woke Lila.

Sarah stroked her daughter's hair, watching her smile curve in the moonlight. "Graham, we'll never forget what was. We have to remember that he brought you back to me. That has to count for something. Judgment isn't for us. Accept the good that he did, let the rest go. For me, Graham, please."

He reached up and ran his hands through her hair that had turned silver under the moon's kiss. "I'll try, for you, but if he comes back, I can't say what I'll do. We have a fresh start. He has a fresh start. Hopefully, what's done is done between us." They pressed their foreheads together and let sleep pull them under once more. This time they did not dream.

22

SARAH SAT ON THE EXAMINING TABLE with her
feet in the stirrups while Graham sat in a chair by her head. He
held her hand with one hand while he kneaded at his lower back
with the other. He'd had a physical therapy session and it was
protesting, but getting stronger.

Sarah stuck her tongue out at him while her doctor did
an internal examination. How embarrassing! One would think
with the current advances in technology that a person would no
longer need to endure such an invasion of privacy. She shook
her head mentally at that thought. There would be *no* dignity
when the baby arrived.

"Sarah, everything looks good here. Your weight is
good, you have nice color. How's the morning sickness?" Dr.
Darlene McDaniels stood up and removed her gloves. She was a
robust, plump woman with a riot of red curls and emerald eyes.
Lively and humorous, she always put them at ease with each
appointment.

Graham raised his hand. "I can field that one. She hasn't
been sick in a week and *I'm* feeling much better, thank you. I

hate that she has to go through all of these changes alone and I can't do anything except sit back and watch."

"Now you know how I felt when you were hurt." Sarah gave his hand a squeeze and directed her attention the doctor. "I'm feeling good. Every now and then there's a little queasiness. Nothing bad." She tried to conceal her impatience while the doctor prepared the gel and wand for the sonogram.

"Well, let's get a look at the little one in here and listen for the heartbeat." All eyes turned to the monitor.

The rapid fluttering, like a hummingbird's wings, filled the room first and an image appeared on the screen. Their little peanut was curled in on itself, thumb tucked in its mouth. Graham's hold tightened on Sarah this time around and when she looked at him, his heart was in his eyes.

Dr. McDaniels wore a wide smile. "I'd say you have a healthy whatchamacallit growing in there. We can't see if this will be a boy or a girl, which you said you want to be a surprise anyway, but you are past the point of danger if you'd like to share the good news."

Graham stood up, shook the doctor's hand, and gave Sarah a hug. "You did it, babe! Let's shout it to the roof tops!" He pulled open the door and called out, "Hey everyone, Sarah's having a baby!" They all started to laugh at his excitement. The doctor cleaned up and took her leave to allow the couple their moment.

Sarah stood but held on to her husband, feeling a little shaky. It was really happening. The image on the screen proved there really was a little person in the making. "I don't know how much *I* did. I'm just a glorified incubator." She rubbed her stomach, only slightly rounded. Loose clothing concealed what would be obvious for the world to see in no time.

Graham lifted a hand to cup her face while the other rested on top of her midsection. "You're much more. Your question mark's whole world and oh, baby, what a wonderful world." He bowed his head to give her a kiss that took their breath away. When they were steady on their feet again, they walked hand in hand out to the car.

It was an incredible day. Officially spring for a little over a week, the weather decided to cooperate. The sun was shining, the air mild, the sky such a bright blue they almost had to close their eyes after staring at its intensity. Upstate New Yorkers knew they were experiencing a tease. The lion of winter could rush back in at any instant. Blizzards had been known to hit as late as April. All the more reason to seize the day.

Sarah climbed in the driver's seat and waited for Graham to force his body to cooperate. Expecting to be stiff after his therapy session, he'd pushed the seat back so he could extend his legs and be more comfortable. As soon as he was settled, she turned the key and pulled out.

"How about a little drive? It's too beautiful to waste and I just want to hold on to this moment a little longer, keep it to ourselves. Does that sound crazy?"

"Absolutely not. Why don't we go by Mayfield Lake and swing around to Mom and Dad's?" Graham turned the radio on and they sang along, giddy over their news.

Sarah reached across and took his hand. She wanted to feel close to him, share the rush, and wondered if his heart was pounding like hers. The relief of making it through the three month waiting period was overshadowed by heady anticipation close on its heels. Their lives would be changing—soon.

The snow was on the way out, the roads quiet. Sarah pulled down the visor to keep the glare out of her eyes. She was humming to the music because she didn't know the words when the lake stretched out beside them. There were some open spots in the ice along the edge, water seeping onto the surface; where it was solid, there was a strange yellow hue, a clear sign that the surface was unsafe. An ice shanty stood in the middle.

"They'd better get that fishing shack out of there before they lose it. That ice isn't going to hold much…"Graham suddenly stiffened and grabbed her leg.

"Stop the car, Sarah!" She pulled over and he was out, walking stick in hand. "Pop the trunk and call 911!" He floundered in the deeper snow that had been plowed to the side and disappeared around the back. There was the sound of his rummaging. He quickly emerged with rope and a blanket.

"Graham, what's wrong?" Sarah fumbled with her phone, fingers shaking.

A glance at the lake answered her question. Two children had emerged from the shanty and stood by it, waving their hands for help. How life could change in a blink! Sarah punched in the numbers when Graham appeared at the passenger side.

"Whatever happens, you stay put. If you or the baby were put in harm's way, I couldn't live with myself." He turned and made his way to the shore.

His steps were shaky and his back had to be screaming. Twice, he slipped on the slope only to pull himself back up with the assistance of Kane's gift. Inadvertently, the woodsman had lent a hand again. There was a solid section of ice. Graham threw the blanket on the shore and tentatively stepped forward. It held and he was on the move, inching his way with caution. Vein-like cracks spread from the strain and he stretched out on his stomach, distributing his weight on a greater surface area.

Sarah prayed fervently while she waited for the dispatcher to answer and described the situation. It was one of the hardest things she ever had to do, waiting in the safety and warmth of her car while three other lives were at stake. She understood Graham's logic. Sarah also knew she would defy him if left no other choice.

He called out to the boys and they lay down as well. A toss of the rope and one boy was dragged across. Graham waited until the first boy stepped on to the shore and tossed again. The second boy was older and a bigger. The ice started to moan as Graham pulled him in. He picked up the pace, racing against time, as the flashing lights of a fire rescue team arrived on the scene.

Sarah motioned to the lake, unable to tear her eyes away from the unfolding scene. Graham was on his feet now, the boy in his arms, crossing the small bridge of ice to shore when it gave, plunging him into the water. Thank God it was only knee deep.

The boy was frightened, drenched by the frigid water, but spared the worst. The rescue workers reached the shore. One took the boy from Graham. Two grabbed Graham's arms and pulled him out of the shallow water. In only a matter of minutes, the crisis was over. Tell that to her heart.

Sarah pressed her forehead to the wheel. *Thank you, dear God, for keeping them safe.* There was a tapping on her window. She looked up to see Danny Rogers standing next to her car. She unrolled it and gave him a quivering smile. "Danny! What are you up to?"

"I was just out for a drive when I saw all the commotion. Are you okay?" He scanned the inside of the car and found nothing amiss. A glance down at the lake and his eyes grew wide. "Is that Graham down there?"

Graham stood with head bowed, hands braced on his knees. Sarah suspected he couldn't take the walk up the bank.

"Yes, that's him. He saw those two boys out on the ice and didn't think twice about helping them. You know Graham. Would you mind giving him a hand getting back up here? He doesn't know the meaning of 'Take it easy.'"

Danny gave her a nod and walked down to her husband, stopping to check on the boys before lending Graham a strong shoulder for the trip back to the car. The assistant ranger made sure his friend was secure. He went on to check on the boys one last time and gave the Scotts a thumbs-up.

Sarah took one good look at her husband, white and shivering beside her, and gave his arm a good whack. "That's for scaring the hell out of me! I know you had to help those boys but let's get one thing straight—if you had been in trouble, you'd better believe I would have been down there. Now, tell me what I can do. You're practically blue and your teeth are chattering."

"First, you can stop yelling at me. Second, how about a hug to warm me up?" He looked so pitiful, Sarah had no choice. She tucked herself under his arms and burrowed close, trying to imagine she was a heater. "Perfect. Now, would you please get me the tallest, hottest cup of coffee you can manage at Stewart's?" Her laughter mingled with her tears.

IT WASN'T THE FIRST TIME that Graham borrowed his father-in-law's pajamas. Upon his mother-in-law's insistence, he took a hot shower to get rid of the chill that had

299

taken residence in his bones after being dunked in the icy, lake waters. She tucked him into bed like he was a child after he came out in red and white striped flannel, looking like nothing other than a giant candy cane.

Why did she pick that pair every time? "Mom, I really don't need to lie down. I'm fine. I didn't even get that wet. Ask Sarah."

Sarah stood beside her mother, hands on her hips. "No arguments. I'm with my mother on this one. All we need is for you to get pneumonia and you'll be miserable, stuck inside for another month. Get toasty, rest, and we'll come get you for dinner." She leaned forward and gave him a kiss.

Her mother linked arms with her and they slipped out before Graham could make a peep. "He's a stubborn one, I'll give you that. Everything is just about ready for dinner. Come on out to the living room and we'll watch a program with Lila."

She gestured for her daughter to sit down on the sofa and returned with hot chocolate for everyone. They watched TV and found time for a round of cards.

Lila set the table. The little girl loved to help in any way that she could. Sarah helped carry out serving dishes and brought dry clothes to Graham. He was already awake, sitting up and rubbing at his face. "Well, hello, sunshine. Did you have a good nap?" He gave her a scowl.

"It would have been better if you were here! You shouldn't have let me sleep. Now I feel like a zombie." He sat a little while longer, but finally forced himself to snap out of it. Pajamas were tossed aside as he slipped into his own clothes, a grimace crossing over his face the instant he put pressure on his back.

Sarah ducked under his arm to offer her support. "Are you all right? You didn't hurt yourself, did you? I saw you fall a few times on your way down the bank." Graham tensed as he tested himself and stood up. She patted his back and handed him the cane.

"I'm okay. Just overdid it, that's all. Nothing's hurt or any worse for the wear. Let's eat. Something smells delicious!" He didn't say another word in complaint while they ate. They had moved on to dessert when Graham caught Sarah's eye, ready to burst with their news. Sarah could see it all over him too. He really was like a book.

Sarah took his hand under the table and gave him a healthy squeeze. "Mom, Dad, Lila—Graham and I have some news." She scanned the faces of the people she loved and took the plunge. "We…that is I…well it really is we…are having a baby!"

Lila let out a squeal and danced around the table. Sally was on her feet, clapping her hands and giving kisses to her daughter, son-in-law, and granddaughter. Steve clapped Graham on the back and gave him a wink. Sarah's father wasn't even able to speak right away, he was so choked up.

Lila jumped up onto her mother's lap and hugged both of her parents around the neck. "Just like Jeanie? Are we gonna get one when Jeanie does? I can't wait! I wonder if it will be a boy or a girl? I don't care as long as I get to be big sister!"

"It will be later than Jeanie's baby, probably around the end of September. You'll have to be patient." Sarah said the words with an understanding smile. It would be hard for all of them to wait.

They finished their evening with huge, hot fudge sundaes to polish off after dinner. Sarah complained that she'd be like a horse, but her mother waved at her dismissively. "You're eating for two now. You might as well enjoy yourself while you can and spoil that little polka dot! I can't believe I'm going to be a grandmother again!"

It was nearing bedtime when they finally climbed into the car. Graham let Sarah drive while Lila fell asleep in her booster seat in the back. Sarah's cheeks were flushed from all of the excitement and her eyes sparkled. "I'm so excited, Graham. I don't feel like I can sleep for the next six months. I want to tell Jeanie, but I'm afraid I'll make her feel bad. She still has to wait and Jeanie's had so many problems. What do you think?"

Graham shrugged, holding up a finger when his cell phone rang. He picked up and there was a pause. "Okay, okay. Just stay calm. We're on our way. We're right here in Johnstown. We'll only be a few minutes. Hang in there."

He disconnected and tapped his fingers on the door, unable to contain a nervous energy. "I don't think Jeanie will be waiting much longer. Jim said she's in labor and they're at Nathan Littauer."

23

WHAT A LAZY DAY. That should have tipped him off. They both slept in, something Jim rarely did but thought, "*Why not?*" He brought breakfast in bed to his bride and shared with her. Jeanie was lit up in a way she hadn't been in he didn't remember how long. Maybe it was the change in the weather, maybe it was because they were laid back, or maybe…just maybe this baby would make it.

Whatever the reason, Jim was happy to see the bloom in her cheeks that had become fuller with pregnancy. Her hair was longer than was her habit, curling around her face to give her a softer look. Her body was like the bud of a flower, about to open for their miracle. Jim never thought her more beautiful than on that day late in March.

The sun was shining, the sky clear, and the air mild enough that he carried Jeanie down to the chaise lounge on the porch. He propped her up with pillows, piled the blankets high, and put the radio on. She insisted he stay with her, to forget about anything that needed doing. It could wait.

Jim slid her over, making a big show over how hard the job was with the size of her baby belly. He received a bop on the head with her pillow in retaliation. They spent the day that way, lazing, dozing off and on, nibbling on a snack, not interested in moving.

Evening approached. He was reading a book about a small town policeman, thinking about the guys at work, while Jeanie read one of her favorite, mushy love stories. He glanced over and saw that her eyes were closed, thought she had drifted off.

A turn of the page and everything changed. There was a jerk of movement and a little cry beside him, her book falling to the floor. Jim turned to see her clutching her side, a look of intense concentration in her eyes. "What is it? What's wrong?"

"It was a contraction. They started a little while ago. I've been waiting them out to see if they would go away. They're not." Her mouth clamped shut and she held her breath as another one hit.

When Jeanie could breathe again, she struggled to stand and fluid spattered at her feet. "It's my water—it broke!" There was the edge of panic in her voice, threatening to pull her under. She made for the door and Jim was by her side, taking her arm.

"Wait! I'll carry you. What do you need?" He put his arm around her shoulders in preparation of lifting her when her hand dug into his other arm, fingernails biting into his skin. He stood still, watching her grow pale with the next pain. "Okay,

okay. Breathe. Remember what they said in the books. Count to ten, slowly. Good. Let it out now."

They hadn't gone to Lamaze because she had to stay in bed. How Jim wished he had brought a Lamaze instructor to her. He'd had CPR and emergency training, even a brief run-down on delivering a baby. He was not prepared, in any way, shape or form, to deliver his *own* baby.

"I have to go to the bathroom, okay? Stop hovering and don't bother carrying me around anymore. That was to keep me from going into labor. It's too late now. I'm not stopping this time, Jimmy."

Her tongue was sharpened by fear. She stepped inside, leaving him waiting outside. He pressed his forehead against the door, hands balling into fists when he heard her scream.

"The hell with this!" Jim burst in to find her leaning against the counter, one hand cupping her belly, her face twisted in pain. He scooped her up, regardless of her orders. "That's it. We're going to the hospital. *Now*. I'm not waiting for you to drop a baby on our bathroom floor. Got it?"

He had the presence of mind to grab their coats and pulled the door shut behind. Jim didn't even lock it. The garage door opened with one press on his key chain, the motor started humming with the help of his remote starter, and Jeanie was buckled in her seat in record time. Jim couldn't have done it faster if he'd timed it.

The tires squealed and they were peeling out onto the road. Nathan Littauer was ten minutes away, five if he pushed it and his foot was itching to do exactly that. *Thank God* the weather was fine.

"Call the doctor, Jimmy. Let them know we're coming and the contractions are two minutes apart." Jeanie's knuckles were white as she gripped the dashboard. She closed her eyes and let out a long, slow breath like air releasing from a balloon.

Two minutes?! Jim hit the button on the dashboard. "Dial Dr. Stonewall." He glanced in the backseat, reassuring himself that Jeanie's bag was there. He'd set that in place a few weeks past. His eyes darted to the clock. Another contraction hit as everything in his wife's body was strung tight like a bow. Less than two minutes, he was sure of it.

Someone picked up the line. "Yes, this is Jim Pedersen. My wife, Jeanie, is having contractions and she's under two minutes right now. We're on our way to the hospital. She's had a difficult pregnancy and it's too early. Will you please notify her doctor and have him meet us there? Thank you."

The line cut off. Jim reached across the seat and took his wife's hand. "We're almost there. It's going to be okay." His next call was to Graham. "It's Jeanie. She's started, fast and hard. There's no stopping it this time. You know my girl. No taking the easy way out. Okay. We'll see you there."

Five minutes later—Jim knew he'd clocked it right after a practice run in his police cruiser with the benefits of lights and the siren—they were in front of the emergency entrance. He was at the passenger side, Jeanie's arms around his neck, and through the door before there was any time to think how terrified he was.

Jim forgot how to breathe and his heart must have stopped with Jeanie's next scream. A nurse took one look, brought a wheel chair over, and they rushed down the hall. Mothers-to-be usually gave birth in the room that they would stay in. However, when the nurse heard about Jeanie's situation, she headed straight for the corridor with delivery rooms, shouting for an administrative assistant to call ahead.

Everything happened fast enough to make Jim dizzy. A room was made ready. Nurses stripped his wife down, gave her a hospital gown, and helped her up onto the table. They put her in a sitting position, nearly folding her in half with her feet in stirrups. A sheet was tossed over her lower half and Jeanie was crying with the pain.

His wife was tough as nails. She never even acknowledged being hurt. One nurse held her hand, Jim had his arm around her shoulders, and another nurse was examining her. "What's going on? Something's wrong, isn't it? She's really hurting. What's wrong?"

Another nurse was setting up monitors. One tracked Jeanie's heart, beating fast like she was running a race. The other followed the rapid, fluttering heartbeat of their baby, soft as a butterfly's wings. The nurse that had completed the internal exam lowered the sheet to cover Jeanie. She gave both parents a smile tinged with anxiety that she fought to keep down. "Nothing's wrong, Mr. and Mrs. Pedersen. This baby is in a hurry to get here, that's all."

Another nurse had Jim by the arm, ushering him out of the room as he glanced back at his wife. "We'll have him back for you in an instant, Mrs. Pedersen. We have to get him dressed properly."

Out in the hallway, the nurse handed him scrubs and a cap. "Here you go, Mr. Pedersen. Get these on, down to the booties to cover your shoes. We have to make sure everything is as sterile as possible. We can't have germs when it comes to your little one, now can we? I'll be back for you in a jiffy." She patted his arm in encouragement and bustled off to take care of other business.

Jim pulled the clothes on and leaned against the wall, letting it do the job of holding him up while his heart threatened to come out of his chest. Too fast, it was all happening too fast. They'd been hanging in limbo all this time with a false sense of security and *WHAM*! Everything kicked into overdrive.

He felt a light slap on the back and Jeanie's doctor went in the delivery room. There were approaching footsteps. Jim looked up and Graham was standing next to him.

"Hey buddy, how are you holding up?" They could have been brothers, similar in features with dark hair and long, lean frames although Graham had the advantage of a couple of inches and wouldn't let Jim forget it.

His eyes were green in contrast to Jim's coffee brown. Calm and steady, an anchor in the storm. Like Graham. "It's going to be all right. *They're* going to be all right. Have faith, okay?" He stepped forward and gathered Jim into a bear hug. They *were* brothers, in every way that mattered.

Jim swallowed hard, unable to speak or he would lose it. The nurse was back. "Let's go, Jim. Your wife told me to stop calling you two Mr. and Mrs. Pedersen because it sounds like old people. It's almost time."

She pushed the door open and another piercing scream spilled out into the hallway. Graham looked stricken as they disappeared inside.

Doctor Stonewall, also covered in scrubs, was in position by Jeanie's feet, bringing to mind a quarterback getting ready to catch a football. It would have been funny if Jim wasn't so scared. "Marie, I need you to get the pediatrician in here along with a premature neo-natal team. Most first deliveries take a while. Not this one."

He gripped Jeanie's knee while she was in between contractions and gave her his best smile. "Well, my girl, we held off as long as we could. I should have known we'd be here this early if this little one is anywhere near as impatient as you."

Jim moved beside his wife and put his arm around her. She was drenched in sweat and shaking as the next pain took her. "I want to push. I've got to push!" She cried out and bore down. She was given a brief respite; the contractions were only a minute apart now.

Jeanie fell back against Jim, crying freely. "When will it be over, Jimmy? It hurts...Oh God, here it comes again!" She closed her eyes, jaw clenched, and her body tightened. It took incredible effort to help a baby meet the world.

More people in scrubs filed in with an incubator while the doctor brought them up to speed. "She's only seven months along. We don't know how well developed the baby's lungs are. The heartbeat's strong, I'll give it that. It's a feisty one, like its mother." Dr. Stonewall returned his attention to Jeanie. "All right, Jeanie. You're crowning now. On the next contraction, give us the biggest push yet."

Jim didn't know how she did it, such a little person doing such a big job. Somehow, she found the strength which shouldn't have surprised him; his wife was stronger than he was. Jeanie screamed again and gave it everything she had. A small, thin wail rose up and the doctor emerged with a little bundle, covered in blood.

"You have a little girl!" A nurse took the baby while he took care of the umbilical cord and the placenta.

Jeanie had her head against Jim's shoulder and they both were crying now. It was over. "Is she all right?" Jeanie reached out to the group of nurses huddled around the baby. A pink blanket was placed in her arms, their daughter squirming with her little face scrunched in protest at the lights and all of the handling. "Oh Jim, look at her. She's beautiful."

"I've never seen anything more beautiful in my life…with the exception of her mother." Jim skimmed the tiny head with his finger, his touch tentative, fearful he would break her. Fine wisps of hair, dark as her mother's covered her little head. Her eyes were the blue of a newborn, but Jim had no doubt they'd be dark snappers too.

Jeanie's eyes met his and he pressed a kiss to her forehead. "You did it. You are the most amazing person I know. *God*, I love you."

Jeanie started to laugh while the tears still flowed. "You're pretty amazing yourself. I love you too."

JIM PUSHED THE CAP OFF OF HIS HEAD, hair dampened by sweat. He didn't know why he was tired. Jeanie did all of the hard work yet it felt like he'd just run a marathon. The Scott family was in the waiting room with Lila sound asleep on the sofa. Sarah and Graham were holding hands, staring blankly at the television when Jim walked in. "Well, it's official. We have a baby girl!"

They were on their feet in an instant. Graham was pounding him on the back and Sarah hung on his neck, kissing his cheek. "Congratulations! Is everyone all right? When can we go in and see them?" Sarah's words ran into each other, she was so excited and relieved after their anxious wait.

Jim gestured to the couch next to Lila's and dropped down, flanked on either side by his friends. "Whew! I am beat. It all happened so fast, but I feel like we've been here forever. They're both fine. Jeanie's a trooper, you all know that. She had me scared though, her contractions were that intense. The baby is okay too. They have her in an incubator and said she'll need to be in it for a week or two. She's strong and healthy, but she has a little catching up to do."

"Thank God. Now tell us the other thing we've been dying to know. What's her name?" Graham stared at him intently, his hold tight on Jim's arm. There had been many discussions around the topic, but they never went anywhere. Jeanie insisted that it would be a surprise.

"Grazia. It's Italian for Grace, our little Gracie. Grazia Stella is the whole thing. Pretty, isn't it? I picked Stella. I've always liked that name. Jeanie picked Grazia because she's God's grace, our little gift brought to us because of Him." No one could speak. They simply gathered Jim up in a hug.

EVERYONE WAS GONE. Jim was dangling between two chairs next to his wife's bed, attempting to sleep. They'd both better get some rest while the getting was good. There was the soft sound of crying and he was sitting on the edge of the bed. "Jeanie-girl, what's wrong?"

"I don't know. I guess it's the let-down. I was so scared, Jimmy. I thought we were going to lose her." She was pale and

313

worn from her ordeal, looking so small in that moment, not much bigger than a child. Jim pulled back the covers and climbed in next to her.

"It's over and she's fine, better than fine. Gracie is fantastic. Now please, won't you try to relax and go to sleep? It will be a big day tomorrow. Droves of visitors will be coming but more importantly, Gracie will be here and you have to rest up for her, okay?" Jeanie reached up to touch his cheek and pressed a kiss to his lips, long and lingering.

"Okay, but only if you sleep here with me." She laid her head down and closed her eyes. Jim didn't have to be told twice. His eyes were heavy, his body heavier. A heartbeat or two later and he was down for the count.

"LET ME SEE THE BAMBINO!" Tony San Giorgio had arrived with Marlene at his side. He filled the doorway while his presence and personality filled the room. An explosion of flowers, balloons, gifts, and cards had been delivered from people who loved them. Word spread fast throughout the police department and amongst friends.

The Andersons and Scotts were gathered around, clearing the way for the first grandparents to arrive. Jeanie's parents had hit the road at the crack of dawn that morning as soon as they had things in order at their business. Jim's parents had to catch a flight; Graham would be picking them up at the airport later that afternoon.

Gracie was tucked in the crook of her mother's arm, a tiny pink cap on her head with a little flower blossom on it, oxygen tubes running from her nose. She was sleeping, her little face exquisite in rest. Jeanie's eyes glowed with a light so bright, she was blinding. "Isn't she beautiful, Pop? Meet Grazia Stella."

The man that was big as a bear, dark and foreboding to anyone who didn't know him, became soft as a teddy. His heart melted and he wore an expression of awe. "She's an angel, that's what she is, an angel from heaven. What a sweetie pie. I'm so proud of you, sweetheart." He gathered his daughter in, careful of the baby, and gave her a kiss.

"Do you want to hold her?" Jeanie asked him shyly. She shifted and Gracie moved ever so slightly. Her little nose wrinkled and then relaxed. She wasn't ready to wake up yet.

Marlene stepped in and gave her daughter a kiss on the forehead. She made the sign of the cross over her granddaughter and began to stroke her little head. "She's incredible, Jitterbug. Are you sure we should be holding her? She looks so tiny and fragile, like she could break. I don't want to hurt her. We've all waited so long. We can wait a little longer to make sure she's safe."

"The doctor said we should hold her as much as possible. Our body heat will help keep her warm and the close contact is important to nurture her when she is so small." Jeanie lifted her bundle, hands extended like an offering, and Tony took her first, taking great care with the wires and tubes attached to the tiny infant. His eyes filled and his lip began to tremble. As if sensing the powerful emotions around her, Gracie let out a pitiful, little cry.

"Oh my goodness! What was that? It sounded like a kitten. Let me have the little peanut, Tony, please." Marlene didn't have to ask twice. Her husband was nervous with this delicate flower of a child. He set her in his wife's capable hands.

"Precious. She is absolutely precious. Who thought of her name?" Everything about Marlene had gone soft, from her face to her words. A minor miracle.

Jim was sitting at the head of the bed, his arm around Jeanie. His wife looked up at him with a smile and his eyes rested on his daughter. "It was a team effort. Jeanie thought of Grazia and I liked Stella. I know it would sound better with a last name like San Giorgio, but it's pretty, isn't it?" Jim didn't think anything could be as pretty as his two girls.

"Very pretty. You did a good job, you two. And Jim," Marlene took his hand and gave it a good squeeze. "You did a phenomenal job taking care of our girl. She wouldn't have made it this long if not for you." Either the world had just ended or hell froze over. Jim almost fell off the edge of the bed.

THE HOUSE WAS PACKED TO THE BRIM. Lila set the table; Graham and Sarah were working together on dinner preparations, stealing kisses in between.

Jim stepped into his kitchen to find Graham's cane against the counter; one hand was on his wife's stomach while the other cupped her neck and their lips did all of the work. "Hey, hey, hey. This is a G-rated household. Besides, the masses are hungry out there. How's it going? Can I do anything to help?"

Graham took hold of his cane and put an arm around Jim's shoulders. "You go out there and spend time with your guests. Your mom and dad really want to catch up with you. Come on." He escorted Jim out so he could return to finish the job of salad, lasagna, and stolen kisses.

Everyone gathered around the dining room table. Both sets of grandparents, the Andersons, the Scotts and of course, Jim, were all there to celebrate the homecoming of the new mother and baby. Jeanie could have come home a week earlier, but there was no dragging her away from Gracie. As soon as their little one was given the all clear, Jeanie was ready too.

Jim sat down at the table, his eyes scanning all the faces he loved, coming to rest on his wife and baby. Gracie was in a stroller, pulled up next to the table. His heart was full to bursting every time he looked at her beautiful, little face. "God bless this family and our precious Grazia Stella, our gift from above!" A cheer rose up around him as everyone raised a glass.

24

THE SNOW HAD FINALLY GONE AWAY. Jim piled
Jeanie and the baby into the car, intent on getting away for a
little while. Their destination: the Scotts' residence. Graham
was out in the yard, doing a little cleanup. He was managing
without his cane, leaning on a rake when he was tired. The pups
were racing around him, nearly adult-sized now and
rambunctious. Dale, the golden retriever, charged and brought
Graham down on a pile of leaves. Jim could hear his laughter
from across the yard.

"I'll rescue Graham and keep the wild beasts at bay.
You go on in to see Sarah and Lila." Jim clapped his hands,
gave a little whistle, and had *two* dogs on top of him in no time.
He wrestled with them until a hand was extended in front of his
face. "I was planning on helping *you* up, not the other way
around." He found himself on his feet with little effort from
Graham.

"I beat you to the punch. Come on inside. We'll have a
beer while the hens cluck." Jim let Graham go ahead, satisfied

to see that the stiffness was nearly gone. They settled outside, on the deck overlooking the lake. It was relatively warm and they were comfortable enough in their jackets.

Graham propped his feet up on the railing and took a long swallow. "So, how's fatherhood treating you? You don't look too rough."

Jim nursed his beer, making it last, savoring the first he'd had since Gracie came home because he was either too busy or too tired to have one. "Good, no—it's the best. Gracie is amazing. There are little changes every day and I'm so glad I've been home to catch them. I'm going to miss it when I go back to work next week, but someone has to pay the bills. What about you? Did you get the okay to go back to work?"

"Two more weeks. It's a good thing or I'd go out of my mind." Graham closed his eyes as the sun beat down on them. They both tipped their faces skyward. The mild turn in the weather felt so good after the long, hard winter. The sliding-glass door opened behind them and little footsteps announced Lila's arrival.

"Daddy, Jim—Mommy wants you to come in. She can't wait any longer!" Lila skipped outside, grabbed them by the hand, and started pulling. "Come on, you two! Jim has to see the surprise!"

Two, grown men let a child drag them inside. Talk about wrapped around her pinky. They stopped outside of a small room that Sarah used as an office. The women were waiting, Sarah practically vibrating with barely contained enthusiasm.

Lila let go and tugged on her mother. "Can I open the door now, Mommy? Please?"

Sarah threw her hands in the air in surrender. "I might as well try to tell the sun not to shine. Go ahead, Ladybug!" Lila didn't have to be told twice. She pushed it open and shouted, "Ta da!"

The space was an office no more. There was a crib in one corner and a changing table, but the walls truly caught the eye. They had been transformed into the One Hundred Acre Wood. Pooh Bear, Eeyore, Piglet, and Christopher Robin had been hand-painted across every surface. A trim of beehives and honey bees bordered the ceiling. There was a pause as the significance sank in.

Jeanie hugged Sarah, tears in her eyes as Jim pounded Graham on the back. "How long have you two been keeping *this* quiet?" Jeanie asked, dabbing at her eyes.

"I'm three months along. We didn't want to say anything until we made it through. You know how that is, holding back until you're out of the woods. I'm so happy we can finally let you in on our news! It's been the hardest secret I've ever kept!" Sarah drew Jeanie in for another hug then started to babble excitedly about new mother talk.

Jim caught Graham slipping out of the room from the corner of his eye. He trailed after him to find him standing by the fireplace, a small wooden carving in his hand. Drawing closer, he saw it clearly. Three deer.

"You all right? We just heard some really good news. We should be celebrating."

The excited chatter of the women spilled out of the room along with Lila's singing to the baby. She made a pass through with the stroller and went on her way. Graham set the carving down and cleared his throat.

"It gets to me, that's all. I love Lila like she's my own. We even finalized her adoption; she'll keep Lee's last name *and* Scott. She's mine now." He picked up the carving again, running his fingers over the smooth lines. "Knowing that we're having another together, that I'll be a part of it..."His voice became thick and he looked down at his hands.

Jim gave his best friend a firm squeeze on the nape of the neck. "I get it, especially now that we have Gracie."

He studied the carving in Graham's hand. Then his eyes travelled to other carvings on the mantle and a wooden walking stick leaning against it. Jim picked up the cane and took a good look at the workmanship, an intricate piece with a wolf howling at the moon for a handle. "Graham, I've been meaning to ask you. Where did the cane and the other pieces come from? The work is amazing."

Graham's hand closed tightly around the deer and he walked out onto the deck. Jim followed to lean against the railing. He had learned to be patient. They both stared out at the lake, the water finally open again.

"Kane Johnson. The deer piece was his calling card after his escape. He gave us the rest on the day I shed my molded body back brace. We took a drive to Blue Mountain Lake. Who do we bump in to?" His laugh was bitter. "I can't seem to shake the man."

"Still hoping for forgiveness?" Jim held out his hand and Graham pressed the tiny, wooden figure in his palm. He tried to picture what he would do if the tables had been turned. Most likely, Jim would have a new home in jail. "How did Sarah handle it?"

Graham shook his head. "That's the thing that really gets me. It was her idea to go out there. She *wanted* to talk to him after she heard about his last visit. Neither of us could say the words he wants to hear. We're not ready. I guess you could say we have a peace treaty. Sometimes, I think I'm crazy for letting him go."

He gripped the railing and stared out at the lake and mountains that stood watch over them. Jim had a feeling that his friend saw something else, *someone* else, and perhaps he always would.

JIM THOUGHT ABOUT GRAHAM'S DILEMMA often in the next week. He didn't know why it crossed his mind on the morning that he prepared to return to work. Maybe it was

323

because he'd be leaving his girls alone. Protective could not begin to describe the way he felt about them. If he were in Graham's shoes, Kane would be dead. Jim pushed those thoughts back. Otherwise, he wouldn't be able to walk out the door. He checked his uniform one more time.

"You look good, like you always do. Are you ready to go back?" Jeanie stood beside him, brushing lint off his sleeve and straightening his collar, little things to keep her hands occupied. She reached up to smooth his hair and there was a tremble in her voice. "You need a haircut. It's more like Graham's now."

Jim turned and tucked her under his chin. "I've been a little too busy these days to see a barber. It's killing me to leave you two. I wish I could stay home forever." Sounds from the nursery pulled them into the next room.

Gracie was awake, staring up, making little cooing noises, the kind that made a parent fall in love all over again. Jeanie scooped her up and handed her to her father. She was warm, soft, giving off the combined scent of baby powder and baby.

Jim held her close, tried to stop time, couldn't take it any longer. "Love you both. Tell me *everything* when I get home." He handed his daughter to his wife, kissed them both on the forehead, and was out the door without looking back.

It was simple, really. Turn the key. Pull out. Drive the few blocks to the station to get his cruiser, except the SUV didn't move. Jim held on to the wheel. It took everything he had to stay put. To not walk back inside and gather his girls in close. To never let go. *Take a deep breath. Close your eyes. Hold your heart together and remember you work for them.* Pulling out of his driveway was one of the hardest things he ever did.

"HEY PEDERSEN. CHIEF MATTHEWS WANTS TO SEE YOU—NOW." Bob Miller, one of Jim's fellow officers, spoke curtly as they passed in the hallway.

Jim tugged on his shirt and ran a hand through his hair. He'd checked in the rearview mirror—his eyes weren't red. The clock told him he had a few minutes to spare. *Great, first day back and I'm already in trouble.*

"Welcome back, Dad!" Familiar voices shouted as he stepped into his chief's office. The small force for the city of Johnstown gathered around a table. Balloons, donuts, coffee, juice, and a few gifts—including beer—were heaped in the middle. Chief Matthews pounded Jim's back, others following suit or giving him a hearty handshake. Someone was snapping pictures, the mood lighthearted.

Bob stepped in, his grin wide. "Sorry I scared you, Pete! How are you hanging in there, old man? It must be tough coming in without your apron or a baby bottle! We figured *you* needed a baby shower." Ripples of laughter broke out around the room.

"Go ahead, have your fun! Most of you guys have dealt with a pregnant wife. Try staying home two months while she's stuck in bed!" He held his hands up in the air. "Don't get me wrong—I'd do it all again and it was all worth it to have Gracie with us. She's an angel from heaven, boys, a real angel!"

Like every proud parent, he had pictures tucked in his pocket. He broke them out and sent them around the room.

With a donut under his belt and a thermos of coffee in his cup holder, Jim was ready to hit the streets again. The lump in his stomach had eased—with a little help from his friends. He resisted the urge to pick up his phone. Jeanie would call if she needed him.

He pulled out and made a sweep of Main Street. All was well. A run through his section for the morning and Jim found himself parked outside the junior high, making his presence known, keeping drivers in line. Since schedules were staggered, he made an appearance at the high school next and moved on to one of the elementary schools last. Other officers covered the remaining schools.

The sun was shining. It didn't take the edge off the chill that morning. The kids were still dressed in heavy coats, many with winter caps. A few defied the weather, determined to dress light and tough it out. Some walked in groups, hamming it up, while others straggled along by themselves. One pair of boys passed a football back and forth. A little girl, probably in kindergarten, trailed behind. She looked up, missed an uneven piece of sidewalk, and ended up sprawled on the ground. The boys were too far ahead, oblivious to the unfolding drama behind them.

Jim was out of the car and across the road in an instant. The little one was crying, holding on to a banged knee. He squatted down beside her and held out his hand. "Are you all right, sweetie? That was a pretty hard fall." He spoke softly, the way he did to Gracie when he rocked her to sleep.

She looked up at him with pitiful, big brown eyes, a head full of brown curls bobbing with each little hiccup. "I hurted my knee...I want my mommy!"

She started wailing in earnest. Calming her took patience and comforting. Eventually, they walked hand in hand to the school, Jim providing a personal escort to the nurse's office.

The rest of the day was routine. A traffic warning here and there, a call to a possible heart attack, luckily a false alarm. Long stretches to sit and wait. That's what being a small town cop was all about. Jim wasn't complaining. Coming home safe every day was the goal. He had chosen to protect and serve his community, but his top priority would always be his family.

At shift's end, he said his good nights, and took the brief drive home. Pulling into the driveway, something inside loosened that had been strung tight from the moment he left. Darkness had just fallen and the living room window was lit.

Jeanie stood looking out, Gracie in her arms. He could breathe again.

"COME ON. GET IN." Jim called from the window of his cruiser, parked in Graham's driveway. It was early. Sarah and Lila had already left for school. Graham pulled the door shut, a look of bewilderment on his face, and walked around to the passenger side. He climbed in and they were already pulling out.

"What's up?" Graham nodded in appreciation as Jim handed him a cup of coffee. He drank it down with a sigh. There was nothing better than a good cup of coffee to start the day. Jeanie's was right up there with Sarah's. Not quite as good, but close enough. The woods flashed by as they booked it back into town.

Jim kept his eye on the clock. He was due in Johnstown in twenty minutes. They'd have to push it. "I know you've been going stir crazy, sitting at home. I thought I'd spring you for a day, give you a drive-along. It might be educational. Most likely, you'll be bored out of your skull, but it's a change of scenery."

The CB crackled, reporting an accident on Johnson Avenue, running past the apple orchard. If they took a short cut, they could make good time. "This is unit 22. I'm on route and will be there in five." Jim hit the lights and turned on the sirens, giving them the freedom to fly.

Graham grabbed his seatbelt and held onto the door. Everything passed them in a blur. "So, this is how fast these babies can go. I've always wondered. Didn't really want to experience it." He closed his eyes on a particularly sharp turn.

"You're looking a little white, Scottie. Don't you remember when we used to take my dad's car out in the country and let it go wide open? We had some pretty good runs." Jim kept his eyes on the road while the adrenalin rush had his heart pumping.

"We were teenagers. We didn't have any fear." Graham sat up straighter when they whipped past three cars and zipped back into their lane, too close to an oncoming truck. "Pete, I know it's important to help out at the accident, but I'd really appreciate it if we get there alive." Staying home didn't sound so bad anymore.

Jim's laughter, always at the ready, filled the car. A few more wild turns, a heart-stopping swerve when a deer jumped out of nowhere, and they were on the scene. Jim was out, practically before the cruiser stopped, going car-side. Graham hung back, staying out of the way, available if needed.

A small, economy car had blown a tire and hit a telephone pole. The driver sat inside, holding his head. He appeared to have smacked it on the window, judging by the spider web of cracks in the glass. "Where are you hurt?"

He had to be in his early twenties and looked like a kid. He gazed up at Jim with blue eyes clouded with pain, blonde hair falling into his face and matted with blood where his forehead smashed into the glass. "It's my head. Feels like it's going to split in half. Deer jumped out and I had nowhere…to go. Man, it hurts."

Graham had slipped in behind them and pressed the first aid kit into Jim's hands. With a nod of thanks, Jim pulled out gloves, a gauze pad, and a cold pack. He'd just pressed them to the man's head, his words soothing, telling him to try and relax when paramedics arrived to take over. They stayed until the driver was in the ambulance and a tow truck arrived.

"No rest for the weary," Jim told his friend with a smile and they moved on.

The rest of the day was true to form—blessedly quiet. They ate a late lunch of sub sandwiches while parked at the side of the road, keeping an eye on traffic. An hour went by and Graham pressed his hands to his eyes with his head against the seat rest. "Pete, how can you stand it? I know my days are slow most of the time too. At least I'm outside and moving."

The sound of the slurp of Jim's straw filled the car. "It's not always this bad. We have some excitement, like this morning. Otherwise, I'm not complaining if it means I come home every day."

He wadded up his sub wrapper, stuffed it in the bag, and tossed everything in the back seat. They both sat, drumming their fingers on the door, sharing stories of the girls, watching the clock. Thirty minutes left.

330

"I appreciate you springing me today, but watching paint dry would be more exciting." Graham gave him a gentle jab in the ribs, ragging on his friend. The radio came to life again, a case of domestic abuse, and the peaceful moment was shattered.

"*Dammit*! I've been to that house before. I *told* the guy he'd regret it if I was ever called back." Jim's knuckles were white on the wheel and his pedal hit the floor.

They made it to a rough part of town and a run-down porch in a matter of minutes. The sound of crying, a woman's and a child's, hit them when they stepped out of the car. "Stay behind me," Jim ordered and pounded on the door. "Mr. and Mrs. Richards, it's Officer Pedersen. Open up."

Graham flanked him, prepared for whatever came their way. "What do you want me to do once we get in there?" The crying continued. Something smashed and there was shouting. Jim's pulse rate kicked it up a notch.

"Watch yourself. Look for the woman and child. They should be our top priority. We have to make sure they're safe. We don't know what we're dealing with when it comes to the husband." Jim pounded the door once more.

"On the count of three, we're coming in if you don't open the door. One…two…three!" He tried the knob; it was locked. A few steps back and Jim rammed his shoulder against the door. It gave, spilling them into the house and chaos.

Jim took everything in at once—the wreckage in every, visible room, the woman huddled in the corner, her mouth bleeding. A little girl was in her arms, the child's face bruised. A film of red washed over Jim's eyes for one moment, clearing at the flash of movement from the next room.

Mr. Richards had seen who came to call and was headed out back. "See to them and call 911. I'll be back as soon as I can." Graham moved quickly to help in whatever way he could, phone already in his hand. Jim was out the door.

The ground was wet from a recent rain, slippery underfoot. Richards pounded down the sidewalk, huffing and puffing. All that drinking, smoking, and beating on his family didn't help him run. Jim cursed himself for not working out. He'd slacked off staying home with Jeanie. A stitch in his side had him gasping, but he pushed to close the gap and launched himself on the guy's back.

They tumbled to the ground. Richards came up swinging. If he was going to go to hell, might as well go all the way. Jim took a few good punches to the face and gut, making him angrier. He popped the guy one good one, flipped him, and cuffed his hands.

"I told you if I was ever called to your place again, you'd pay for it. I don't give a *damn* if your wife presses charges or not. You assaulted an officer and I'm hauling you in. You have the right to remain silent." Jim stopped to catch his breath and spit out a mouthful of blood. Lucky he didn't lose a tooth. "You have the right to an attorney."

Flashing lights washed over them with the arrival of a police car. Bob Miller got out of the car, assessed the situation, and stood back until the Miranda was completed. "Let me take him in for you, Jim. You all right? You're going to have a shiner and you've already got a fat lip."

"I'm fine. Tell the chief I'll be in to press charges once things are taken care of with his wife. Thanks, Bob."

The walk back gave Jim some time to cool off and rein in his emotions. One good look at the damage inflicted on Mrs. Richards and the child made his head ready to explode with an instant migraine. Jim started to pace on the sidewalk. They were not fit to be questioned nor was he fit to ask questions.

The ambulance arrived and Graham talked quietly to the mother, comforting her daughter. His best friend had a way about him that set others at ease. He stepped back to allow the paramedics to close the doors and pull away.

Graham let out a low whistle when he caught sight of Jim's face. "I hope the other guy looks worse. They're going to be all right. The mother might have a mild concussion and it looks like only bruises for the little girl. They're being checked out as a precaution."

Jim stomped back and forth, hair standing on end from where he ran his fingers through it. "*Only* bruises! Heaven help me I want to kill the guy for laying hands on that little girl, and the mother for that matter. I don't trust myself to face him at the station. *How* have you managed to hold civilized conversations with Kane?"

Graham slung an arm around Jim's shoulders and pointed him in the direction of his cruiser. "I'll give you a little advice from a wise woman. Sarah says you have to learn to let it go. We'll go to the station, you'll get off work, and we'll stop for a beer. When you are able to unwind, you'll go home and enjoy your family." He walked around to his side of the car and waited for Jim to start the engine.

"There's one problem with this plan." Jim stared straight ahead, a grin tugging at the corner of his mouth. "How are *you* getting home to *your* family?" They headed out, only a few blocks to the station. Once the engine was turned off, he gave his full attention to Graham.

Graham shrugged. "We'll worry about that later. Let's follow the plan: let it go—your anger that is, not that bastard. Get some beer. Go home. Maybe I'll hitchhike." They fell into step, side by side, with a small hesitation at the door.

Jim squared his shoulders and held his head high. "There's no way in hell you're going to hitch. Jeanie and Sarah would kill me. You'll stay for dinner and I'll be sober enough to drive by then. If not, there's always the couch."

THAT NIGHT, JIM LINGERED OVER HIS DAUGHTER'S CRIB. The moonlight fell across her face, so peaceful in sleep. He gave thanks that she was safe. For his beautiful wife. For a friend like Graham. He said a prayer for Mrs. Richards and her daughter, for himself to never lose his sense of reason. Jeanie called to him from the doorway. He dropped a butterfly kiss on Gracie's cheek and followed Graham's advice. He let it go.

25

SPRING WAS SHY, SHOWING HERSELF A LITTLE AT A TIME. Kane's father had always compared it to a bride teasing at what was to come on her wedding night. The nights had lost their bitter edge. The days stretched out a little longer. The geese cried overhead and more animals started to make an appearance. The land was coming alive again after a long winter's sleep. Kane could spend more time in the Adirondacks' heart. Breathe deeper. Rest easier.

Change was coming to Kane as well, gradually, easing its way in. His last visit to his childhood home had sealed the door on the past. He wouldn't be going back. His new home had become a haven and his shack had a sense of permanency. Whatever life had in store, Kane would meet it on his own terms. He would not open himself to exposure again.

The wind in the trees lulled him to sleep, gathering him in. A splash of red, a cardinal against the receding snow, mesmerized him to drink it in. The deer in the meadow, nuzzling the first, tender shoots, made him become still. It was not so much being back in the Adirondacks as Kane letting *them* back in to his heart. In the embrace of the wilderness, he was never truly alone.

There was a conscious effort to steer clear of memories, to grab hold of the present and take each day, one at a time. This was *his* life, a new life. He immersed himself in the outdoors. Filled his eyes. Filled his soul. He kept his hands busy, tired his body with work and walks. He read his small collection of books and tried his hand at keeping a journal. Mama had kept one. Why couldn't he?

His carvings became a passion. They accumulated in his little cabin to the point of spilling out into a storage area he fashioned in a cave. Lord knew what he'd do with them, but they soothed him. As the pieces took shape in his hands, memories from his past played out in his mind—the bear that had taken up residence near his home when he was growing up, the raccoon that had been his pet when he rescued it as a baby, the robins that brought back spring, the busy chipmunk, a reminder of all that had to be done in a day, the deer—steady, peaceful, beautiful.

Kane even found himself etching designs randomly in the trees on his journeys throughout the wilderness. No one shared his life. No one might ever know of his existence, yet he'd leave his mark and contribute something to the earth gifted to him by the grace of God.

Kane's last conversation with Graham Scott made an irrevocable mark on his life, the greatest impetus for change.

The compulsion to seek out the ranger, take the risk of being captured or spurned, drove him to that other world like the animals he'd once seen flushed out by a forest fire, taking flight.

He had been but a boy, perhaps ten-years-old. His parents had taken him for a day-long excursion, venturing away from home to see a breathtaking waterfall near Northville. It was mid-summer, the forest caught in the grips of a dry, hot spell. Skirting around a makeshift campsite in the woods, they found disaster—a campfire left unattended and flames licking the trees.

It was too late to stop it. The Johnson family was forced to flee as surely as the wildlife. Kane would never forget the dark, heavy smoke. The intense heat. The fear that emanated from all of the living creatures and made his own heart hammer.

Strange. Creatures usually moved away from a threat, yet Kane moved toward it. There was no denying that in Graham Scott, injured or no, he'd met a formidable foe. That Kane had saved his life was no guarantee that the favor would be returned indefinitely. Still, he *had* to go, had to reassure himself that Graham was well.

The ranger's restoration to health was key in restoring Kane's soul. He could never erase what he had done to Sarah. At least he could prove his regret, share his yearning to make amends. He sought out Graham to heal the wound that festered within all them.

It was said that for every action, there was an equal reaction. When Kane stole Sarah from all she had known, eventually it came back on him to rob him of his world. He hoped the same could be said of the moment he saved Graham's life. Would it save his own?

Kane returned home from his attempt at reconciliation, exhausted, and slept like the dead. The sun was high in the sky, shaking him out of bed when he finally came awake. There was a new sense of lightness about him. It didn't matter that he slept in or missed the sunrise. There would be plenty more. God willing, a lifetime more.

Kane stoked the fire and made himself tea, sweetened with honey salvaged from the time before. Soon, the bees would hum. He could follow them, restock, relish holding a honeycomb in his hands. Many a time he had broken off a piece, let the liquid gold run over his fingers, and sucked it dry.

A step outside made him smile. It was unseasonably warm. A good wash day. His father's army duffel came in handy, filled with clothes and homemade soap. Kane tossed in a handful of venison jerky, some nuts, and set off.

It was a day meant to watch, listen, and feel. Animal tracks were easy to follow in the last of the snow and where mud was brewing. He could have hunted, but decided to let it be. There was enough to get by. Live and let live. The rest of the forest had the same idea, bursting with activity on that fine day.

Kane actually worked up a sweat by the time he emerged by the lake's shore. It was a remote section, far from any residences or prying eyes. He stripped down and laid his clothing on a rock to be warmed by the sun. Experience taught him he'd need it.

He took a deep breath, gathered his resolve, and ran into the water. It was like ice and would have driven the faint of heart back to shore. Kane forged on and dove in, completely submerging himself. His shout echoed against the mountain when he shot to the surface. A mad flurry of strokes made his blood start pumping again. The water was so cold, his insides hurt and felt like they were shriveling. Times like these, he missed the bathhouse that Daddy had made. Kane could make one himself, but this made him feel *alive*.

A few more strokes and he went to where it was shallow enough to get his feet under him. He picked up the soap, lying next to his clothes, and scrubbed every part of his body, including his hair. The clothes were next until they were all laid out on the rocks and his teeth were chattering. Kane didn't stop shaking until long after he'd pulled his dry clothes back on and wrapped himself in the blanket he'd brought as an afterthought. There was nothing to do now except wait until everything dried.

Moments of rest—they were rare in the natural world where the need for survival meant never-ending effort. Kane allowed himself to relish a moment of tranquility. He leaned back against the rocks, taking advantage of the opportunity to be still. Slowly, the warmth of the sun seeped into his bones from the warm stones and his body went loose.

He worked Mama's brush through his hair. It had become quite long and tangled until it was a bother. Peering at his reflection at the water's edge, his hand ran through the unruly strands and traveled to his heavy beard. It was the way he'd looked for as long as he could remember and suddenly tired him. Kane no longer wanted to be *that* man.

Don't think. Just do. He had his pocket knife, kept dangerously sharp, tucked in his flannel shirt. Gripping his hair, Kane began to saw away until it just brushed his collar. He contemplated his face, deliberating, pushed ahead. He'd watched Daddy and knew it could be done if he was careful. He lathered some soap into his beard and scraped the blade against it, careful of the angle. Bit by bit, bare skin, reddened by his efforts, appeared. When he was done, a stranger peered back at him.

The passage of time was stripped away by about twenty years, his honey eyes catching the light, the wind lifting the hair away from his face. A face he hadn't had a good look at in a long time, very similar to two others that he had lost a short time ago. A tide of emotion threatened to drag Kane under. He looked like his mother, when she was young and strong, and Caroga before illness struck.

He sat that way for a long time, remembering those sweet women and what they had given to him. His cheeks were wet with tears when he turned away and set himself to the task of gathering his clothes. They were not tears of pain this time. They were an expression of gratitude for the women who gave him life and love.

Kane sat by the fire that night, chewing jerky, hands working on a piece of wood. He was restless. There was something more for him to do, if he was ready for it. A week. He needed that many days to find his nerve.

He woke early, before the dawn, as was his habit. Careful with his choice in dress, Kane wore jeans and a red flannel shirt, clothing that was worn but not frayed. Nothing to draw notice. Face scrubbed until it was almost raw, hair as tamed as it ever would be, he deemed himself presentable. His pack was already set from the night before when he'd built himself up. He *would* do this.

Walking up the mountain felt good. Winter had lost its grip, giving way to spring and the snow was almost gone. Bird chatter filled his ears, the air mild, holding a hint of possibility. Kane made the peak, sat cross-legged on a flat stretch of rock, and let the morning take him. The colors seeped into the sky, trickled into him, settled him. Time to move forward. From now on, always forward. There was nothing for him in the past except memories, pain and regret.

Down the mountain, back through the forest. A pair of deer grazed in a small clearing, nipping at the first, sweet grass of the season and peeling bark from the white birch. Wonder stopped him. Always had, always would. Kane considered it a good omen for the day. The anxiety, buzzing below the surface, died down to a low hum. Pushing on, the trees were met by the black snake of the road.

The last time Kane left the shelter of the trees was his meeting with Graham; otherwise, he no longer sought contact with the outside world. Today, that would change. It was a mile trek along a quiet stretch. A few cars passed and he fought the urge to let the woods take him back. *Stay calm. Walk slowly. Lift a hand in a wave.*

Just another nature lover, out for a walk. Up ahead, a small building stood by the side of the road. Little more than a shed, it had a covered porch to protect a display of tourist pamphlets and a bench for travelers in need of rest. Perfect.

Four months had gone by since his life had been thrown into upheaval. Losing Sarah. Enduring captivity. Leaving his childhood home by force. Starting over.

Four months gave him the opportunity to think about his life and mistakes, to heal, to change. To realize he needed something more than living alone in his tiny shack. Kane was his father's son, finding comfort in the woods, but he was also his mother's child, craving contact with others.

He kept coming back to advice from Sarah. He couldn't expect the world to come to him nor take it by force again. The passing of time, his encounter with Graham, and a change in appearance gave him the confidence to follow her advice.

With care and deliberation, the contents of Kane's pack were set on the railings and on the bench with a carved sign, "Hand-crafted Woodwork—For Sale." The animals of the woodland peeked out at the road, captured forever by the work of his hands, life-like in detail. Nothing left to do but wait, he dropped down on the steps. Open for business, Kane contemplated the possibilities—no one would come or he'd have success. If he did, what next? Go into town, mingle, enter a shop or buy a cup of coffee, maybe a sweet dessert? *No, not ready. One step at a time.*

It was early. The occasional passerby with long gaps of silence allowed a slow unwinding of his insides that had been pulled tight on his way out of the woods. Kane reached inside his back and grabbed a handful of jerky. He needed something to quiet a rumbling stomach. He was working on a mouthful when a car pulled off the road, forcing him to choke it down and get to his feet.

Relaxed. Casual. Like it was normal to be around others. What was the expression Mama used to say? Just a walk in the park. Kane gave a slight nod and propped himself up against the wall.

"Fine morning, isn't it?" He said softly as an elderly couple peered at his work. They made niceties back, fingering his carvings, commenting on its craftsmanship.

"Hank, the grandchildren would love these, don't you think? They could put them on their shelf or in the window at

344

the camp. You know how Brenda just loves deer and Brandon is always going on about wolves." The woman was quite animated, picking up several pieces and showing them to her husband. She handed them over and started digging in her purse.

Hank gave Kane a long-suffering roll of the eyes. "We could be a while. My Martha has everything but the kitchen-sink in that handbag of hers. It's a wonder she can carry it. Honey, you want me to pay the man? You can sift through that catchall some other time."

"Now, Hank, you could take a lesson from this fine, young man. Look how patiently he's waiting. Not a peep out of him. There, I've found my wallet. How much will it be for these three pieces, young man?" The woman, Martha, was a little bird of a woman, dressed in a pale yellow sweater and dress with a straw hat and gold-framed glasses. She tipped her head up and gave Kane the sweetest smile, waiting expectantly.

A grandma. She reminded him of a goldfinch. With a pang, Kane realized Mama and Daddy had denied him the opportunity to get to know his grandmothers or grandfathers. What had they thought about his parents' decision to take to the woods? Had they known about their grandson or granddaughter?

The man cleared his throat, forcing Kane to pay attention. "That will be five dollars for each piece, if that's all right, mam."

Her eyes widened and she raised a hand to her lips. "My stars, child, that's nothing. You go into the little shops in these towns out here and it would be at least ten dollars each. Did you do all of these yourself? They're lovely, quite lovely." She fumbled with her wallet and pulled out the money. "Here, young man. I'm getting one more for Hank and I, that pair of sweet sparrows."

Kane's head was a muddle, unaccustomed to so many words coming at once. He was rusty, had never been one for talking much anyway. He ran the money through his hand, pocketed it, and dug out a response. "Thank you kindly, mam, and yes, I made them myself. I hope you enjoy them. Have a nice day."

He raised a hand as they drove away, hoped his smile covered how shaky he felt inside. Kane made it about an hour that first day.

It was all he could do not to run back to the woods. When he reached his home, it was a cool drink to a man in the desert. Kane didn't venture far from his shack for several days, except to hunt and get water, lying on his back at night, eyes wide. The roadside stand, the little, old couple, the exposure away from the protection of the forest, kept playing out in his mind. Each time he envisioned going back, his heart picked up the pace and his stomach began to churn. He wasn't ready.

Several infinite days later, he was restless again. Unable to find contentment in anything. Lonely. It was the lonesomeness that pushed Kane out again, past the edge of the forest, past his limits, back to the stand. He stayed two hours. Watched a little boy, face shining like the sun, when his father bought him a carving of a bear. Kane thought he'd die with missing his own father. It was a struggle to maintain his composure and he went home soon after they left.

Unwilling to go back to his empty cabin, Kane made his way to the lake. Knees drawn to his chin, he stared out at the water, taking out his box of memories. Why had his parents done this to him? Had they never realized how devastated he would be without them? Even Daddy needed Mama before he came to the forest. They raised Kane, loved him well, then left him bereft and unprepared.

Craving that little bit of human contact, a candle in the night of his existence, he began to make the trek back to the stand every other day. The time of day and the length of stay varied. Kane did not want to draw undue attention or make anyone ask questions. The authorities hadn't passed by yet. He hoped to continue to be fortunate, that they would avoid one another completely.

A pile of money grew in a box that he made. It remained to be seen what Kane would do with it. He didn't care for the profit. The brush with others, however light, *that* was his intention.

His life was turned upside down on a clear, blue, cloudless day. Mild, with little traffic, Kane thought about

347

packing it up and climbing the mountain when a car pulled in. A couple got out. A man with dark hair, limping heavily. A woman, with the sky in her eyes and sun in her hair.

Kane's mouth went dry until a twist in his stomach was strong enough to make him taste his breakfast. He swallowed hard and waited as they came closer. He resisted the strong urge to run by gaining his feet and clinging to the post. "Sarah?" The word was out and couldn't be pulled back in.

Graham held her hand. Kane wasn't sure if he did so for Sarah's sake or to restrain himself. The ranger's eyes bore into Kane, would flay him to the bone if any harm was done to his wife, of that there was no doubt. And Sarah...she was as Kane remembered, hair falling past her shoulders, shielding her face when she turned to look at her husband. The ranger had gone white and held himself stiffly. Strong. Ready. Brave.

Only a few words passed between them. Kane couldn't say more. After all this time, finding his way, finding his home, finding himself...to lose it all again. Unthinkable.

Minutes passed, a blink, and then the unconceivable. Sarah set him free.

Still holding Graham's hand—they were an extension of one another, like Mama and Daddy—she walked back to the car. It pulled away, taking a piece of Kane's heart with it, the piece that belonged to Sarah. The steps caught him again and his head pressed to his knees. Peace...he had felt glimmers, might really have it one day. It would be hard-won.

26

ANOTHER WEEK PASSED BEFORE KANE RETURNED TO HIS STAND. Seeing Sarah and Graham had rattled him. He drew comfort from the woods. Walked farther than he ever had before, pushing himself to the limit. Climbed the mountain. Swam in the lake. Watched. Listened.

He took pleasure in food again. Kane considered braving town to find some luxuries, sugar, spices, flour. At night, he let his shack settle him. Staring into the fire, the warmth seeped in, touching the raw places. He let sleep take him when it wanted to, slept long and hard. A few dawns went by without him on the mountain. There would be more.

Sarah's words had made him feel free in a way he hadn't ever before. Made him ready for…more. Refreshed, with a new-found healing, Kane ventured out again. He made small talk with a straggling of customers. Sat on the step and soaked in the sun. Breathed in deep of the fresh air.

He was leaning against the step, eyes closed, when footsteps approached. "Hello. You've got beautiful work here. I'll take everything."

A female voice pulled Kane to his feet, making his blood hum. Willowy and tall like the pines, she was a woman with dark hair and eyes. He knew her. Jillian Martin. *No, Jill.*

"Everything? You're sure, mam? That will be one hundred dollars, a fair amount of change." He looked down at his feet, a rush of heat flooding his face. What was wrong with him?

"Oh my God! John, is that you? I wouldn't have known you except by your voice. I've heard it many times in my mind, remembering the day you helped me down the mountain." She set her hand on his and his skin burned from her touch.

"You've got me. What brings you back, Jill?" He turned and gathered the pieces, to busy his hands and slow his heart. Having brought nothing else, Kane placed them in the sack he'd made of deer skin, handed them to her, and took the hundred dollar bill. It was a fight to breathe again when he looked into those eyes, brown like a doe's.

She took the sack and gave him a smile in return. "Well, I loved it so much here this winter that I couldn't stand the city any more. I sold my condo, quit my job, and I've bought a little cabin in town. I've started a shop downstairs and I hope you don't mind, but I'm going to put some of your work in it. People love this stuff!"

As if sensing his hurt, she reached out and took his hand. "I love it too. I'll be keeping my favorites for me. Listen,

I still owe you a cup of coffee from the first time we met. What do you say? I promise that I won't bite."

Kane eyed her car, glanced back at the woods that led the way home. His carvings were gone, his day done. Jill waited expectantly, unaware that she'd made a mess of him. Heart pounding, cold sweat breaking out, his lungs squeezed until Kane didn't think he could breathe.

He closed his eyes, swallowed hard, and took the plunge. "I'd…like that."

They walked together, Kane remembering something he saw in a drive-in movie once with his parents and opening her driver's side door. He walked around and sank into a soft seat of black leather in a sleek black car that was nothing like Daddy's army jeep. It hardly made a sound once they were on the road, engine running on a low hum, tires smoothly hugging the surface. Kane held onto the handle, because it gave him an anchor and would let him go if he needed to escape.

"Relax, John. It's just a cup of coffee. We're not getting married!" Jill's eyes were mischievous, white teeth flashing with her smile.

She turned on the radio and a soft, mellow music filled the car. Heat blew from the vents and washed over him. Her soft chatter, about the wilderness, about her business, about her life— worked on Kane. His grip eased up on the door.

It was a short drive into the small town of Blue Mountain Lake and blessedly quiet. The tourists wouldn't be coming for another couple of months. Kane wasn't sure what he would do then. The need to protect his privacy was strong. Still, a part of him wanted to be around others.

Too much time amongst the townspeople would raise questions. Best to continue as he had, occasional visits to the stand. Maybe he'd come back to town, like today. They stopped outside a quaint cabin made out of logs, The Cozy Cup. "Come on in, John. They've got really good coffee and their pie is to die for."

Getting out of the car took considerable force of will. A part of him would rather take cover like a turtle in its shell. He scanned the surrounding shops, the light posts along the road. The posters of Sarah were long gone and there were no wanted posters either. If they'd been on the look-out for his face, the face he used to wear, it was old news now.

Take a deep breath. Get out. Walk by the side of a woman, in a town, to a diner. No police officers came on the run, no rangers descended from behind the building. No one took notice at all except perhaps to smile in appreciation. Jillian was fine to look at and…so was he.

Kane held the door and let her go in first, pausing at the entryway. She turned to look at him, a puzzled expression on her face. Walking in, sitting down at a table, like normal people…it was something he'd never done. His trips into town with Mama and Daddy had been brief, with the exception of fireworks and the drive-in movie. But to join others in a diner? Never.

He closed his eyes to still the butterflies in his stomach, opened them, and followed Jillian. Once seated, Kane cleared his throat. "I'm sorry. I keep to myself a lot. I haven't been here…in a long time." *Or ever.*

She handled it with ease, a cool breeze on a summer day, picking up the conversation where others might have been awkward. Jill started with small talk, the inconsequential, focusing on herself before moving in the other direction.

Her hand seemed to float in the air and rested on his. "I have to be honest. I've thought about you a lot since that day. I didn't expect to find you but I hoped, and now, well, you're almost too pretty to look at."

An ember that had been burning deep down in the pit of his stomach flared at her touch, her words. Kane let out the breath he'd been holding with a little catch in it. *"You're* too pretty. Got my tongue tangled in knots."

Watching this woman across the table, it hit him what Sarah had been trying to tell him all those months he'd kept her. He burned for this woman, saw the reflection of that fire in her eyes. With Sarah, it had been comfort, companionship, the normal hunger of a man for a woman. Not this heat that traveled between them in a touch and a look. Another first.

A waitress came to the table, handed them menus, and filled their coffee cups. Kane added a generous helping of cream, let the sugar pour, gloried in its sweetness. Jillian tipped her head back and laughed, making a clear bell of a sound.

"Goodness, John. You'd think it was your first cup of coffee." She sipped her own, equally light and sweet.

"Not my first, I'm just not used to other than black. It's been a while since I've made it into town to get the fixings." He tried to make it last, but shouldn't have worried. The waitress refilled his cup when she came to take their order.

The menu. He was supposed to choose something. Kane had never ordered anything from a menu. There were so many choices, many he'd never had. What to have? What would he like? What if he never came again?

"What will it be, honey? I don't have all day." Alice, or at least that's what her name tag read, tapped a foot and pulled a pencil from behind her ear.

Black hair, streaked with white, was pulled tightly in a bun and black-framed glasses perched on the end of her nose. Her feet were tired, her back ached, and she was too old for this. If she was a few years younger, she'd be sweet on the taste of honey at her table. Lucky girl.

Jill tapped the desserts and handed the menu to Alice. "I'd love a piece of that apple pie with a scoop of vanilla ice cream. Is it homemade?"

One doe's eye winked at Kane and he felt a foot nudging his under the table. He dropped his menu with fingers suddenly gone numb and sat up straighter.

"Sure is, sweetheart. I did the baking early this morning. My Joe is busy at the grill. Only the taste of home when you come in the Cozy Cup. Now, how about you, darlin'?" She turned and gave her attention to Kane. He could swear he saw the woman bat her eyes at him and give a little twitch of her hips.

Say something. Sound civilized. Breathe. "I'll have the chocolate pie."

On a day of firsts, he chose a pastry he'd never tasted. He'd had chocolate candy before. When he was little, Mama picked a Hershey's bar off of the shelf at the tiny store near Canada Lake. He and his parents sat on the bench out on the porch and the three of them shared it. A little bit of heaven. One bar and he was hooked. Kane bought some most every time he went in once he made the trips as an adult, always saving half for Caroga.

The last time he'd shopped in town was October, when he bought the trinkets and other extras to appease Sarah, as well as a gift for his sister to lift her spirits even as she was slipping away from him. The waitress cleared her throat, reminding Kane of where he was. She took his menu and went off to take another customer.

There was hardly time to search for something to say when two generous slices of pie arrived. Kane picked up his fork, took a tentative bite of the chocolate with whipped cream heaped on top, and his eyes closed in ecstasy. The hum of conversation, the bustle of activity—so different from the woods and nature's pace—receded.

There were only the two of them, the sweet treat, and time to savor it. *A man could get used to this. Something good to eat. The attention of a woman. Having someone know and care that he was alive.*

"You want to swap? The apple pie is pretty good and that chocolate looks worth gaining ten pounds." Jill's eyebrows raised questioningly.

She slid her plate across and he did the same. Each sampled the other's. Her eyes closed and her smile told of obvious pleasure. "That *is* good. How do you like mine?"

Kane swallowed, took another bite, scooping some of the ice cream with it. He could count the number of times he'd had the frozen dessert on one hand. "My mama made the best apple pie I ever had. This is a close second. Not as good as that chocolate. I've never had that before." Why did he let that slip?

"Never had chocolate pie? Where have you been living—under a rock? Now that I think about it, I don't know anything about you. Why don't you tell me about yourself?" Jill drained her coffee cup and propped her chin on her hands.

Kane slowly chewed the last of his pie. Watched the swirl of cream in his coffee and drank it down. Kept his eyes trained on the table. Breathed in. Breathed out.

Talk about his life? Not all of it. He couldn't give her all of it or she'd run away screaming. He didn't want her to run away. He looked up into Jill's deep, brown eyes and gave a nod. "You won't believe a word I say."

Kane had meant to skirt around it, to only tell her of his unconventional upbringing in the woods. In the end, his tongue loosened and like a flood gate that had burst, the words spilled out, everything up to Sarah and beyond because if there was any hope of traveling down this path with Jill, she had to know the truth. In so doing, he destroyed any chances at all. She stood up without a word, crossed the room, and walked out.

What would one expect? Fleeing was the only sane reaction. Kane dropped his head into his hands and tried to find some solace. The home fire of his parents' devotion. The comforting candle of his sister's unswerving affection. A spark of compassion from Sarah. The hint of a bonfire with Jill. Perhaps those were the only flames of affection God would dole out in his lifetime.

The sound of footsteps and the chair scraping across the floor said otherwise. "Explain it to me. Make me see. *Help me to understand.*" Jillian's voice was soft, her hand gentle as it rested on his. Kane looked up and saw...a second chance.

THEY WENT TO HER HOUSE and sat at her kitchen table in the apartment above her shop. Kane told her his story from beginning to end, not an easy task for a taciturn man who said few words throughout his life. She sat still as the oaks in the forest, her chocolate eyes never wavering from his face; he suspected Jill was equally as strong as those mighty trees.

Finally, as darkness fell, the words ran out. He was hoarse, parched, and drained in the telling. Kane stood and raised a hand. "Don't say a word. Don't make up your mind. Think on it. My father always told me for any decision in life, big or small, you need to mull it over because the road you take may not have any way back. If you want to find me, you know where I'll be." He kissed the top of her head and walked out the door. Kane didn't look back.

27

IT WAS LILA'S SIXTH BIRTHDAY. Graham took pictures with his mind, catching memories. They hosted a party with her friends from school, scampering around in the backyard at Nana's and Pop Pop's because most of the children lived in town. Sarah came up with a carnival theme. There was a cotton candy machine, a popcorn maker, hot dogs on a roller, even a slushie maker. Graham dressed as a clown, comical with a big, red nose and a riot of curls in rainbow colors. His wife was adorable in a smart, red jacket, black pants, boots, and a top hat.

Playing the role of the ringmaster, she'd drawn and ring around his heart and made his head swim. Graham wanted nothing more than to strip those clothes off of her. A look of understanding passed between them several times that afternoon. Waiting would make it that much better. The day ended with little ones sprawled on the grass as they watched a movie, courtesy of a projector that threw the image up on the side of the garage. Everyone went home full of cake and ice cream. Sticky. Tired. Happy.

The family party came next, on Pleasant Lake. Summer was on its way in early, bringing warmth and sunshine. The grass had turned a deep green, there was an explosion of flowers, and Sarah's gardening talents trimmed their home. They had a backyard barbecue with the Andersons, Graham's mother, and the Pedersens.

Steve volunteered to man the grill, a master when it came to outdoor cooking, which allowed Graham to sit back in an Adirondack chair and get an eyeful of his wife. Blooming was the best way to describe it. Nearly halfway through her pregnancy, there was a small swelling of her belly that was nowhere near the size of his pride, close to bursting. He'd never seen her more beautiful and the thought that a life was growing inside her, one they had made together and would share, squeezed his heart every time.

Sarah sat next to Jim's wife, ogling the baby. It felt good to see Jeanie, cheeks blooming and fire in her eyes. The little mother watched Gracie like a she-bear and was back to her normal speed—hurricane.

"They look good enough to eat, don't they?" Jim handed Graham a beer and they clinked bottles in a toast.

He dropped down in the chair next to his best friend with a sigh. He was tired, but it was a good tired. Taking care of Gracie was a full time job for both of them. Jim pulled his weight and took over when he came home from work. He didn't mind. They'd been through so much to have her and didn't know if they'd ever have another. She was worth it, whatever the cost.

"You've got that right, brother." Graham took a long swallow. The cold beer felt good going down. He was being lazy and it was a new experience. He'd been wound tight with tension, like a spring ready to release, for nearly a year. First, there had been Sarah's abduction and the all-consuming search, then Kane's escape, the catastrophe on Blue Mountain, and a lengthy recuperation that wore him down.

Finally, the knots had come untied inside of him. Sarah was back where she belonged and he'd started to believe it was for good. A shaky peace had been made with Kane. Graham was back on a job that was like air to him. Life was good.

Jim patted him on the back and he was up, chasing Lila and swinging her round and round. More snapshots. All the people Graham loved, gathered around the picnic table, smiling, laughing, living. Free to hope again.

Lila's smile stretched from ear to ear when Sarah brought out the cake. Her little mouth was soon covered in frosting and ice cream. Her giggles rang out as she ran around the yard with a handful of balloons until Graham caught her. He lifted her to his shoulders, wishing he could freeze that moment in time.

The film kept rolling, moved into fast forward that night when Lila told them what she wanted for a present. A camping trip to Blue Mountain Lake. Her friend, Paige, had told them about it at school for show and tell. Lila was insistent.

With the stubbornness only known to a child, there was no budging. Graham forced himself to stay calm while he tucked her in and told her they'd see what they could do. He pressed a kiss to her forehead and left Sarah alone to say goodnight. The deck was calling to him.

He had to get outside, needed the cool, night air. Graham took in big gulps, trying to clear his head. His hands gripped the railing and helped to ground him There was the sound of the door opening and closing; hands wrapped around his waist and Sarah pressed up against him.

Graham could feel her trembling. "We don't have to go. We can take her someplace else, tell her we're in Blue Mountain Lake."

"I'm not going to lie to her, Sarah. I know I'm being irrational, but the thought of going there—it's all tangled together, the accident, Kane, what he did to you. Do you think I'll ever be able to think back on that time without my stomach burning and my heart pounding? To say, 'Oh, that. It was a long time ago. We're over it.' I don't know if I'll ever be over it! I can only imagine how it must be for you." Graham's head bowed and he closed his eyes to keep himself from falling apart.

Sarah ducked under his arms and placed her hands on his cheeks. They were cool and when he opened his eyes, hers were a calm place to land. "It *is* hard. I don't know if we'll ever be *over* it, but we'll learn to cope and it will get easier. Seeing Kane, that last time, talking to him, understanding him

363

better…it went a long way toward healing me. I'm not afraid of him anymore. We shouldn't stay away from Blue Mountain just because he's there. I'm not going to let anyone or anything keep us from doing something we want to do. Besides, what are the odds of seeing him?"

A bark of laughter without humor echoed in the night, bouncing off the mountains hovering on the other side of the lake. Graham pulled her in close and rested his chin on her head. "I know by experience that Kane Johnson defies all odds."

There was a movement between them, a sharp jabbing in his stomach, making him pull back. Eyes wide with wonder, Graham laid his hand on Sarah's belly. He watched it rise and fall with another punch or kick. "Someone has something to say. What do you think she's trying to tell us?"

"It could be a boy, you know." At the shake of Graham's head, she could only smile. He was convinced that he was destined to be surrounded by girls because they made his world go round. "I think she's telling us to relax. Be happy. Have faith. It will be all right. It's a camping trip, something you love more than any of us, in a beautiful place. There's nothing bad about it in Lila's mind. Let's try looking at it through her eyes."

Graham felt the hard, warmth of Sarah's stomach and saw the light shining in her eyes. Once again, she helped him to beat down the panic. He pulled out some hope and grabbed hold of some of *her* faith. She had more than enough to go around. Sarah simply amazed him, every day. "All right. No promises, but I'll try."

In the middle of the night, when he couldn't sleep, he went to the kitchen. Filled a glass with cold water. Pressed it to his forehead first to ease a splitting headache. Drank it down with a few aspirin. The lake drew Graham back outside.

Barefoot, with the grass cool on the bottom of his feet, he let it tangle around his toes. A few more steps and he was on the dock. He dropped down and let his legs dangle over the edge. It was cold, a shock to the system, but not unpleasant. The sound of the water lapping against the shore and an easy breeze soothed him enough to go back inside. He'd give sleep another try.

There was one stop along the way. Graham leaned up against Lila's door and watched her while she slept. Sarah had said to look through a child's eyes. Sometimes, he thought he would give anything to go back to those days. Innocence. Pure delight. Play. The world of pretend.

Graham whispered a prayer to keep his little girl safe and let him see life the way she did. Lila had been through a world of trouble yet she was resilient, like all young people were. Graham could learn a lesson from her.

There was a slight shift under the covers when he slipped into bed. Sarah didn't come awake, but her arm came across his chest and a leg wrapped around his. Spoon style, his body finally relaxed and grew heavy. Like a sigh, sleep tiptoed in and carried him away. Graham's eyes didn't open again until the sun was high in the sky.

They left on the Friday before Memorial Day weekend for four days at the public campsite in Blue Mountain Lake. There was no fear of Kane being *there*. They'd made it past the stand where he'd been before. There was nothing besides pamphlets this time around. Maybe the odds would be in their favor.

The weather was fine and unseasonably hot, the perfect present for Lila. She played at the beach, splashed in the water, and rode her bike with Graham and Sarah around the campsites. They took a row boat out on the lake, Graham carrying them wherever they wanted to go with powerful strokes. Once in the middle, they dropped their fishing lines and caught some sunnies. Night time meant sitting around the fire, making s'mores, playing cards. They stayed up late, got up early. Caught the sunrise. Listened to the magic of the loons. Closed the door on the past and opened a window to the future.

On their last day, packed up and ready to go home, they were reluctant to leave. It happened on every vacation, that desire to make it last a little bit longer. Graham pulled into the parking area for the Blue Mountain trail. His wife took his hand. Lila was buzzing with excitement, oblivious of the tension running between them; the adults were rigid, faces tight.

Sarah whispered softly, "You're sure you pick this path?"

The memories were difficult for her as well. She'd never forget her terror when she didn't know where he was or if he was all right. Much worse was that glimpse of Kane at the moment she found Graham by the side of the road and didn't know if the woodsman had hurt him, then the drive to the hospital, wondering if they'd make it in time.

"I'm sure. I need to go back up there so I can put it behind me. You ready, Ladybug?" Graham tapped Lila on the nose. She wrapped her arms around his neck and held on tight as he climbed out of the truck.

"Come on, Daddy! Come on, Mommy! Let's go!" He set her down, and she raced to the sign-in area, a wriggling ball of energy. They waited patiently while Lila wrote down all of their names.

Job completed, she grabbed hold of their hands and started tugging on them. "Come on! We haven't gone on a hike in forever. This is how we found Graham, 'member, Mommy?"

The little girl's excitement was contagious, taking the edge off the anxiety, just under the surface. "I seem to remember it was the other way around. *I* found *you*!" Graham couldn't resist.

He glanced at Sarah, counted to three, and they swung the little girl in the air between them. Laughter—everyone's— mingled with the sounds of the forest.

"Really, I was the one, 'member, Daddy? I went looking for help and I bumped right into you. Ms. Ashley said it was destiny. We have a girl in my class named Destiny and she told us that her name means what's meant to be or a dream come true and that's you, Daddy."

Lila's smile was big, her touch on his hand warm. Graham thought his heart couldn't hold any more love than it did in that moment. He glanced at Sarah, her palm resting on her belly, and he knew—there was room for more. Always room for more love.

They took their time, stretching out their last day before going home. Enjoyed the birdsong. Caught a flash of a blue jay in a pine. Stopped to watch a chipmunk nibbling on an acorn. Stood statue still as a doe and her fawn crossed the path. The view from the peak was worth the climb. It stole their breath away and made them feel like they were on top of the world. Sarah and Lila sat on a boulder, drinking down their water bottles, while Graham approached the edge.

He knew the spot, could find it with his eyes closed. Life-altering places were like that. The ridge made his legs shake and his mouth go dry. Forced him to sit down, try to rein in his pounding heart. He could remember everything about that day, the urgency to find the lost men, the elements fighting against him, his lack of caution. That sickening freefall off the ledge and the *THUD* that jolted all of his bones.

Strange how a chain of events could lead a man one way. Although his intentions had been only the best, his emotions had nearly been his undoing. It was a long way down. Graham could still feel the free-fall, the bloom of pain, hear the sickening snap and the thud. He swallowed. Drew in one breath. And another.

Graham thought about what came after and it sucked his lungs dry with the stunning realization; without Kane, he wouldn't be here with his family. Wouldn't see the little one on the way. Wouldn't be taking in the fresh air or feeling the sun. Wouldn't be living out this day.

There was the touch of a hand on his back and another on his shoulder, smaller and lighter, a feather. "Are you all right?" Sarah's voice trembled.

She knew the place well. It had been stamped in her memory when she nearly followed Graham's example and saw his pack hanging on that limb. Sitting there now felt like dangling high on a branch, ready to snap. She peered over the edge, closed her eyes, and buried her head in her husband's shoulder. *Thank you, God, for saving him for me. Thank you for bringing Kane that day.*

Understanding bloomed. Kane was in her life for a reason. First, as a torment. Then full circle, to give back her life by saving her husband. Her child yet to be born would not have known its father without Kane. Yes, the woodsman had taken much. That he had given so much more, without measure, tipped the scales in the opposite direction. To have Graham, safe and whole, by her side, Sarah would have relived every part of it. Without a moment's hesitation.

Lila held on tightly to his waist. "Is this where you fell, Daddy? That's really far. You must have been scared. Are you okay?" Her eyes were wide and she snuggled in closer. This little girl could never get close enough.

Graham tucked both of his girls against his chest and slowly stood up. He looked down once more than out at the incredible view, grateful to be able to see it and enjoy it with his family. "I'm fine with you two here. There's something I have to do before we go. Are you two up for a walk in the woods?"

At nods from both his girls, they started on the downward path before branching off into the forest. Everything was changed without the snow covering the land, but Graham let his instincts guide him. Pain non-withstanding, he'd still paid attention to the landmarks around him.

He remembered that odd rock formation, the tree that had been split down the middle by lightning, the small stand of pines that stood in a ring. Time stood still when they stopped by a small shack, run-down by all outward appearances. Graham knew that it was livable with the basic comforts held within, maybe even more so now.

"Look Daddy! A little house! Do you think it's like the seven dwarves and their cottage where Snow White lived?" Lila piped up, always bubbling over with curiosity. They pulled up short as all three studied the little building and let their imaginations run.

Sarah held on to Graham's arm, giving and taking strength. "It's his place, isn't it?"

She stepped in closer, letting him be her shelter. Saying Kane was behind her and truly believing it were two different things. A small part of Sarah might always be locked in that other cabin in the woods with the woodsman.

There was a flicker of movement and the snap of a branch as Kane emerged from the back of his cabin. He'd given them fair warning. The woodsman's stealth was such that he could have circled around them and the Scotts would never know they were being watched. With the exception of Graham.

"Can I help you? You look lost." Kane's smile was wide, his honey eyes warm. His voice was gentle. Kind.

Everything about him took them off guard, made them almost forget what Kane had cost them. He didn't even look like the same person. There was an openness about him, welcoming them in. Before, he would have shut the door to himself.

Graham cleared his throat, unable to speak for a moment. Finally, he found the words. "We were just on a walk. I'm Graham Scott. This is my wife, Sarah, and daughter, Lila. We took a trip off the beaten path. We're sorry to bother you." He held out a hand in greeting.

Kane accepted what he knew was being offered. The words hadn't been said out loud, but the gift of forgiveness was finally his. His voice was choked. "I'm John Benson, pleased to meet you. Would you like a drink, something to eat? I made some cinnamon bread just this morning and there's some tea, still warm, on the fire. I could bring it out to my table—right there." He gestured to a table with benches, tucked in against the side. They looked lightweight, easy to be concealed if necessary.

"We'd like that. It's a long walk back." Sarah followed her husband's example and gave Kane her hand with a nod. She felt a shaking that matched her own and let go. Graham's arm came around her and held her steady. Her rock.

Lila skipped forward and stuck out her hand. "Nice to meet you, Mr. Benson. Do you live here in the woods all of the time?" She tipped her head up and the blue in her eyes flashed brightly. She stopped Kane in his tracks. She had the power to do that to anyone.

He squatted down and gave her hand a shake, looking her square in the eye. "I do live here come summer. All year round, I love to spend time in the forest; it's my best friend. I can tell that you love it too. You all go sit down and I'll be right out." He stood and turned away but not before Graham and Sarah could see tears in his eyes.

They sat at the table. The four of them. Together. Like friends. It was a tea party, according to Lila. The strange

372

ensemble enjoyed the sweet bread and tea, a natural blend. There was a new-found ease about the woodsman, his former reticence gone. Kane told Lila stories of the animals in the woods and some of his adventures while Graham and Sarah listened, held hands, and mended hearts.

When it was time to leave, before the approaching sundown, Kane hurried inside and returned with carvings. For Lila, a chickadee, as spirited as the little girl. For Sarah, a doe, gentle and sweet. For Graham, a mountain lion, fierce and protective. "Take them and enjoy. Have a safe journey back home. Maybe I'll see you again someday."

Perhaps. The prospect no longer made Graham burn with anger or fuel the flames of resentment. A welcome idea? Doubtful. Would he seek Kane out again? Probably not. Turn the man away? No.

Graham offered his hand once more to give a firm shake. "You never know. Thank you again, for everything."

The two men took pause, staring at each other's reflection in their eyes. For a brief moment, they saw a mirror of what was good in each man. Sarah gave her thanks as well, followed by Lila, and they began the trip out of the wilderness.

Graham felt himself grow lighter with every step. Something inside of him that had weighed him down broke loose, let go. Lila was singing, swinging her hand with her mother. The sun turned their hair to gold as it headed on the downward slope to the horizon, another Adirondack sundown that would never cease to amaze. The wind picked up and brushed their skin, setting the trees to sighing.

The feeling of passing a barrier couldn't be denied. Graham fought it, tooth and nail, but the bridge to forgiveness hadn't been that hard to cross. With Sarah and Lila by his side, they'd made it. He was strong enough.

Dedicated to my mother, Betty Pedersen Churchill, who has taught me strength and in memory of my father, Stephen Smith Pedersen, strong enough to hold me close, watch me soar, and let me go. Daddy, you have my heart forever.

Coming Soon:

Against the Grain

Paulie Goodwin has pushed his limits in life. As a photojournalist, he goes wherever the wind blows, and has been around the world and back again, seeing its many faces and places through the lens of his camera.

When his most recent assignment as a photojournalist lands him in Afghanistan on an army base with the American soldier, his life is turned upside down. A young serviceman gives his life to save Paulie's, sending the photographer reeling. He'll come back home to his family to heal from a severe injury in the small town of Cordial Creek. He's gone against the grain all of his life, choosing the road less traveled, but this time the mountain of guilt may be too hard to climb.

Anna Peters has lived in Cordial Creek for all of her life. A teacher of fifteen years, she's always been content with her predictable routine, but lately has felt a need for something new in her life, some kind of spark. Change will literally run smack dab into her when she sweeps Paulie Goodwin off his feet at the airport. Once high school sweethearts, they've remained friends throughout the years, catching up whenever he's breezed in to town. This time, he's here to stay and ready to fall to pieces. Anna may be the only one who can help put Humpty Dumpty together again.

Sunrise Over Indian Lake

Book Three in the Lost in the Adirondacks Series

Looking for me?

You can follow me on Facebook at Heidi Sprouse Writer. I'm also on Twitter, Heidi Sprouse Author @heidi_sprouse. Find me on the web at heidisprouse.wix.com/heidi-sprouse.

39491145R00226

Made in the USA
Middletown, DE
20 January 2017